A PLACE
FOR THE WICKED

NOVELS BY
ELLESTON TREVOR

Chorus of Echoes
Tiger Street
Redfern's Miracle
A Blaze of Roses
The Passion and the Pity
The Big Pick-Up
Squadron Airborne
The Killing-Ground
Gale Force
The Pillars of Midnight
The V.I.P.
The Billboard Madonna
The Burning Shore
The Flight of The Phoenix
The Shoot
The Freebooters
A Place for the Wicked
Bury Him Among Kings

A PLACE
FOR THE WICKED

Elleston Trevor

HEINEMANN : LONDON

William Heinemann Ltd
15 Queen Street, Mayfair. London W1X 8BE

LONDON MELBOURNE TORONTO
JOHANNESBURG AUCKLAND

First published in Great Britain in 1968
This edition 1972
Copyright © Elleston Trevor, 1968
434 79306 x

10332971

Reproduced and Printed in Great Britain by
Redwood Press Limited, Trowbridge & London

For

NOËL HOOD

CHAPTER I

It began on a late May evening but as often happens with terrible events they did not know it was beginning, because there was nothing different about this particular evening.

They spent it as they had spent so many others here at Alec's place, drinking and talking a bit and joking a lot, wading in on the cold chicken or whatever it was that Laura had got for them and listening to some of Alec's records until the talk broke out again and he turned off the music. On this particular evening they all had a good time as usual and no one got tight or stayed too late but between their coming and their going it had begun.

Ron had arrived first. He was still shaking with excitement although he'd walked all the way from Victoria to get over it so as they wouldn't notice anything. Chris wasn't with him because Friday was her afternoon for going along to St Dunstan's and sometimes the kids there kept her hanging on. Otherwise he couldn't have done it – she would have known straight away by his face and his hands. He'd told her he'd given it up but he hadn't.

Alec was alone when he opened the door but that wasn't unusual: Laura often went down to Stan's for a hairdo before they all met up at Alec's place for one of their evenings.

'Come on in,' Alec said. There was some music on the player, something he'd dug up from the back of the shop; you'd never hear the pops in this place.

Ron went in with his hands stuck hard in his pockets

because of the shaking. He couldn't tell if Alec had noticed anything in his face because he wouldn't say so anyway: he was dead quiet, Alec, whatever was going on, not dim-witted or moody or anything like that, just quiet. Chris had said once: 'What's so nice about Alec is that you can never tell what he's thinking, but you never feel he's thinking anything you wouldn't like.'

'Name it, Ron.'

'I wouldn't say no to a glass of beer.'

It was a nice flat and as he looked round the room he felt steadier because there was so much to see, though it was funny because you could never say it was overcrowded, just a few deep chairs and a big sofa to match, with soft-coloured wood covering the whole of one wall, not shiny but with a waxy glow about it, and a few big pictures without any glass on showing reeds and birds with long beaks, Chinese, you could tell that.

He felt better already, looking round the room, as if he was one of those puppet things that had been jerking about and now the strings had gone slack. It was a quiet place, like Alec. Perhaps it was because Alec was here that he felt calm again, not because of the room so much.

'Cheers,' Alec said and gave him a glass. It was Scotch.

Ron always asked for beer because he couldn't afford Scotch in his own place and he didn't see why he should ask for it here. Usually Alec would give him a beer but this evening it was Scotch in a big dumpy glass, heavy and thick at the bottom, with chiselling round it and going thinner all the way up and so wonderfully thin at the top that you'd think they'd get broken, glasses like these, the first time you washed them up. There was ice in it, what Stan called 'on the rocks'.

He thought perhaps Alec had given him Scotch because he looked as if he needed one, quick. It was the kind of thing Alec would do, without saying anything. But it was all right now. He felt great. Great.

They sat down with their drinks, not talking because the music was on. Ron didn't want to talk but he knew that if he started saying anything Alec would quietly reach across to the switch and sit listening to him, nodding his long head and taking a lot of interest. Alec said if music wasn't good enough to listen to without talking it wasn't worth putting on the player. He called it 'audible wallpaper', the bad stuff, and Ron took him to mean it was always there but you didn't really hear it. Alec had a lot of words like that and Ron remembered them and told them to other people, but he always told them it was Alec who'd made them up, not him.

The record on now was sort of weird, with thin pipes and little tinkly bits that put you in mind of the pictures on the wall. It was catching enough but Ron was glad the others would soon be here because he wouldn't want to go on listening to it for too long.

He watched the ice floating in the yellow-coloured Scotch and felt very calm now, not upset at all; it was a kind of singing calmness, like the music. He could think about it now and enjoy it all over again without that shaky feeling.

From across the room Alec saw that the kid was relaxed now and that if Chris came she wouldn't notice anything. He always thought of Ron as a 'kid' although there were only a few years between them. He knew that the others felt the same way; it wasn't a question of age. Ron was smaller than Mike and Stan and himself, and there was also something puckish about his face and a nervousness about his movements that reminded you of a nipper ready for mischief at every turn. Ron was a grown man now; he must be what, twenty-four, twenty-five? But however long he lived you'd still be able to see the boy in him, the cocky little mudlark shining in an old man's eyes.

Alec finished his drink. May Ron and his kind live for ever; they could do with a bit of eternal youth about the place.

They heard a car pulling up below the open windows.

'Stan,' Ron said at once. He knew his exhaust-notes; he worked with them every day.

Alec nodded and got up, putting his tumbler on the bar and picking up the small blue slipper that had found its way half under one of the chairs. The other one was afloat in the bath upstairs with a leaf torn off the calendar for a sail and he'd had to carry Toops out of the bathroom with urgent cries of *Abandon Ship!* to avoid even stormier scenes on the way to bed. Mandy would be reading to him now and it had better be something good because his head would still be full of thoughts on how to bribe her to go into the bathroom and give the slipper a push and report back to him on its performance.

'This is where the action is!'

Stan was in the doorway, black Homburg lifted high above his head, pink shirt glowing and white teeth shining in a Sunless-tanned face. The scent of Old Spice was already in the room and the music on the player seemed fainter although no one had turned it down. Laura was ushered in with courtly bows from Stan, who then skimmed the Homburg neatly across to Ron. Ron caught it without a blink and dropped it on to his head, where it half-covered his eyes.

The evening had started. These evenings never started until the moment when Stan arrived.

'Hello, sweet,' Alec said.

'Hello, darling.'

'I like your hair.'

Laura grimaced. 'It's still filthy – Stan's got a new shampooer and I've been telling him to sack her but he says she's got an aged mother or something.'

'Stan should hire the mother – she might be a better shampooer.'

They weren't touching but he could feel her warmth; he had felt it even on the day they had first met, a winter day when she'd been shivering at a bus stop. Her eyes were bright now, flicking away from him, but she didn't look at Stan. The question came into Alec's mind again but it didn't bother him because it would never be asked aloud, so it would have to die away of its own accord and good riddance. He turned away to switch off the record-player but she followed him.

'Are they all right?'

'They're fine.' The arm settled on to its cradle and the record stopped turning. *Bamboo Shadaws*. She took the slipper from him and he said: 'The other one's in the bath, when you go up.'

'Is the tooth out yet?'

'No.' Mandy had a loose milk-tooth, the last of them, working its way out. 'She's been shoring it up with chewing-gum on the sly —'

'Oh, Alec. You said you'd take it out.'

'I know.'

'It wouldn't hurt her.'

'She thinks it will, that's the trouble —'

'Well if it comes out in the night and she swallows it it'll be your fault.'

'I've got my money on the Wrigley's.'

She went upstairs and he heard Stan saying: 'On the rocks – what's the hold-up?'

'How's it going, Stan?'

'Bloody wicked. Two permers home with the curse, a

short-circuit in one of the dryers and a stand-up fight with a queen of tarts all eager for a pint of peroxide when the stuff was coming out in handfuls already – wouldn't let me cut it, not that you'd need scissors, you could break it off like spaghetti, said she'd never go there again so I said she'd got the wrong address to start with. I was a hairdresser not a haymaker, Christ you should have heard her go out, the place sounded like a launching-pad! Took me all my time to calm the other clients down, I don't mind telling you.' He accepted the big tumbler and held it up to the light and shook it gently until the ice tinkled. 'That's my baby. Thank the Lord our Laura was one of them, did a marvellous job, making out she didn't know me and turning on the sympathy for talented hair-stylists who found themselves at the mercy of anyone with a couple of pounds in their bag, that sort of angle, you know – Christ, she broke their hearts while they sat there and when they left I could have passed the hat round and done a bomb!'

The signet ring on his right hand caught the light as he pulled a Stuyvesant from a gold case without offering one to Alec because Alec didn't smoke.

'Lousy today, lucky tomorrow.'

'You must be joking!' Stan said. 'It's like that every day.' He lit up and looked around, glad to be here if only to get away from the stink of the setting-lotion, though there was more to it than that. This place suited him. Alec had something it was hard to put your finger on but easy enough to name. Style. It was the same down at the Club and it wasn't just in the furnishings, the soft lights and the good-class music; there was something extra in both places and it was Alec who'd put it there.

Stan had been struck by it the first time he'd gone into Alec's club and when he'd opened up as a crimper he'd tried to do the same thing, decorating the salon and supervising the work himself to make sure everything was plumb on. He'd called it 'Crowning Glory' and had it put up in gold letters above the window in a panel of black glass with a curl of plaster hair making the big C and the big G and a miniature crown making the dot for the 'i' – took a lot of trouble and worked through the night for three weeks before the opening, champagne reception and the Press and all that. But it didn't work. Everyone called it 'Stan's place' just as if it was a ten-and-six touch and no extras down the Mile End Road. The money poured in all right and he'd doubled the staff in three months but that was because he was a good crimper and treated the clients like countesses so long as they weren't bloody whores like that one who'd blown in today. No, it was a big success and you couldn't argue: eighteen months and he'd got a flat in Knightsbridge and a Jag at the door. But there was one thing missing. Style.

Alec had the touch.

'How's the Club?'

'No problems.'

That was a lie, Stan knew. It was all very well having style but it didn't pull in the lolly.

'Cut your losses, boy. Turn it in and come in with me. You'd carve 'em up as manager, a bloke with your kind of style.'

'I don't get on with people,' Alec said. 'Unless I like them.'

Stan had been trying to persuade him to take over the salon for a long time now but he knew the idea wasn't so much to boost the business as to let Stan out.

'The thing is for people to like *you*. In your case that's a cert.'

Alec gave a slow smile, his large eyes narrowing. 'Go

and kiss someone else's. You're fed up to the back teeth with that place, right?'

'That's a beautiful understatement.'

'Then sell it and set up something new.'

'What like, for Christ's sake? All I know is crimping!'

'You didn't know crimping once.'

It was all Alec was going to say. One of the quickest ways to lose a friend was by giving him advice. In any case Stan had no problem in his life. With his amount of vitality he'd open up in some new direction and make another success and maybe marry again and maybe make it last the second time. Stan was ready to go and all he had to worry about was where.

It had sometimes occurred to Alec that Stan Sedgeman was almost his exact opposite: vital, restless, impulsive, a dynamo of a man. Just as little Ron Webber was different from them both: mischievous, imaginative, driven along by his nerves so fast that it got him nowhere because it was the pace he lived for and not the objective. The attraction of opposites in close friendship – and they were all close friends who'd be here tonight – was a fascinating subject for study but to Alec's mind it was also dangerous. Go too far in discovering your friends and you'd start learning a few things about yourself, and Alec Bromley had long believed that there were a few things about himself he didn't want to know.

They were really swinging now and the girls were taking the wreckage of a York ham out to the kitchen and the cork was off the brandy. All you could hear above the talking was the buzz of the coffee-grinder.

Mike and Fay had picked up Chris on their way and now they were complete. None of them thought about this consciously but their actions had expressed it in small ways: Alec had put his arm round Chris to welcome her and Stan fixed himself another drink and Laura slid one of the chairs nearer the settee to make a clear gangway for the trolley. There had always been this sense of completeness when the seven of them came together, and it had happened in many places, mostly here at Alec's but sometimes at Stan's after the divorce and exactly three times at the Villa Mimosa in Antibes.

Mike Owen was probably the only one of them whom Alec – if he had let himself analyse their friendship – might have called a composite of the three other men, Alec himself included.

With the looks of a farmer, red-haired and sideburned, stocky and check-suited, Mike possessed a nervous energy belying his resemblance to a man who worked the earth and waited on the seasons for a living: it was the kind of energy seen in Stan Sedgeman, though it was not so near the surface. The blunt weathered face was the opposite of Ron Webber's in every feature; but the sudden spark leaping in the close-set eyes in moments when his imagination was fired could sometimes be seen in the younger eyes of Ron. For all this there was a restraint about him, an ability to listen to the others for a long time without a word put in, that Alec recognized in himself. The rest was Mike, identifiable less by the way he looked than by what he said, and by what he didn't say; his reaction to most things was usually silent, expressed by the sudden spark in the eyes, a quick and rather devilish smile, a pursing of the mouth in a soundless whistle. Pressed to comment, the most he would give you would be 'Well I never,' or 'Is that a fact?'

Mike had been the last of them to join the group and Fay had naturally come with him. That was four years ago and the introduction had been precipitate: Alec had just opened his club and a bunch of protection boys had come in to soften him up for the squeeze. He'd been expecting them because nobody opened a club inside the five-mile ring from Piccadilly without getting a visit, so his barman had put through a prearranged call to Stan Sedgeman and Ron Webber. They were quickly there and brought a third man, a stranger to Alec.

From the moment Mike Owen was inside the place there wasn't much to do except stand around and watch. Mike looked as strong a man as he was and the protection boys stepped back an arm's length and stayed there with their guns on show. Mike gave them his quick smile that flicked his rust-red eyebrows up into two little horns.

'We'll have a drink,' he said. 'My friend here is going to give us a drink.' He turned his back on them and leaned at the bar and Alec took his cue and set up the glasses. It seemed to have gone very quiet. The mobsters didn't move at first and Mike jerked a look at them. 'You're not on the wagon, I hope?' Then they moved up to the bar. It wasn't what he'd said or the way he'd said it; there was something about the man that made people do what he asked. Perhaps it was the situation, too, that sent them out of their depth: they'd come here ready for action and there wasn't going to be any. One thing was quite clear to Alec: these boys didn't think the red-haired man was going to do a deal with them. He didn't look like a man to do a deal with anyone.

Little Ron and Stan came up to the bar because Alec had poured a drink for them too but the atmosphere changed subtly and Mike said at once – 'Don't make a crowd, now, we don't want to breathe down each other's necks, do we? This is a nice big place and there's room for everyone.' The protection boys relaxed again as Ron and Stan moved away and kept their distance. The barman, who had never worked in a club before, had gone white in the face when they'd shown their guns, and now he stood right at the end watching Alec in case there were any orders. At some time in the proceedings the blue lamp over the door came on and the barman looked at Alec but Alec just told him: 'We're shut.'

They took a sip at their drinks and then Mike began talking.

'You know Jack, do you? Jack Tango?' They were watching him and said nothing, holding their drinks in their left hands. 'Come on, you know Jack, you've heard of Jack. The South-West boys.'

One of them looked suddenly nervous and said that he knew Jack. The red-haired man jerked round and said very quickly —

'You've got nothing to say against Jack, have you, against Jack Tango? Eh?'

They said no, nothing. They spoke as quickly as Mike Owen. He seemed satisfied. Then he went on talking about other people, dropping a name or two, and they found themselves holding their drinks in their right hands, perhaps from habit. Mike talked to them in a crooning tone, sometimes giving them his quick little smile. Everyone was relaxed now and the barman had got some of his colour back.

Alec didn't remember anything in detail afterwards: no one could have, any more than you can remember an accident clearly. They were all standing there with the glasses in their hands one minute and the next minute one of the protection boys was doubling up and another had a streak of red across his cheek and the third was tilting slowly backwards as Mike brought one hand across his face in a flipping motion that made a sound like an enormous razor being stropped. He went at them in turn, starting on the first one again and talking to them in precisely the same tone, crooning to them – 'Mind that carpet now, we don't want blood on it' – and a glass smashed somewhere – 'Don't do that, don't you try that, will you –' and Stan had to dodge back as a man went down with his head lolling – 'You're turning nasty now and I don't like it, you're a nasty boy, I can see that –' and he dragged the one with the gashed cheek away from the carpet because of the blood.

They were still half-conscious and he talked to them again, telling them not to come here in the future, telling them not to go near Jack Tango or Willy the Whiff or Big Busby because if those people knew they'd come here they wouldn't like it, they wouldn't like it at all. Then he helped them up and took them to the door, telling them to go out quietly because this was a nice place, a nice respectable club.

He had followed them out and didn't come back, and Ron explained to Alec that it was to avoid being thanked because he didn't like being thanked for anything, but Alec had asked Ron where the man could be found and had gone to see him the next day, and now he was sitting on the floor here four years later in his farmer's tweeds with a plate of York ham on his lap and sharing the jar of pickles with Fay. Mike and Fay could go through a half-pound jar of pickles in one night, so Laura always kept a stock.

The rest of them knew much more about Mike after four years of evenings like this and three trips to Antibes on what they called the Old Firm's Annual Outing, and one thing they knew about him – it had come up quite by chance – was never mentioned. He wouldn't have minded, but just the same it was never mentioned.

CHAPTER 2

Later they danced, Mike and Fay. It was how they had met, dancing.

The plates had been cleared away and when the coffee was brought in there was a lull in the talking and Alec had put on the other side of *Bamboo Shadows* but it wasn't long before he turned it off again because Stan was going through one of his acts, telling them what he was planning to do down at Antibes.

They had booked a night flight for a week from now, a Friday. That was what they always did, or at least what they had done three times before. The Villa Mimosa was booked already; they'd got into the routine of giving Madame Dupont a deposit every time they left there at the end of their holiday, making sure of it. The place was shabby enough but big and near the sea and although some of them – Stan especially – could afford a smarter place these days they never thought of staying anywhere else. Every holiday at the Villa Mimosa had been memorable but the first one was just a dream, and the big shabby house with its palm trees and peeling balconies had become part of the completeness they felt when they were together.

Stan had written a song about it soon after their first time there – *Down at the old Villa Mim*, to the tune of *Down at the Old Bull and Bush* – but the girls started throwing cushions at him whenever he tried to sing it because the Villa Mimosa was far away from the East End pubs and they didn't want to think of it differently from what it was: a house in the sun by the blue sea with a real mimosa tree actually growing in the garden. Fay especially had hated the song when Stan had first sung it; she thought 'mimosa' was one of the most beautiful words she had ever heard, and didn't like it shortened to 'mim'. But that was just Stan, a wonderful person when you knew him but none too sensitive. Fay had sometimes thought that it had been the real reason for the divorce, because his wife – she couldn't remember her name now – had seemed to be a girl with instinctive good taste, what little she'd seen of her before they'd broken it up. The grounds had been the usual, of course, but Fay had thought the marriage might have held up and become valuable to them both if there hadn't been deeper differences, if Stan had been more sensitive or his wife less. There were plenty of women who'd count themselves lucky with a handsome and successful man like Stan Sedgeman for a husband once they'd seen that with his brand of high-powered energy they'd just have to let him have what he'd call 'a little bit on the side' now and again.

Dancing with Mike to a record she hadn't heard before, Fay looked across his shoulder and saw Stan for a moment against the charcoal-grey curtains talking to Laura, his face serious as it always was when he talked to her. Fay sometimes wondered if they talked alone together and if that was all they did. She had asked Mike once: 'If anything bad happened to Alec, Stan would make a go for Laura, wouldn't he?' Mike had pursed his mouth for a bit and then said: 'If anything bad was going to happen to Alec, Stan would be the first one to try stopping it.'

Mike always said a lot in a few words like that. He didn't only mean that Stan wouldn't wait for his chance without doing anything for Alec – that would make Stan a thorough bastard and he was far from that. He meant that Stan would never have a go at Laura all the time Alec was around because that would amount to 'something bad' happening to Alec.

Fay had been secretly worried the first time they had decided to go to Antibes, because the divorce had gone through some time before and Stan was on his own again and it was going to be difficult for him down there with the hot sun and the warm nights and the holiday feeling over them all; but Stan had found a girl to 'make up the number' and it was all right. Since then he'd found a new girl every time they went down there and this year he'd fixed himself up with someone called Dolly. They hadn't met her yet because she was on a modelling course and was going to join them in Antibes the day after they got there. Stan sounded extra keen on this one.

'You've got distemper in your hair,' Fay said.

The music was slow.

'Is that a fact?'

You wouldn't have thought Mike could dance like this; he was such a big man. She'd been a hostess at the Flower Bowl in Streatham fifteen years ago, March 10, a Tuesday (it had said under Taurus, 'Emotional matters will be in the foreground and a cool head must be kept'), and when she'd seen him coming across to her she'd felt her feet sort of wincing.

They danced now just as they'd danced then. It was when she felt closest, and least frightened.

'You'll look distinguished one day, with white hair.'

Their cheeks were together and she felt him smiling. He'd been three days doing out the bathroom of Charlie's house down the road because Charlie wasn't young and he'd laid himself out doing the rest of the place and the bathroom hadn't been touched. Mike hadn't ever spoken to Charlie before; he'd just been a neighbour, but Fay had talked to the wife sometimes at the Co-op and heard about Charlie knocking himself up through working at the house all night to get it finished by his wife's birthday as he'd promised; so she'd told Mike and he'd shut the office and put on some overalls.

That was why there was still distemper in his hair: there hadn't been time to wash it. She didn't really think he'd look distinguished one day with white hair; it was burning red like a fire and she didn't want to see it go like ash, ever.

'I'd be lost without you.'

She could only say things like that when they were dancing, when she felt closest and least frightened.

Fay couldn't remember if life had frightened her before the day at the store. She'd been nineteen. The store was called Weymark's and it had closed down later. She'd never done such a thing before and it would make her feel sick to think of ever doing it again. There was a fat manager there, bald and pink, with bright-looking glasses with no frames, and he'd just followed her out to the street.

'Would you allow me to look in your handbag, Miss?'

The whole street had seemed to lean inwards suddenly and the buses roared at her and he had to grab at her before she fell. Then they were in the café next door. She never remembered going in there but she remembered the café so clearly even now after twelve years that she sometimes dreamed about it, the crack across the corner of the marble table and the hair sprouting from a mole on the waitress's neck but most of all his face, the manager's, his eyes through the bright glasses.

'You're all right now.'

He'd ordered coffee and although she could remember the pattern of the cups and the way the handle on hers had a little bubble in the glazing, she hadn't at the time known what it was doing there in front of her or why the man was there.

'But I'll have to take a look in your bag, you see.'

She gave it to him without thinking. She felt empty, aching with an emptiness, not just in her stomach but right through her body and through her bones. She saw him open her bag.

'Are you going on holiday?'

He didn't smile. He was breathing rather heavily and sometimes looked quickly around the café but he looked most of the time at her face and down at her body with little glances.

'No.' She supposed it was her own voice.

'Then why did you want it?'

'I didn't want it.'

He suddenly put it into his pocket and passed her handbag back and then sipped at his coffee. She saw his cup trembling.

'Then why did you take it?'

She said: 'I don't know.'

A bus went past and the café window buzzed, but there was no roar from the bus like before, and the street outside was all right again. She felt normal, though a bit cold. She had passed through something and was out on the other side, normal again except that nothing mattered or meant anything; she had left something behind, life itself. She felt dead.

'Of course, this is a very serious matter.'

'Yes.'

Nothing could touch her now.

'Well I'm glad you seem to appreciate that.'

His bright eyes flickered down and up again to her face.

Someone came into the café, one of the girls from the store, and tried to ask him something; but he spoke to her sharply with his little red mouth and she went out in a huff.

In a minute he said: 'Now what are we going to do about this, eh?'

'I don't mind.'

'You don't *mind*?'

'No.'

Then he talked a lot about it being his duty to the proprietors of the store and the general public to report her to a constable ... couldn't have people taking a fancy to whatever they saw in a shop ... where would everyone be if this kind of thing got out of hand ...

She remembered that phrase: 'out of hand'.

'Do you lack money?'

'No.'

He looked sort of disappointed.

'You didn't intend to take this to a pawnbroker?'

'No.'

Suddenly he got impatient and said: 'I want your name and address.' She gave it to him and he wrote it down in a very small thick book. His hand wasn't very steady.

'Drink your coffee.'

She obeyed and because she was dead and everything was unreal she didn't think about whether the coffee might be too hot still, and scalded her lip and spilt some, and that woke her up all right. The pain seemed to bring all the life back and she could feel tears starting.

'How old are you?'

'Nineteen.'

Today it had said under Taurus: 'Various matters require careful adjustment, but you can count on help.'

'Nineteen, eh? Quite a young woman, then. And

quite old enough to know better.' His bright eyes moved about on her. 'If you were younger I'd have to go and talk to your parents. Do you live with your parents, still?'

'Yes.'

He looked disappointed again.

'Well, I'm not going to embarrass you. I'm going to give you a chance. Now what do you think of that?'

'I'm glad.'

The tears had been because of the scalded lip, nothing else, so they hadn't got worse. She had never cried, even when Miss Hacker had gone on at her in front of the other girls to 'make an example' of her, even when she grew old enough to know what Dad was doing to Mum behind the thin closed door when he 'broke out'.

'And grateful, I'd hope.' He seemed to make a point of that, so she just said:

'Yes.'

He nodded, drumming his short pink fingers on the marble, breathing heavily. 'Now you know what I'm going to do? I'm going to keep this matter a secret between us. You're a very nice-looking young lady and I wouldn't like to get you in trouble.' He smiled for the first time, very slowly. 'I wouldn't like to bruise a young butterfly's wings, eh?'

She wished he hadn't smiled like that.

'So I'm going to put you on what you might call probation for a while. How would you like that?'

She didn't know what the word meant; she knew it was something to do with being caught, but he said he wasn't going to tell anyone, so it couldn't be that.

'All right,' she said.

He nodded and his fingers drummed faster. 'I'll make a point of seeing you once a week, you understand? Just the two of us. That'll enable me to – to tell you a little about the world and how we ought to behave in it. Like a father, you follow me? I'll talk to you like a father.' The slow smile came again and he whispered low across the table – 'A father *confessor*.'

Someone came into the café again and he jerked round but it was nobody from the store apparently. All the same he beckoned the waitress with the mole on her neck and paid for the coffee, apologizing for the puddle beside Fay's cup – 'A little accident, Betty, for which I humbly crave pardon.' He was very perky now, as if he was glad the waitress had seen him in here with a strange 'young lady'.

Then it was all settled and they got up. He would park his car outside the doors of Fenning's Repository in the narrow street off the High at seven o'clock the next evening and she would go there to meet him.

'If you don't come,' he said with his voice low and his small red mouth near her face, 'I would have to bring certain matters to the notice of the police, you follow. But I'm sure you'll decide to be sensible, an intelligent young girl like you, eh?'

She hardly recognized the street when they went out on to the pavement; it was just the same but it seemed so long ago: it was as if she'd been away somewhere. He took her elbow and she felt the trembling of his fingers.

'Until tomorrow, then – Fay.'

She wished he hadn't used her name with his small red mouth. It felt like spittle on her.

Then she walked all the rest of the day and found herself in strange places, a chemist's asking for aspirins and a glass of water, a seat in the playground at Balham, a bus going to Dulwich where she knew no one. And it came to her for the first time in her life that she knew no one anywhere, not Dulwich or anywhere. There was no one she could tell or ask for help, what to do. Mum had enough to do as it was with Dad in the house; to tell her a thing like this would be like hitting her and she got enough of that. If she told Dad he'd just sling her out. There was no one else.

So she went to Fenning's Repository in the narrow dark street off the High the next evening and waited there an hour but the man didn't come and it was a long time, years, before she learned enough about people to realize that he hadn't had the guts, that if he had to get a girl this way it would be more than his life was worth if it ever came out that he'd been with one.

The manager at Weymark's had become the first person in the world she'd known pity for.

Ron was talking to Alec when the phone rang.

Laura picked it up and said, 'Yes, he's here,' and gave the receiver to Alec.

'Yes,' Alec said after a minute.

Ron watched his long quiet face and knew someone was in trouble. Anyone in trouble rang up Alec. That was why Ron had got Mike along to the Club that time; it had made a nice change for Alec to want help and Mike was the bloke to call in.

'You'll have to,' Alec said.

Ron looked away because he didn't want it to seem as if he was listening. He hoped it was big trouble because then Alec would want to do something about it and they'd go across the room to Stan and Mike and just give them a jerk of the head and they'd all be off, piling into one of the cars and on their way without saying anything, like they did on the pictures. Ron enjoyed that sort of thing.

The girls would be left together wondering what was on and if there was any danger and he enjoyed thinking about that too.

Alec was doing a lot of listening and Ron had nothing to go on so he watched Mike and Fay dancing, marvellous they were, and thought about the smell of the leather and the way she'd kicked when he'd put his foot down along the Brompton Road. It was the first GT6 he'd ever driven. He always went for new models and never took the same one twice.

She was a dream, all-white with blue leather, covered grab-handles, matt-black dials, floor-stick manual and a fly-off handbrake. There wasn't time to look under the bonnet but he knew what was there: twin side-draught Strombergs and an o.h.v. head with a $9.5:1$ compression ratio – he'd mugged it up ever since she'd come on the market because there was no fun driving a rod you didn't know anything about.

It was the first for three weeks and he'd been itching for it. The minute he saw it pull up at the meter he knew it was on, because Chris was down at the Blind Home and he'd have nearly an hour between work and going home to change for coming on here to Alec's place. It was the best heist he could remember for a long time.

Of course it wasn't a heist but he thought of it like that. A heist was when you took a motor with the idea of doing a repaint and flogging it with a bent log-book you'd got from a breaker. That was a crime, what Stan would call the 'big-time stuff'. (Of course Stan didn't know he nicked motors now and again, none of them knew except perhaps Alec and he wouldn't split.)

There was nothing wrong with nicking a motor if you looked after it.

This afternoon the bloke had got out with a briefcase and put a full hour on the clock which meant he wouldn't miss the GT for that amount of time. She was ready and willing. He'd given it ten minutes and then got in and had a quick fiddle under the dash to join the wires and taken her away with the seat-belt on and a warm engine and half a tankful on the dial. You always had to take a dekko at the dials because you'd look a proper lemon if she was out of juice and conked out in sight of where you'd taken her from.

One time he'd nicked a nice little 4-4 and the minute he started up the oil warning-light came on so he just got out and left a bit of paper under the wiper-blade saying 'You're clean out of oil'. Some blokes didn't deserve to have motors, they didn't know how to look after them.

But the GT6 was a dream, a lovely whip to her on corners with hardly any noise from the tyres, and inside a minute he'd got the revs just right for the changes and settled down for the ride. A thought took him of a sudden and he'd turned off Brompton and gone down through South Ken into the Fulham Road where his aunt lived, doubling twice round the square to go past her place again out of devilment, knowing she'd have a fit if she knew, the silly old bitch!

You'd never think Mum could have had a sister like that. After Mum had gone there was no one else to look after them except Aunty Miriam. He'd never known his Dad – there was a bit of a mystery there if you felt inclined to put a few questions but he'd never asked Mum anything because by the time he was old enough to worry about it he was old enough to know it'd make Mum miserable if he pestered her.

Once she'd said: 'You never seem to want to know about your Dad, do you?'

He'd said: 'I don't suppose there's much to know, is there?'

'Not much.'

They never mentioned it again and although he knew it was better that way he felt sad for a time because if Dad was dead she'd have told him out straight. That meant he must be alive somewhere, perhaps somewhere round where they lived, and it was sad to think he might pass his own father in the street without knowing him. He'd stayed awake a lot in the next week, trying to get it off his mind.

His Dad might have been someone nice, because Mum would never have taken up with anyone rotten. His Dad might have been someone like Alec.

He knew who his Mum was, all right. She was the most wonderful woman he had ever known. Of course all kids thought this at first but he'd gradually got to realize she'd be a wonderful woman even if she hadn't been his Mum. It wasn't because she'd been soft with him, having no Dad: he'd fetched many a quick clip on the ear when he'd played her up; but, looking back, it was only when he'd lost his manners, cheeked her or cheeked someone in the same street or even strangers. Bust a window or tear his drawers or chuck a brick at the cat next door and she'd just say, 'Well you've got *that* off your chest an' I hope you enjoyed it.' (Everyone hated that Tom next door, including its owner Mr Balcock, who'd invite anyone's dog in the back yard, especially Alsatians, in the hope they'd go for the cat and kill it, though he could never do anything *himself*, as he always told you. The cat had one ear torn off and a bad squint and all the fur gone from one side of its arse and three yellow teeth and a limp and not from dogs either, it was from the fights it picked among the other cats. It always won, though, and after a bit all the other cats began looking in much the same state. When it was on heat it had a voice like an air-raid warning shut up in an empty dustbin and that was why everyone threw bricks at it. Mr Balcock put up a little greenhouse in his back yard but it didn't last five minutes.)

His Mum had been bed-ridden the year before she passed away but it didn't make any difference in the place except there was more work for him and his two sisters. Mum ran the house like the captain on a boat, calling down the stairs telling them what she wanted done and how she wanted them to do it, and they wore out the newel-post at the bottom of the stairs, swinging on it while they listened to what they had to do next.

'That's all for now, you can go out an' play.'

'I don't want to, Mum.'

'Of course you want to!'

'No, honest. Think of somethin' I can do next.'

They'd hear her going '*Tch-tch-tch!*' through the open door of the bedroom and they'd grin at each other and it was always Florry, the eldest, who'd have to ask.

'Mum!'

'What is it now?'

'Can we come up an' talk to you?'

And there was always a pause before she answered.

'If you've got nothing better to do.'

They'd always had to ask. Up there in that poky little room day in, day out for eleven months, yet she'd never *ask* them to go up and see her. Never.

Then it was December and they didn't swing on the newel-post any more.

Aunty Miriam came and lived there and Florry the eldest got a job in Woolworth's quick as she could, and his other sister Marge only stayed till he was old enough to earn his keep at Cosgrove's Fruit-Bottling down at Bow and find some digs.

Aunty Miriam (whose real name was Ermyntrude, as they all knew, and a much better name it was for a silly bitch like her) had got married for the second time and gone up in the world and now she lived in the Fulham Road. She couldn't help being a cross between a piss-pot and a parrot and she had at least tried to look after them all, so he still took her a bunch of flowers now and then and stayed for a chat because she said she was lonely: her old man was a commercial traveller, picked up the job soon after they were married even though the money was less.

But today there were no flowers: he'd gone past twice, coming out of the corner from the square in second gear with a bit of a squeal on the tyres and the exhaust singing up so she'd hear him even if she didn't chance to be at the window and see him. Faint right off if she knew!

Then he forgot about Aunty Miriam and sat with the thin leather-covered wheel in his hands, feeling the shiver of the suspension over the manholes and the sudden pull of the discs when the lights went red and the shove in the back from the seat-squab when she got away and kept ahead of the others before the next set of lights. She was dreamy, the GT, and the streets looked wider and the trees looked greener and there was a sweet smell in the air and he breathed it in, his whole body breathing it in, not just his nose; and he felt a liking for everyone he saw no matter who they were, an old dear on the crossing (somebody's Mum), the conductor on the platform of a bus (poor sod, what a living!) and even the copper on the corner by the Oratory with his head turning slowly as the white GT went by, as if he wished it was his.

Ron hadn't always liked coppers.

It had been a Vauxhall, a nice enough motor though nothing special. It was soon after he'd got the job at the garage and funnily enough the day was his birthday. Everyone knew he was mad on motors and he got a lot of friends very soon because they were all mad on them round that district. A bloke he hadn't seen before told him there was a Vaux always stuck outside Maple's every day and would he like to deliver it to a mate of his?

Of course he'd asked what he meant exactly and the bloke said his mate just wanted to have a look at it.

'It's fifty for you.'

Ron had picked up the Vaux and they'd got him in the Edgware Road. They'd come up so quick that he never saw them in the mirror; there was the bell tinkling and the blue arm and the white glove swinging out of the window to slow him down and he was sitting there trying to think straight when they got out and came over, one on each side.

Up to that minute he hadn't let himself think what he was doing. There'd been nothing much to it: this bloke had told him about the Vaux and it was an easy fifty and anyone would be a fool not to pick it up, seven weeks' wages in half an hour, you'd be a lemon.

Now he started thinking, stuck in the seat with them coming over one on each side, and he'd thought: I couldn't have done it, this is what they call crime, I'm only Ron Webber and it can't have happened to me.

'Can I see your driving-licence?'

They hardly took their eyes off him. Log-book, insurance, all that.

'Are you the owner of this car?'

'No.'

'How do you come to be driving it?'

'I don't know.'

They looked at him again but it was God's truth, he didn't know. He knew he'd picked it up outside Maple's of course and that he was turning it in for fifty quid but he didn't know how he could have come to do such a thing without even giving it a minute's thought.

'All right, we're taking you along.'

He wasn't scared or anything and he gave no trouble. He was kind of waiting to wake up. Everything seemed just as usual; there were a few people stopping to have a look when the coppers put him into their Wolseley but they had ordinary faces and he nearly called out to one of them, a fat woman with a big black handbag, 'I won't be long!' It was a funny kind of dream.

Then gradually, with the worn steps of the police-station and the polished floor and green-shaded lamps and the crumpled-looking charge-book and their eyes under their peaked caps and the way they didn't smile, gradually he began knowing what he'd done and what it meant.

'I won't be long!' he'd nearly called out to the fat woman, but it was six months before he saw a girl again, or a bicycle, or a bunch of flowers.

They pulled in the whole gang and at first they thought he was one of them but Mr Clarke, a thin young feller with a lot of pens along his pocket, got the others to admit they'd tipped him off to do it because they knew he was young and mad about motors and would have done it for a dare without the fifty quid. They were all youngsters in that mob, kids almost. The bloke that had tipped him off had a funny name, Fagin or some such name as that. He was the ringleader and Mr Clarke said in the court: 'We have read about this man somewhere, haven't we? I would say his name was Fagin.'

Everyone was very pleasant and the magistrate had a kind sort of tone, though of course he was severe with it. 'It may well be that you are young and that you did this thing because someone else tempted you to do it, but the fact remains that the unlawful taking away of property is a serious thing for anyone to do, and unless you are given a sharp lesson you will be tempted to do it again. So I am going to send you to prison for six months.'

It didn't sound so bad even then, though it was springtime and the daffodils were out in the park. He'd seen Brixton often enough, it was part of the town, part of the skyline. But inside it wasn't part of anything.

It had all stopped.

All the people and shops and traffic and flowers and pigeons and frying tonight and the football. Stopped.

Stones. Under your feet, by your side, above your head, stones. Bars. In the window, in the door, along the galleries, bars. Cold. The stones, the bars, the bucket-handles, the water and the air, cold.

But the worst was inside your head.

What you doin' tomorrow, mate?
Nothing.
Where are you goin' next —
Nowhere.
When are you —
Never.
Are you thinkin' of —
No. No! I'm not thinking of anything so shut up sod you shut up will you for Christ's sake shut up!

Outside you did things but here you did nothing and went nowhere and six months meant never. You'd lost time. People outside could see this place but from inside it you couldn't see people. You'd lost people. You saw yourself with different faces on, waxy, shifty, the same garb with its itch at the back of the neck, the same hands with the skin blue at the knuckles, the same feet with their canvas on going down and back, along and back, up and down and in and out and back, *always back.*

They say there's —
Stop talking! That you talking, three-five-nine?
No, sir!
You'd lost your name.
What's your name, mate?
Three-five-nine.
Come off it, I mean what's your name?
It's three-five-nine sod you isn't that bloody good enough for you leave me alone will you!

He'd screamed the first night but they said a lot of them did that the first night.

There was this door, see, and it was shut, and when you tried it you found it was locked, but you went on thinking like you'd always thought when there was a locked door – here listen, who locked this bloody door? You got the key, have you? Then who's got it, who's got the key? Come on, I'm late as it is. Well, where's the caretaker then, eh, he'll have a key, he's bound to. Now don't mess me about, go and find the key.

The first night he'd sort of been two people, Ron Webber and three-five-nine, the boy asking for the key and the thing in its itchy garb shaking at the handle and knowing it couldn't get out and screaming *I can't stand this you got to let me out I can't stand this!*

Two of them had dragged him away and he'd hit out and they'd slugged him and the screws had come and thrown water on him and he'd seen the window, first, and thought it was morning. Then he saw the bars and remembered it didn't make any difference if it was morning or not.

Six months and this was the first night.

It was a long time after that, he didn't know how long, when the Governor's cat got in. Not close, he only caught sight of it down the end of the gallery, but it looked soft and warm even from that distance and he began shaking with excitement and he said to one of the screws:

'I've seen a cat!'

The screw looked at him out of his metal eyes.

'It'll be pink elephants next. Come on, sharp with that bucket now.'

Cats weren't for in here.

That had been the worst.

They met him when he came out, Florry the eldest and Marge. Aunty Miriam couldn't come, they said. They looked at him sort of queer as if something had happened to his face. He got rid of them as quick as he could and stayed in the park all day, moving when people came near so they couldn't look at him. That night he picked up a tart in Lisle Street and gave her all the money Florry had brought him, four pound seven and six, and the tart said it wasn't enough but he said it was all he'd got. He never touched her, it wasn't for that; he wanted someone to hold him, someone who wasn't sorry for him like his sisters were. The tart held him in her fat powdery arms like he told her to, and asked him if he was in some kind of trouble, but he said no, he wasn't in any kind of trouble. After he left her he found the notes back in his pocket, four quid, and thought sod it, I don't want people sorry for me.

A couple of nights later when he was walking down past Hyde Park he stopped dead with a kind of laugh inside him. There were black iron railings along the pavement, which was deserted except for the cat. He went up slowly so as not to frighten it but it wasn't a bit frightened of him and when he crouched down it got up on its back legs and pushed its head against his fingers with its eyes shut and he could feel it was purring.

It was weeks before he could look at the skyline when he went through Brixton. It didn't look the same, and he knew that it never would. And he knew another thing: whatever happened, no matter what happened to him, they'd never get him inside there again.

CHAPTER 3

Chris was the hit of the evening and when she came downstairs they gathered around her.

'Did she fight back?'
'Where is it?'
'Is the patient making rapid recovery?'
'It's more than I could've done . . .'
'Well let's have a look!'
'We put it down the loo,' said Laura and lit a cigarette. 'It was covered in chewing-gum.'

Alec got himself another drink. He'd been more worried than he knew; the idea of Mandy being hurt by anything made him depressed because it recalled a nightmare he'd once had: someone had been hurting her and he couldn't go to help her because someone else was holding him back.

'Go up, will you, darling?' Laura said.
'Sure. She crying?'
'Of course she's not.'
'Is it bleeding?'

Chris said indignantly: 'Are you calling me an amateur?'

Alec went upstairs, taking his drink with him: the full story of the operation would take much longer than the job itself.

Laura shut the door after him because there was some music on and Toops – having sensed drama – wasn't properly asleep yet. He would cut up rough in the morning when they couldn't show him the tooth.

Seeing the pink-and-white blob sinking through the

water she had thought, That's odd – there goes a bit of Mandy.

'On behalf of all those present . . .' Stan was calling above the music . . . 'I would like to extend my deep-felt thanks to Miss Florence Nightingale for her devotion to duty in this, our greatest hour of need. And I am sure she would forgive my adding —'

'Give it a rest, will you, Stan?'

Chris turned away and left him caught in a gesture suddenly foolish instead of funny; the only sound was the record playing, its tune meaningless.

They all looked at each other, their drinks, their hands, anywhere neutral. Stan gave a rueful grin and said nothing. Fay stepped in smoothly, saying to Laura: 'Poor old Alec, he's so relieved . . .'

Ron said: 'You heard Johnnie Delany sing this one, Stan? He really carves it up.'

Then they were all talking and Chris dropped into one of the deep chairs and closed her eyes as if she was listening to the record. She hadn't realized she was touchy about that subject: she had snubbed Stan without meaning to, without knowing she was going to do it.

It had seemed so worth while at the time and she'd worked like mad, they all had, straight out of school and into the PTS for three months as a student – preliminary introduction to Anatomy, Physiology, Hygiene, Public Health – it was a new world and a big one and she got distinctions in the Prelim. Training exams and then went on the wards. That was the most exciting day: she'd almost fainted. The long polished floor and the rows of beds, all those people to look after.

At the end of the first six months quite a lot of the other girls were falling by the wayside but she didn't see why; the only bad time for her was when Mr Johnson had died;

she was on duty that night and had to report it and help lay him out and she couldn't sort of understand what had happened to him. She saw now that death was a difference, but so big that there was no relationship between Before and After. First there'd been Mr Johnson with his chart and his crosswords and his two sons coming to see him every week and his stories of how he and the boys had 'done it on Jerry' in Normandy; then there was the cold white shape in pyjamas, heavy and with trapped gases escaping and the wrist-watch still ticking.

'Come along, there's nothing to be frightened of.'

'I'm not frightened, Sister.'

'Arms to the middle, then, and don't wake the others up.'

There was a kind of singing in her ears and the air went cold and her scalp felt tight and she heard herself saying, 'But where's Mr Johnson?'

'You can go to your room, Nurse.'

'I'm all right, but —'

'You will go to your room at once.'

On the way out of the ward she hit something, walked into it, and there were bruises when she woke up the next morning.

That was the only bad time; the rest was slave labour and sluice-cleaning in the surgical wards and listening to the other girls in the dining-room. About half of them had just wandered into nursing for the want of anything else to do; they were the ones who fell by the wayside; the others were the tough ones who slowly got the idea that the patients were there for use as basic material for advancement.

She would have stuck it out if it hadn't been for the discipline. She'd thought at first that it was designed to make nursing more efficient, to help the only people who counted – the patients. Then she saw that the discipline existed for its own sake.

'I think you know, Nurse, that the wearing of earrings is strictly forbidden.'

'*They're* pretty,' Mr Johnson had said in a whisper. 'Who gave them to you? Go on, tell me his name so I can think about him giving them to you.'

Mr Johnson didn't get much to think about in all those months.

A girl called Mavis had worked it out in exact figures. 'Ten of them are full-blown Lesbians – including Sister Gibbs, though you'd never believe it but I happen to know – and seven of those are males and the rest female. Five of them are pathological sadists, mental cruelty type, and we've got one shoe-fetishist – you know who *that* is. I'm not sure about Sister Hobbs but she spends a lot of time with her finger up the taps to make sure they're not furring, so she says. Any day now Sister Smith is going to chase Sister Chapman into a broom-cupboard with a No. 2 Bancroft enema and that will be the day, my little Christine, when I shall hand in my cards before I go stark raving bonkers like the rest of them.'

Chris had left the Hospital at the beginning of her third year when she was just coming up for her 'strings'. The big world she'd discovered had been getting smaller every day under her eyes and now it was suffocating and she had to get out.

She hadn't known, the day before she went to see Matron, that she was going. That evening the ward was very quiet and she was alone on duty; the long polished floor made a dull glow under the night-lamps and nearly all the patients were asleep. Being asleep they weren't in pain, and there was a stillness about them that forced her to lean at the doorway and keep still herself, just looking down the ward past the shadowy beds, listening.

'Are you comfy, Mr Allsop?'

'Jim. I'm fine. Call me Jim.'

It was so quiet that even the traffic sounded miles away.

'If there wasn't a chance, they'd tell me, wouldn't they?'

'Of course, Mr Maclean. You've no reason to worry, it's slow going, that's all.'

The wax flowers made blobs of colour halfway down the ward, blue and yellow in the pale light.

'There's none of them tucks me in like what you do.'

'We all try our best.'

'You're different. You're too good for this place.'

Moonlight from the windows came through a gap in the curtains and glowed in a glass.

She had resigned the next day because the next day would be like all the others and the peace she had known – the peace she had known for *them* – would be broken up on the sharpness of tongues and the indifference of eyes and the carping whine of Sister Romford's voice that put fear into the nurses and fear into the patients. The next day would be a charade like all the others with the staff parading their hates and intrigues in front of an unwilling audience of people who had been brought in here for healing and couldn't escape because they couldn't walk, couldn't wash themselves, couldn't refuse the disgusting food or tell the sisters that if they wanted to take it out on these young girls they should do it in private or go on the stage, one or the other.

She hadn't minded the interview with Matron. The woman's lips were set in a silent grimace of dismissal – *another broken reed!* – and she didn't trouble herself to comment on Nurse Compton's reasons; her only remark was time-worn and a standing joke in the dining-room: 'Well, you still have a great deal to learn, and I'm sorry you're choosing to deny yourself the opportunity.'

They decided you were responsible enough to be left in sole charge of a tracheotomy patient whose life depended on the tube you had to keep clear of phlegm but the minute you made a decision for yourself they realized you were a moron.

The interview hadn't upset her, and saying goodbye to the sisters had been an itching kind of pleasure; but from the day she left, the feeling that she had let them down – the people who counted, the patients – began and got worse as the weeks went on, and she had to talk to her friends about it before it gradually passed to the back of her mind and she could stop thinking about it.

But it would always be there.

The music had stopped and the automatic arm was swinging out of the way of the next record; she heard it clicking, and opened her eyes.

Stan was squatting on his haunches drawing something invisibly on the carpet to show Ron – a boat, it looked like. She got up and went over to them.

'I'm sorry, Stan.'

'What for, my love?'

'You touched a raw spot, that's all.'

'Oh, we've all got them. I can't tell you where mine is but look at the way I'm sitting!'

They both straightened up and Stan looked for Mike to tell him about the boat he'd seen for sale down at Antibes last year; he'd got ideas about that but so far no one seemed very keen.

'I keep telling you,' Ron said quietly to Chris, 'you can stop thinking about that bloody hospital. They were lucky to have you there for all that time, just you remember that.

Don't you do enough for people as it is, what with St Dunstan's and cooking for the Old People's Home every Sunday and that?' He stroked the curve of her ear in the way he had. 'Compared with you Florence Nightingale was dead selfish. Anyway Stan never meant it —'

'I know.'

'You think Florry'd go back there? You'd never get her near the place!'

'I know,' Chris said again, and wished Stan hadn't left them; she didn't want to talk about it.

Florry had been one of the few girls she'd got on with; they'd slipped over the wall at the Nurses' Home some evenings, the part where the laburnum tree was, and brought back some fish and chips to share with the other juniors. Then Florry had got fed up with the discipline and living in, and took a post as assistant to a midwife in Clapham where she had a bed-sitter, and that was where Chris went to see her some time later, to tell her she'd left the Hospital too. She'd met Marge there, Florry's younger sister, and the three of them had gone out together, the pictures and dances and things like that, for three or four months before she knew they had a brother.

He was there one night when she called in with a geranium in a pot for them because they'd never think about gaying the place up for themselves. They introduced him awkwardly.

'Your brother?'

It was too late to do anything about the surprise in her voice; it seemed to go on echoing all round the walls. But it wasn't really her fault: they'd never talked about him.

He wasn't much taller than she was, a wiry boy with a pallor and nervy eyes.

'That's a nice flower,' he said, and they all looked at the

geranium. Marge pulled off a leaf that had turned yellow. 'It's a lovely colour,' he said. Florry and Marge went on looking at it because they couldn't think of anywhere else, but their young brother seemed to be drinking it in, the bright crimson colour, as if he couldn't see enough of it.

'I was passing the shop,' Chris said, 'that's all.'

It was too soon to look at her watch; she'd only been here two minutes.

'I've been away.'

He was looking at her now, not at the geranium.

She thought he must have known his sisters had never talked about him; that was why he felt he should tell her he'd been away.

'Have you?'

Florry was putting the kettle on, though it was seven o'clock and they never had tea when she called: they either went round to the corner for some fish and chips or stayed here and had a rummage in the cupboard.

He was looking at her as he'd looked at the geranium, as if he'd never seen a girl's face before. His bright eyes were screwed up a little as if the light was too strong.

The gas popped and Florry turned it off and blew across the ring and Marge went to help her.

Instinctively Chris knew that she mustn't ask the usual polite questions, where had he been and was it a good trip.

'Are you glad to be back?'

He nodded quickly and his sharp strained face relaxed a little and she remembered a mongrel she'd rescued from some barbed wire once on a waste-ground; it had been frightened when she'd come up and then when she'd managed to get some of the fur free it had stopped trembling and she had seen trust come into its eyes.

40

'We thought we'd have some tea,' Florry said and lit the gas properly this time.

'I've got to go,' Chris said, and looked at her watch.

'Don't go.' He couldn't look away from her.

Marge was getting the cups and saucers from the long cupboard with the transfer on the door, a rose with ribbon round it.

'All right.'

She was able to smile for the first time, no longer worried that she shouldn't have come and shouldn't be here because whatever was wrong it was a family affair.

'I suppose we *want* tea?' said Marge doubtfully.

'Why don't we go down to the corner,' Chris suggested, 'and have a tuck-in instead?'

'There's some tins in the cupboard,' said Florry quickly, and Chris knew they didn't want to go out, or their brother didn't. The top corner of the cupboard door took a bit more plaster out of the wall as it always did.

The gas had stopped hissing and Marge gave a nervous laugh. 'The shilling's run out anyway.'

Chris picked up her bag. 'I'll go down for some fish and chips to make up the weight.' She could see there was nothing in the cupboard except sardines.

'I'll go with you,' their brother said and Florry turned her head and Chris looked at him in surprise; and in that half-second his courage and his trust had gone again. 'Shall I?'

'Well for the Lord's sake,' Florry said, 'if *you're* going why don't we all go?'

He looked at them in turn, uncertain, wondering what he'd started.

Chris took his hand – 'Come on then, the first there gets the best fish!' – and felt his hand jerk as she enclosed it and took him to the door; but by the time they reached the corner and the big sign on the window, *Frying Tonight*, it was the other way round and her hand was enclosed in his and she knew his courage had come back.

He didn't tell her until a whole year after, but of course she'd realized long before then.

In that year they'd seen a lot of each other and after the first few times when they'd spent an evening together he'd slowly changed and become the person he'd been before they'd met; she hadn't seen a new Ron emerging from the scared little sharp-faced animal, but the old Ron she'd never known – warm, confident, ready for anything. It was only when he'd called for her one night in the car he had borrowed from the garage where he worked that she saw him for a few minutes as he'd been the first time, his face nervy and his bright eyes narrowed while he told her about it.

She'd been sitting in for Alec and Laura again and when she reached the pavement Ron got out of the little car and held the door open for her.

'Milady's carriage awaits!' He had his best suit on.

'But Ronnie – where did you get it?'

'Borrowed it!' He gave an odd little laugh. 'Honest!'

She got in and shut the door and he came round to the other side.

'But who from?' It was almost new.

'Customer. She wants testing – I've had the head off and back in one day and she goes like a bird!'

These were his usual good spirits, yet tonight there was something forced about them as if he was having to play the part of his normal self, and when they pulled into the kerb in the park and he switched off the engine she knew there was something serious he had to do.

'There's a couple of things you've got to know, Chris.'

He didn't dramatize anything and he didn't blame anyone except himself. 'Everyone was quite fair and I've nothing to say against them.' He talked about the warders and although he didn't say anything bitter she had a clear enough picture of what it must have been like, especially for a sensitive boy like Ronnie. 'Of course, if those places were worth living in you'd have half the population bashing the other half on the head just to get sent in there, the grub's free and there's no taxes, after all.'

When he had finished she listened to the delicate tick of the clock on the dashboard, and a tremor passed across her mind and for an instant she was sad and frightened; either it was remembering Mr Johnson's wrist-watch or thinking what it must have been like for Ronnie in a cell.

'I knew about it,' she said, 'a long time ago.'

It was coming on to drizzle and the shiny black bonnet of the car turned slowly grey.

'You did?'

'Yes.' He was very quiet and she added: 'They didn't tell me, don't think that.' He would know she meant Florry and Marge. 'Nobody told me.'

The drizzle swirled in veils past the tall lamps. In the distance by the park gates a policeman was putting on his cape.

'Dear oh dear,' Ron said, 'I don't *look* like an ex-con, do I?'

He said it with so much alarm that she laughed and turned to him and looked at his impish face with its sharp strong nose and perky mouth and the intense light in his eyes.

'No,' she said.

'Well thank the Lord for that!'

Still with the laughter in her voice she said: 'What was the other thing?'

'What other thing?'

'You said there were a couple of things you wanted me to know.'

He nodded. 'That's right. I'd like to marry you. That was the other thing.'

It was so sudden that it didn't mean anything for a time. She knew he'd said it brusquely like that, almost defiantly, because he'd put himself on the defensive against a rebuff. And she knew that although this was the more important thing he had had to tell her, the other thing had come first because it would have been too late afterwards.

'You did it the hard way, Ronnie.'

'There wasn't any option, was there?'

'Yes.'

'Well I don't think there was.'

'I know.'

'There's no need – I mean you don't have to answer now, I mean not tonight.'

In a minute she said: 'Do you think you're ready for it, Ronnie?'

'Look here, I didn't tell you I wanted to marry you just because there was an awkward silence! I could've said it was coming on to rain, couldn't I?'

She felt laughter rising to her throat again because of his quick indignation and because this was the opposite of the way it should be, holding hands and talking softly and gazing into each other's eyes and all that; she wanted to laugh partly out of gladness because this way was much more real, more serious.

'You mean,' she said, 'you've thought about it first?'

'*Thought* about it? Dear oh dear, I haven't had a proper night's sleep for weeks!'

His hands were shaking and he realized it and held them

together but she could feel the whole of his body shaking with nerves; the whole car seemed to be vibrating.

'When I said did you think you were ready for it, I wasn't just being —'

'No, that's all right, it's hard to know what to —'

'I mean just being practical or —'

'Of course not, it was sprung on you, wasn't it – they put me inside for six months for knocking off a motor and will you marry me, that's what it must've sounded —'

'I couldn't care *less* about the bloody prison part of it!' She was suddenly impatient with him for not understanding and the next minute he was holding her and she was sobbing against him and even then, even with the hot welling up of her heart shaking her unbearably, she knew she had to tell him quickly or he'd think it was because the idea frightened her or shocked her because of the prison thing so she said, 'I'd like that,' but it got lost in all the other noise and she had to try again, 'I'd like that —'

'Like what?'

'Marry,' was the best she could do between sobs.

'Marry me? Us? Us marry?'

The words lost any meaning because any words did if you kept saying them over and over again but it wasn't the words he said that were funny, it was the tone of astonishment he said them with that finished her off.

His voice sounded far away – 'Well you don't sound very happy about it!'

All she knew after that was that laughter and tears were the same thing, otherwise you could never feel both of them at once.

The evening had reached the stage when the ashtrays were getting full and a glass had gone over and the record-player was going through the same sides for the second time because no one had turned them over and Alec was still upstairs.

The album was down from the shelf: the evening had reached that stage too. It didn't always happen but it usually started about this time or a bit earlier; their excitement about the coming holiday reminded them of the other years down at the Villa Mimosa, and someone would say, 'Do you remember when —' and someone else would say, 'Alec took a wonderful picture of that!' and they'd get the album down and open it on the floor and sprawl round it.

There was more laughter now and Stan was funnier because he'd had a few drinks and wasn't trying so hard, and Laura was thinking that she'd willingly go to bed with any of the men here if the chance came, not that it ever would – she'd make quite sure of that – so it was interesting to think about.

There was one of them all down at Antibes the first time: Chris looking very cool and sylph-like in a white swimsuit setting off her neat black hair, Ron standing on the tip of a plastic gondola because he was shorter than the other men in the group, Fay looking rather withdrawn but smiling – she never laughed easily – and Mike looking out of place in a pair of baggy shorts, more like a Victorian wrestler with all that hair on his chest.

Alec came down and dropped something into the wastepaper basket and turned off the record-player.

One of Stan standing on a deserted rock with one hand shading his eyes and the other holding an oar aloft with someone's panties hooked over the top. Alec had put the title underneath: *Another good girl gone wrong.*

'She all right, darling?'

'Nearly asleep.'

He dropped on to the floor between Laura and Fay.

'Who rang?'

'When?'

'A time ago.'

'Oh. Henry.'

One with Laura looking sulphurous, stretched out on the sand with her long hair dark from the sea and the sun in her eyes.

'What did he want?'

'Someone was getting tight. I had to tell Henry to throw him out with as much tact as possible.'

Laura laughed, and Stan idly watched the movement of her diaphragm and wished to Christ he didn't like old Alec so much.

Laura had laughed because Henry was the new barman at the Club, a practical soul who believed that an awkward member should leave the premises quietly and that the most tactful way of persuading him was to give him a sly rabbit-chop when no one was looking.

'What did you throw in the basket?' she asked through a yawn.

'Another *Bash!*'

'Oh. I didn't see her with it.'

When Alec had found the first one, Mandy had seemed so impressed by his lecture that they'd thought he'd sold her the general idea pretty well: 'Well that's a funny name for a comic – *Bash*! Now what makes them call it that?' Mandy had narrowed her large eyes, concentrating, just as Alec sometimes did. 'A comic's meant to make us laugh, but all I can see here is people hitting and shooting each other. Can't we be happy without bashing things? Look at this poor young man here, with someone driving a motor-car at him on purpose – now suppose that was poor little Toops being bashed up . . .' She hadn't even murmured when they'd taken the thing downstairs.

'It was under the bedclothes,' Alec said.

'We'll have to ask Chris to have a go at her.'

Her elbow was getting sore on the carpet. She looked at Chris, whose dark head was bent over the album; she didn't look much older than Mandy. 'I'm afraid I can't come any more,' Chris had said to them suddenly one night. 'I'm getting married.'

They'd both laughed, Laura and Alec, because she'd looked even younger, then.

Chris always made sudden decisions, Laura knew now. Leaving home, throwing up the nursing career, getting married – she'd never even mentioned Ronnie before that night.

'You can't leave Mandy now,' Alec had said. 'She'd break her heart.' Chris had been coming here on odd evenings to see Mandy anyway, even when they were staying in, and Laura would cook for three, or sometimes Chris would cook for them.

'I know.'

'You'll have to bring Mister Chris along with you, if you can get him to come.'

'All right.'

It was somewhere in the album, a big photo filling the whole page, Ronnie looking shined up like a kid on a school treat, Chris not so recognizable because the veil took away the intense blackness of her hair, Alec standing there like a duke with his topper gleaming, Mandy as a bridesmaid smiling prettily (without the gap that was there now). They hadn't known Mike and Fay then; they weren't complete.

'There she blows, my hearties!' Stan was tapping the colour-snap of a small blue boat beached in the shade of a palm tree with a notice on it: *A Vendre.* 'Now I reckon that if we club together and do her up a bit we've got ourselves a poor man's millionaire's yacht for peanuts!'

'I'd be sick,' Fay said.

'We'd feed you up on Quells, my love!'

Laura said deliberately, 'You'll have Dolly down there with you. There'll be no time for boats.'

Stan looked at her with one eyebrow lecherously cocked.

'It's got a cabin, hasn't it?' That drew a laugh because of the way he said it.

'And the rest of us can sit on the roof,' said Ron, 'and talk in loud voices about what nice weather we're getting for this time of the year!' And that got a bigger laugh because it brought them all into the act.

Laura sat up and rubbed her elbow and Chris said: 'Ronnie, we've got work in the morning.' She brushed a lock of hair back and looked at him thoughtfully for a moment because the album always reminded her of their first years together; this room reminded her too; it was here she'd first told anyone, and Alec and Laura had laughed, she still didn't know why.

She'd been wrong, thinking Ronnie might not be ready for it. 'It's just that you didn't play much when you were a kid,' she had said to him.

'I didn't?'

'You've told me yourself, so have Florry and Marge – you had to look after the place all the time —'

'But we enjoyed it.'

'I know, because you were doing it for your Mum. But you still didn't play, like most kids. What I mean is, perhaps you ought to do a bit now, and get it out of your system.'

'All right, I'll go and stick a bed-pan on Nelson's Column an' let a few tyres down on the taxi-rank an' drop a banana skin outside Buckingham Palace, won't take me long and it's dead easy – in the old days they had to go an' slay monsters, proper rough it was.'

She didn't know if he'd understood what she was trying to say, about playing, or if he'd decided it wasn't important; she knew that she'd never laughed so easily before she'd met him, and that might be more important to them both.

Alec got up and turned on the record-player as he always did at this time, to show he didn't want them to go; he'd never failed to do this even when it had been a tough day at the Club and he was dog-tired.

He caught sight of the comic in the waste-paper basket and wished Mandy hadn't put it under the bedclothes like that.

Laura picked up the photograph album and slid it into the bookcase between the Ronald Searle and *The Decameron*, taking away a glass someone had left on the top shelf.

Then they were all talking, saying goodnight, with Chris going '*Shhh!*' because of waking Mandy and Toops. The men were in a group near the door and Alec was fetching coats.

'It was a lovely evening, Laura.' Fay, rather formal.

Someone's cigarettes and lighter.

'I'll give you a ring if I don't hear.'

'A Twiggy, you can tell that.'

The record was *Something Stupid*, turned down low.

'Aren't they nice?'

'No, that's mine, Alec.'

Near the door Ron heard Mike saying, 'Not Friday. I've got something lined up.'

He was talking to Stan.

Ron turned his head in a little jerk to make sure the

girls weren't listening; then he looked at Mike again, his eyes sparkling with interest. 'Friday? But that's when we're going!'

Under his breath Stan was intoning, "Allo, 'allo, 'allo ...'

'You're kidding,' Ron said.

'Me?' Mike gave his quick smile.

'Well you're cutting it fine then.' Ron's sharp face was alive with mischief.

Then the girls were coming over and Stan said loudly – 'Alec! Where've you put my Hamburger?'

It was what he always called his hat; it was part of the 'Stan patter'.

'Come on, Ronnie,' said Chris and took his hand in hers.

They were the first to go.

And now on this late May evening the first words had been spoken and it had begun.

CHAPTER 4

Alec had been ten minutes in the Calidarium and the sweat had got into his eyes. He sat letting them water.

Someone came in, his rubber sandals squelching.

Through the doorway Alec could hear one of the regulars – the big man with the birthmark – sounding off about losing a packet on the dogs. Nobody was answering him; nobody ever did. Maybe they'd be more interested if he told them he'd won something.

Alec sat with the half-thoughts ebbing and flowing through his mind. He ought to sack Henry, or give him a final talk; he couldn't go on treating the members like that, it wasn't that kind of club . . . It was going to be as hot as this down there, with any luck, but dry, not like this; how would they talk old Stan out of buying that boat? It didn't look seaworthy . . . Better get Laura's mother something for when she arrived, crystallized fruit or something . . .

The chap who'd come in went squelching out again, couldn't take it.

The showers hissed.

Fifteen minutes, must be a record. Overdoing it.

Alec slopped across the marble floor and sat down in the main hall. Throbbing behind the eyes.

They wandered about in their towels with nothing to do but wait till they'd had enough.

The masseur was slapping the hell out of someone.

'How's tricks, Alec?'

His eyes were still watering and he wiped them.

'Oh hello, Jim. How's it going?'

'Mustn't complain.'

They were silent for a time.

Jim was in 'D' Division, coming up for sergeant. They'd been at the East Cheam Grammar together, swopped catapults for liquorice, it didn't want thinking about how many years ago. Alec had bought the record-player from Jim when Jim had gone for the telly.

'I thought Friday was your day?'

'We're off on Friday night,' Alec said. 'There'll be packing, and seeing to the Club.'

'Lucky bugger.'

'You get holidays, don't you?'

'Not starting Friday. How's Laura?'

'Fine.' He slid the sweat from his arms.

'Taking the nippers, are you?'

'Not this trip, it's adults only. Laura's fetching her mother up from Brighton. It makes a change for her to see a bit of London. Then we'll take the kids down there in September.'

They did the same thing every year.

The fat man passed them, wiping himself with his towel; he looked like an overblown Caesar in the Forum.

'Strewth,' Jim muttered, 'that bloke's well-hung.'

'You're a very observant young officer of the law.'

'Well I wouldn't need a telescope, would I?'

Alec snorted in amusement. Jim's tone had put on just the right degree of mild shock to make it funny.

'How's Phyllis?'

'All right. Tired. The kids, you know.'

'I can imagine.'

Jim and Phyllis had four.

'How's business?'

'Gets on my tits,' said Jim, 'sometimes.' He mopped his

face and neck. 'Look at last week. Case came up, a young chap I'd pulled in, took a bloke's wallet. A quid, I ask you, not even lucky. Know what they've done? Put him on probation.'

In a minute Alec said: 'Well that gives him a chance, doesn't it?'

'That's what they all think. Give the lad a fair chance, it's his first offence. It fair makes me puke. That lad's got no chance. His old man's an epileptic, brings home ten quid a week working in a rehabilitation centre, the only job he can find. His old woman does a part-time job at a laundry, brings in another two-pound-ten. Our lucky lad's got two brothers and a sister, all younger than him an' none of them earning, not left school. Six of them. Twelve-pound-ten.'

He was silent for a time, feeling it worse than Alec because he hadn't been into the Calidarium yet.

'Mr Bates!' an attendant called. 'Three on the dot!'

A boxer went past, playing his muscles, admiring them, the sweat shining on them.

'Eighteen meals a day, every day. Clothes, chemist – you can add up, Alec. This lad was half-starved when I ran him in. I sent out for buns while he was bein' charged. Now they've put him on probation – sporting chance. My arse. That lad's going to pinch again and he'll be run in again.' He kept his voice low but its tone now grew intense. 'It's not so much that the family's on the borderline – there's close on a million homes like that in London – hand to mouth and often as not the hand's got nothing in it. It's that the probation officers don't *know* this kid's background, haven't troubled to find out, like I have. Now what the bloody hell's the good of giving a lad like that a chance of mending his ways? That was what the Beak said: a chance of "mending his ways". The poor little sod's not even got a chance to eat!' He mopped his neck, pulling the towel over his head and his wet hair over his face. His voice was muffled. 'An' he lives inside a couple o' miles of Buckingham fucking Palace.'

They sat for minutes not talking.

A steam-pipe was leaking somewhere, making a noise like a never-ending fart.

'That's what gets on my tits. Next time it'll be six months and they'll say he's already been given a fair chance an' won't learn. Won't learn.'

'Never mind, Jim. They say mustard yellow's going to be all the rage this year at Ascot.'

Jim got up after a while. 'Well, remember me to Laura, eh?'

'I will. Same to Phyllis.'

Jim drifted off towards the hot-room.

Alec finished with a cold shower.

Lying on the bed with his eyes shut, he started worrying again about Laura. Her mother could easily get on a train but Laura always fetched her in the Cortina. She'd take her time on the run back – her mother was nervous – but she'd drive too fast on her way down, alone. She drove well – did everything well, Laura, had a lot of style – but these days out on the road you were out on a limb.

Worrying got you nowhere. She'd be all right.

He'd begun sweating again, getting his clothes on.

When he took his things from the box on his way out he asked for an envelope and tucked a couple of pounds in it with a pencilled note for Jim to pick up when he left.

Give it to the kid, will you? Keep smiling, Alec.

They knew where to find him because he was on probation.

Not that he was fooling himself. In the long run it wouldn't do the kid any good; he was just buying off his own conscience.

Ron Webber didn't come to the Club often because of a lot of reasons. Chris got home before six most evenings and they'd have a meal in or go to a flick or pop across to see her Mum and Dad, take something; and the Club was a bit swish and his nails were always black, you couldn't help it; and although Alec had made him an Honorary Member – it sounded great, that, Honorary Member, good as a title – he still couldn't really afford the drinks because it always meant a couple of rounds and no one wanted a beer, Scotch was the thing of course, being a club.

But he liked coming here, once he'd made up his mind, because he'd never seen anywhere done up as good as this, lovely woodwork everywhere – Alec was keen on wood, like in his flat – and dark, well not dark, subdued lighting, they called it, and plenty of room to walk about in, you weren't pushed up in the corner like at the Bow Bells, nothing like that, you could stroll about, take your drink with you, and the people were interesting, talked very quiet, you could imagine there was a lot going on in this place, underneath the talk – you could just see Sean Connery coming in here or Michael Caine, not saying anything, just walking in quietly and all the talk stopping suddenly, dying away, and heads turning, till someone would say 'How'd it go?' and he'd say 'Terrifico . . .' and you'd know there'd been something big on. That was the sort of place it was.

Ron only ever came here when Chris was out late; she was the staff nurse at England's, the Oxford Street branch, and sometimes she'd look in on one of the girls if they'd been sent off home during the day, to see if they were getting on all right.

It had been rough today at the garage; first he'd wrung off a sump stud and taken nearly an hour to drill it out; then Woodhouse had come in – the son, he was a proper young tearaway – with his S.U.'s off-balance, and they were a real swine because he'd got the works to fit them up with hydraulic linkage to stop lumpy running and of course it wasn't standard – you could tune a pair of S.U.'s inside five minutes in the ordinary way but young Woodhouse was always on to the gadgets and then complained when his motor sounded like porridge on the boil; finally he'd let the hoist down on his foot and was lucky to get away with nothing broken.

He'd been thinking, on and off all day, about seeing Mike, couldn't get it out of his mind; perhaps that was why he'd been all fingers and thumbs. So when Chris had given him a tinkle and said she'd be later tonight he'd not been sorry in a way, just for once.

He'd come in quietly, taking it slow, not looking at anyone, just lighting up a cigarette and blowing out the smoke, and some of them had turned their heads to see who'd come in.

Honorary Member.

'You pranged a banger, have you, Ron?'

'What, me? No. Why?'

Mike looked at Alec, meaning a drink for Ron.

'I thought you were limping.'

'Oh, that. No, I was standing too near the hoist. Hello, Alec.'

'How's it going, Ron?'

'Not so bad. Is that for me?'

'On Mike.'

'That's handsome. My turn next.'

He knew he shouldn't have said it; he wouldn't have said it down at the Bow, you took it for granted that when someone gave you a drink, you'd give them one back; it was just this place, he wanted them to know he could stand his turns even in this place. He'd have to stop saying it.

They'd been talking about Stan's boat and he joined in and watched their faces, trying to see if they'd been talking about the other thing; but he couldn't tell; they were both the quiet sort, Alec and Mike.

But he *had* to know.

Alec left the bar to talk to someone who'd come in, and Ron looked into his Scotch and said:

'Something big, is it?'

Mike had his quick smile on and his bushy red eyebrows went up into two little horns. 'Well well. I didn't think you'd be interested.'

They looked at each other and had a quiet chuckle. They understood each other.

Ron was suddenly thinking of Chris because this one was strictly for the boys. Last night after they'd left Alec's place she'd asked him what they'd been talking about near the door; she didn't say what made her ask, but of course he knew it was because she'd noticed their heads together, the three of them (Alec had been fetching coats). He'd just said it was Stan talking about one of his women – she knew what Stan was.

'I wouldn't say big,' Mike told him.

There was no one near them.

'What would you call it then?'

'A pushover.'

Ron screwed his face up in frustration, eager to understand. 'But why *Friday*?'

'Quite a few good reasons. You could think of one.'

Ron swung the Scotch around in his glass. This was great. This was what the others did, stood in little groups talking quietly under the dim lights, a drink in their hands. Great.

'Yes,' he said. 'You'll be skipping out right afterwards.'
'That's it.'

The thing they all knew about Mike – not the people here at the Club, just Alec and Stan and the girls – was that Mike was a professional. Well, not exactly a professional, because he ran a small house-agency business, that was his living, his actual profession. But he'd done a few jobs, professionally. Put it like this: he didn't just go after *anything*, hit or miss, in the hope of getting away with it; no, he'd plan a job, set it up, carry it out and come away clean, just like a doctor with a bit of surgery to do, or like a mechanic with a motor to fix up, put it that way. Professional.

So when he said he'd got 'something lined up', that was what he meant. It was a job.

Of course they never talked about it. It was his business. They never even knew when he was 'working', because as far as Mike was concerned there was nothing to it. That's why it had come out so casual last night – Stan had asked him round for a drink or something (Ron hadn't heard that part), and Mike had just said not Friday, he'd got something lined up (that was the part Ron had heard). But it was interesting, and that was why Ron had been thinking about it on and off all day. It was the first time he'd ever heard Mike say such a thing – just as anyone might say not Friday, I'm going to the dentist – and it was interesting to know there was the date fixed and everything.

And it was obvious now why he'd picked on Friday. The plane they'd booked up was a night flight – reduced fare, night-time, that was why they always did it – and

Mike would be off out of the country right after he'd done his little job.

Ron felt a kind of tickling inside him and it made him laugh, though he brought it out quietly because everyone was quiet in here, it was that sort of place.

'You really are a terror,' he said, 'oh dear oh dear...'

'Is that a fact?' Mike could obviously see the funny side of it too.

It was Ron's turn and he asked Henry the barman to give them the same again.

'You're gaining on me,' Mike said.

Ron saw that he still had some Scotch in his glass. He'd finished his own already, perhaps because he was used to beer, or because he felt excited.

'You don't have to hurry,' he said. He didn't suppose Mike felt excited at all, that was the funny thing.

He wanted to go on talking about it but didn't like to; it was Mike's business after all.

They talked about Fay, and Mike said she was here, hadn't he seen her when he'd come in? And Ron looked round and saw her sitting alone at the end of the banquette against the wall where there was the great big blown-up photo of Monte Carlo – 'Mount Charles', as Alec called it because that's what it meant. Then they talked about Barney, who was Mike's son by his first marriage, rising nineteen now and in the Merchant Navy; Mike often brought postcards round to Alec's place to show them all, ones Barney had sent him from places like Buenos Aires and Sydney and that.

Then without knowing it was in his mind Ron was saying:

'What makes it such a pushover, then?'

Mike nearly choked on his drink, laughing.

He didn't have an ordinary kind of laugh, out loud –

his eyebrows sort of jerked up and down and all you could hear was a kind of whimpering noise, bottled up. That was when he really let himself go, like he did now.

'I'm just interested,' Ron said, 'that's all.' He felt a bit narked, because he didn't see what was so funny.

'You are?' Mike said.

'Well of course. I mean you're a chum of mine, and that.'

'You can come in on it if you like.'

Mike was only smiling now, watching him as you might watch a kid you'd just bought an ice-cream for. They all treated him like that because he was the shortest, that was the trouble, they wouldn't take him seriously.

'All right.'

There was only ice now in the bottom of the glass.

That was the second one. He'd have to stop now.

'You can drive a car,' Mike said, 'so they tell me.'

That was a compliment, by the way he said it. It was one thing they all admitted: he might be a short-arse but he could take a motor through the eye of a needle without touching the sides.

It didn't matter now, the way Mike had laughed, before.

'What's the set-up?'

It was one of the phrases he'd got from Alec. It sounded good. Especially in a place like this.

The tickling had changed to a sort of tingling now – oh, there was a difference all right, this was going right through him, all down his veins, warm and kind of gold-coloured. He could feel how straight his shoulders were, without moving them, very strong they felt, and his feet were firm on the ground.

'We'll meet up,' Mike said.

'Not at my place.'

'No.'

'Where then?'

'You name it.'

'I don't know.'

He just couldn't think of anywhere. It had all come so quick.

'Alvin's?'

That was the garage where Ron worked. Mike always got his petrol there.

'Next door,' Ron said. 'The café. I go for my dinner there.'

'Fair enough. I've got to look in tomorrow anyway for a service.'

'All right.' He wanted to go now. He wanted to stop talking about it.

'What about another one?'

'That's my lot, Mike, thanks.'

Mike seemed to know he had to go. 'Chris out late tonight, is she?'

'She'll be back by now.'

'Give her my love.'

'I will.'

He went across to spend a minute with Fay, sitting alone under the great big photo.

'You're looking great,' he said. She really was.

'That's nice of you, Ronnie. Have you hurt your leg?'

'Eh? No. My foot, that's all. A bit.'

'Chris'll fix it up.'

'Oh, yes.' He couldn't see Alec anywhere. He ought to say goodnight to him. 'I've been talking to Mike.'

'Have you?'

She was watching him, her slow brown eyes looking all over his face. Perhaps she was wondering how bad his foot was, if it hurt.

'Yes.'

He wanted to go.

'It's quiet here tonight,' she said.

'Yes. Look, when you see Alec, tell him goodnight for me, will you?' He'd seemed to say it all in a rush.

'Of course.' She sounded surprised.

'I can't see him anywhere.'

'Never mind. I'll tell him.'

'Will you?'

'Of course.'

'Well, goodnight, Fay.'

'Goodnight, Ronnie.'

And out.

CHAPTER 5

The week seemed to go quickly.

With the holiday getting near there was more to think about than usual. Laura spent a lot of time on the phone; she was organizing the trip and the others let her look after them because she was good at that kind of thing. On Wednesday she rang Fay to make sure her passport hadn't run out and of course it had, Fay being Fay, and Laura whipped round there in the car and took her off to the Passport Office to fix it up.

Alec was busy checking stores at the Club and briefing George, his brother, who was going to take over while he was away. They never saw much of each other: George lived out of London and their wives had never quite hit it off, but he was in the catering business and his head was well screwed on and Alec could trust him to see that everything went on running smoothly. Henry the barman had been given a 'final' talk by Alec and seemed to take it the right way; he didn't yet realize that the most important people at the Club were the members but he was dead honest and would never touch the till or the booze, which made up for a lot of things.

Chris got home later than Ron every evening this week because she had to show her replacement the ropes – a girl with a slightly cleft palate and the name of Henrietta, both of which were a bit off-putting (she wouldn't even call herself Hetty); but she was a first-class nurse and Chris had nothing to worry about on that score. England's was a big place, twenty-five main departments on five floors, and the important thing Chris had to do was more or less introduce Henrietta – always as 'Miss Wanstead' or some of them would have laughed outright – to the rest of the staff and then warn her in private that quite a few of them would be trying it on with her so as to get off work; she even gave her the secretly-filed list of menstruation dates so that none of them could swing that one on her. Henrietta seemed to be taking it all in so far, and from the girl's starchy approach Chris was already beginning to think that England's would turn out to be the fittest store in town by the time she got back from the holiday.

She didn't like getting home after Ron because it was her place to cook the supper; but he said she worked as hard all day as he did, so where did she get that idea? Whoever got home first had the job, that was the fairest way. He was so good about it and he knew what a saucepan was for and could prove it.

Tuesday night he looked upset about something; he said he'd had a rough day – someone's carburettors had got the wrong way round or something – and she'd had to massage his foot, which was bruised. He said there wasn't anything else on his mind at all and she didn't persist: he'd gone along to the Club, not feeling like getting the meal, and it was probably the whisky – it didn't suit him. They got in about the same time and went straight out again for a pizza down at the coffee-bar; he said why shouldn't they live it up a bit when they'd had a hard day? He was wonderful company, even when his foot hurt and everything.

This week didn't seem to be going so quickly for Stan.

On Wednesday he hit the roof. One of the girls had cheeked a client – Mrs Davenport, a nice woman who'd been coming for months – and when he'd blown her up in the privacy of the staff-room she'd burst into tears, a thing he couldn't stand because they only did it to make you lay off and you had to lay off even though you knew that, because you couldn't keep on piling into them when they were carrying on like a bloody fountain.

He walked out in the end, got into the Jag and went like a bat out of hell up the road to see if Mike was in; he sometimes did that; it was only a couple of miles and Mike could pull him out of a mood in five minutes flat without even trying.

Mike was alone in the front office so he dropped into a chair and put his feet on the desk where the three-colour stand-up cut-out said *Your Home is Here* and let out a long whistling breath.

'You know what women are for? Poking and shooting, in that order.'

'Is that a fact?' Mike got up and shut the door of Mrs Hallowes's office. 'You're as bad as Dan MacDory.'

'Who the hell's he?'

Mike slid the chrome cigarette-box across. 'He was a big tough Yank who joined a trading-company up near the North Pole, and the boys there said he had to do three things to prove how tough he was – drink a bottle of corn-whisky, shoot a polar bear and poke an Eskimo girl in that order. Well Dan MacDory knocked off the bottle and staggered out into the snow and came staggering back in ten minutes with his gun smoking and hollered out – "Okay, now where'sh the bear?"'

Stan began feeling better already but he still had to get it off his chest and Mike sat there listening to it.

'Look, I'm a hair-stylist and I'm good at it, worked hard at it, got five diplomas and two international gold medals though one was a fiddle but never mind, say it myself

I'm the best, give me ten minutes with a sheepskin rug and you'll be asking it for the next dance, I'm not big-headed I'm just telling you – but these sooty-eyed little cows that come to me for training are enough to drive me up the wall and round the bend! Eighteen months I've spent with one of them and you can take that look off your face, I wouldn't go as far as the top of the stairs with her even if she had a sack over her head – eighteen months, cutting, setting, tinting, perming, the lot, shown her all I know, and d'you think she's learned anything? If Madame Pompadour ever walks in there she'll go out looking like a lavatory-brush. Tactful with the clients, too – oh, she's the soul of tact I can tell you – we had a Mrs Davenport in today, a fine woman, you'd go for her, python shoes and a Bentley outside, but charming, very charming, and she mentioned very quietly that one of the towels wasn't clean, and what does this soppy little cow go and tell her? "Well, it was clean when I put it on, Mrs Devonport!" – couldn't even get her name right!'

Stan's deep voice hardly ever rose into even the medium register; it was like the bass string of a 'cello and sometimes Mike, sitting here with him on similar occasions, had heard the Marley Tile ashtray vibrate on the desk. He sat listening with the amusement compressed inside him while Stan's indignation reached its peak and began subsiding. Stan was like most men of his type: handsome, virile, devoted womanizers, their biggest trouble in life were the women they adored.

When the tirade was over he stubbed out his cigarette and took another from the chrome box.

'You'll get ulcers,' Mike said.

'I've got 'em.'

'Never mind. Friday's coming.'

'I'm bored stiff with crimping, you know. Bored stiff.' He blew out a stream of smoke.

'You'll give it up one day, Stan.'

'One day. Too true.' He took his polished shoes off the display desk. 'Well, how's it with you?'

'Getting near the off.'

The casual way he said it reminded Stan and he looked at the inner door and lowered his tone. 'What is it you've got lined up?'

'Only the usual. A peter.'

Good boy. What's in it?'

'Six grand or so.'

Stan gave one of his short low whistles. 'That'll keep the wolf from the door.'

'I shan't get all of it away.' He watched a young man and his girl through the glass door; they seemed interested in the Bijou 68 down in the corner; everyone was, it was a smashing little design.

They didn't come in. They went off, her hand in his arm.

'Why not?' asked Stan.

'Because it'll be mostly in ones. Ones and fives. It's a district where I wouldn't carry a case at night.'

Stan wanted to laugh because old Mike took the whole thing so casually. Anyone looking through the glass door would think they were talking about weather-proofing and rateable values.

'Well there must be an answer, Mike.' It was a bloody shame to leave any of it behind.

'Not really. I don't want to push my luck.'

Mike was gazing at him blankly and Stan could see his mind was a long way off, trying to work out the problem. Stan knew him pretty well and it struck him that the others – Ron and Alec – probably wouldn't have gone as far as this in the conversation. Stan thought that Mike probably wouldn't have let them.

'Well isn't there something *I* can do?' It worried him to think of Mike going to all the trouble of cracking the thing and then having to leave some of the stuff behind. He wouldn't have known about this job at all if Mike hadn't mentioned the other evening that he'd got 'something lined up'. Now that he knew a bit more he might as well show willing. It wasn't called the Old Firm for nothing.

'I wouldn't like to ask you,' Mike said.

The liveliness had come back into his eyes and they had that glint of amusement again as he looked at Stan.

'You haven't asked. It was my idea.'

Stan wasn't a fool. If he was going to lend a hand with this job it would have to be on Mike's terms: and Mike's terms would be that Stan would be coming in as a volunteer responsible for himself whatever happened. And he didn't want Mike to have to tell him that.

'Well I should forget it,' Mike said.

'I've only just thought of it!' He flicked ash off his cigarette and cocked one eyebrow again at the door of Mrs Hallowes's office. She was typing. 'Give me the drift, then I'll know what the bloody hell you're talking about.'

Mike opened a drawer and took out a nail file and began picking at his nails, his head down and his double chin appearing. Stan knew that he was trying to decide whether to let him in or not; Mike was a pro and very efficient – meticulous was the word; and he couldn't afford to monkey about. He'd never talked to Stan on this subject but Stan felt pretty sure he always did a job on his own and was quite ready even to leave some of the stuff behind him rather than bring someone else in to help.

'It's in the City. You know what it's like there after closing hours.'

'Like a graveyard.'

'That's right. This place is an alley where you can't get a car – it's the back entrance. I wouldn't even want to park a car anywhere near there, not for any time. So I was going to walk it down as far as the Bank and then find a taxi. And it's not a district where I'd want to carry anything: a briefcase wouldn't look so bad but it'd be too small. So it's a question of pockets.'

He didn't look up.

Stan wanted to bust out laughing again. It seemed a long time ago when he'd walked in here worrying his guts out about that wet little cow and Mrs Davenport.

He said: 'Well I'll bring my camel-hair. It's got pockets like rucksacks.'

Mike looked up now.

'It'll be a cold night if this weather keeps in.'

And now Stan laughed, deep in his chest.

'I'll bet you even study the weather reports!'

Leaning forward Mike said seriously: 'You go down Threadneedle Street in a camel-hair coat on a warm night and you're running a risk.'

'Okay,' Stan said, 'I've got a lot of respect for you.'

'I don't like risks, see?'

'That makes two of us,' Stan said. 'Now where do we take the stuff?'

'Over the Channel.'

'Goes with us all the way, does it?'

'That's right. I know a man down there. He takes twenty-five and there's no one in London who'll do it for less than forty. It's worth it to him because the Swiss frontier's not far, and it's worth it to me because once I've got francs there's no trace.' He beamed gently. 'No risk.'

Stan was eyeing him sideways now. 'You do this every year, do you then? Every Old Firm's Outing?'

'Do what?' asked Mike, and Stan laughed again.

'Well stone those bloody crows . . .'

The phone rang and Mike pressed a switch and it went on ringing in the other office until his secretary picked it up.

'I've got to go and show someone a house.' He looked at his watch.

'Sod it,' Stan grunted. It had been getting interesting.

'They told me they'd ring sharp at twelve if they'd made up their minds to view.' He beamed suddenly. 'They're nice people and it's a nice house.'

'Then I hope they buy it. They're in good hands, I'll say that much.' Mike was the most honest estate agent in the business and there weren't so many.

Mrs Hallowes came out of her office and said something about the Parkinsons and Mike told her he'd go and pick them up. When she'd gone away Stan said quietly:

'We'd better fix a date. To talk.'

'All right, Stan.' He got up and took his raincoat off the peg; the sky had turned dark while they'd been talking.

'We tell the others?' Mike would know he didn't mean the girls.

'Ron knows.'

'Oh, does he?' That was a disappointment: there'd been a nice exclusive feeling about helping Mike on a job.

'He was dying to come in on it but I shan't let him – he'd get too excited.'

They both laughed about that. Ron was like a wagon-load of monkeys.

Mike shrugged his raincoat on. 'But he's coming for the

ride – he'd have broken his heart otherwise. He can pick us up, save us finding a taxi.'

Stan got his black Homburg. 'You know something? I feel a bloody sight more cheerful now than when I came in here a few minutes ago!'

Mike shone his quick little smile.

'We always try to please.'

CHAPTER 6

Suddenly it was Friday and even though they had all been preparing for it throughout the week there still seemed a lot to do.

At breakfast Alec asked when Laura expected to be back with her mother and she said:

'About tea-time. It depends when I can start off from here.'

'Start early.'

'That's easily said.' She got up and brought the coffee in. 'I haven't seen the newsagent yet – Mother always likes the *Express* and we don't want anything to keep on coming – or do we? What about your *Newsweek*, do you want to have it sent just the same?'

'I can get it down there. Leave things like that till you get back from Brighton.'

Rain was hitting the windows.

'There won't be time, with Mother here.' Half impatiently she said: 'I won't drive fast.'

'You always do, and the roads are wet.'

'For God's sake, I've driven in the rain before now, Alec.'

She didn't like being protected.

'Did you get the screen-washer fixed?'

'Yesterday. Ronnie did it himself.' She poured coffee for him. 'Is he all right?'

'Ron?'

'Yes.'

'How d'you mean, "all right"?'

73

'He seemed – I don't know – tense.'

'Really? I'll give him a ring.'

'What have I said?' She sipped her coffee and grimaced and put some sugar in. 'He's all right.' Ronnie didn't want protecting any more than she did, but you only had to say a thing like that to Alec and he was ready to lay down his life for someone or other. 'You should have joined the Boy Scouts – you'd have been a big success.'

His smile was slow. 'You think the uniform would suit me?'

They'd had almost a row about it once: he'd got someone out of a jam and finished up the loser and she'd told him exactly what she thought, surprising herself by her own vehemence. Her view was that the only people worth helping in life were those who'd never ask for it; the others would leech on to you and suck you dry. She'd even brought Chris into it – this was soon after Chris had begun sitting in for them and they hadn't known her very well – and Alec had said finally:

'Look, there's nothing wrong in a girl visiting the kids at St Dunstan's once a week or cooking a meal for the Old People's Home. The reason why most of us can't stomach that kind of goodwill is because we know we ought to be doing the same thing now and again, and we resent them for showing us we're a thoroughly useless bunch of egocentrics.'

'That hardly includes you, does it?'

'Certainly it does. All my time is spent in looking after Number One, planning how to get what I want, or what I think I want – a more comfortable flat, a new car, good clothes, expensive pictures, Scotch in cut-glass to hand to my friends so that they can see how well I'm doing —'

'Well thank God you're *human*!'

'Oh, sure. That's always the perfect excuse. That's what the word really means, doesn't it? It means weak, selfish, greedy – it never means anything good.'

They'd closed the argument, both intelligent enough to know that basic convictions could never be changed by the opposition of mere words, but only deepened.

A film was forming on the surface of the coffee in the percolator.

'More?'

'No thanks.'

'I shouldn't have said that about the Boy Scouts.'

'So I don't qualify after all?' He pretended to look hurt.

'You qualify all right.'

He never minded her getting at him on this subject; for one thing he knew perfectly well that the idea of helping others was praiseworthy in some people but suspect in himself – it was too easy to slap your conscience down by a good deed deliberately planned; for another thing he knew she was impatient with him because – or partly because – she was trying to come to terms with her upbringing, as most people were. In her case she'd been blessed with a father once described by a divorce judge as 'a drinker, lecher and seducer of young women', and although she loyally pretended to see him as a gay Lothario she secretly knew he was a mess.

That was why her mother's visits usually began with a resentful attack on Alec's 'goodness'. He didn't mind.

She asked: 'Will you be here this afternoon?'

She knew of course that he would; she had asked to show that it wasn't taken for granted.

'With your mother coming?'

'She wouldn't expect it, Alec.'

'That's why I want to be here.'

Laura's mother had stopped expecting to be considered a long time ago; she would date it from the first month of her marriage.

'She knows you'll have things to see to at the Club.'

'I'm going back there tonight anyway. Ron's giving me a hand – some crates are being delivered some time about six and I can't leave it all to George.'

She pushed her chair back, picking up her napkin from the floor. 'Well keep an eye on the time, Alec. Airport Terminal, 11.20.' She went over to the telephone.

'If I'm held up,' he said, 'you go on ahead. And don't worry, I'll be there for the plane.'

She was checking the list of people who had to be phoned – laundry, grocer, dairy – and he didn't know if she'd registered what he'd just said.

'All right, Alec.'

He would tell her again this afternoon.

The rain had stopped by midday but the air and the streets were still wet and people on the pavements kept away from the kerb because the buses were sending up spray. Umbrellas were drying in doorways with dark rivulets coming from them.

Alec spent all morning at the Club, checking the stock of spirits. His brother George hadn't arrived yet. He didn't phone Ron because he'd known since yesterday what he was looking 'tense' about.

Yesterday he'd filled up at Alvin's so that Laura would have a full tank for the run to Brighton, and he'd had the same impression as she had: there was something on Ron's mind. He'd said something about the rendezvous at the Terminal tonight and Ron had said:

'I might be going straight to the Airport in Stan's Jag. Him and Mike are probably going straight there, so I might as well go with them, mightn't I, save hanging about. Chris says she might be kept late, seeing two old people she's been looking after, pensioners, all on their own.'

Alec got it at once. There were too many 'mights' about all this. Ron was so honest that whenever he brought out a white lie it looked as black as sin. The other night when he'd been fetching the girls' coats he'd heard Mike saying he'd got 'something lined up'. That was all he'd heard because he was busy helping the girls, but he knew Mike could only mean one thing. Soon afterwards Stan had called out for his 'Hamburger' with just that degree of heartiness that didn't ring true.

He'd thought no more about it until now. Now it clicked. Ron was too ready to explain himself.

'What's the problem, then, with the others?'

The petrol-vapour made a bloom on the cellulose of the Cortina above the filler-hole.

'Mike says he's got to settle something before he leaves tomorrow night – some people called Parkinson are buying a house. If he doesn't sign it up he might miss the sale, see, that's understandable, isn't it? You don't sell a house every day, I suppose, and if you —'

'Sure.'

'Eh?'

'Sure. It's understandable.'

The pump droned.

He didn't ask what the problem was with Stan; there'd be a detailed explanation for that too. He'd just gone straight round to see Mike and they'd talked it over.

Now it was all fixed. There wasn't any question of trying to talk Ron out of it or to ask Mike to change his plans.

The best way of losing a friend was to give him unasked-for advice. It was their business and there was only one thing he could do about it now.

Fay felt that time was rushing on her and knew that it always seemed like that when she was going away. She didn't go away often: once a year to Antibes and sometimes to the coast for a weekend with Mike, nothing more. It was the packing that made her feel like this.

Are you going on holiday? his small red mouth had said.

Sunburn lotion – that was the most important. Her skin was too fair to stand the sun. Marzine – that was important too, the most important, really, because she'd always had a fear of embarrassing the others in the plane. (Mike had said once, 'You've never been air-sick, have you?' She'd said, 'No, this stuff stops it completely.' Nothing ever bothered Mike; he was too healthy. 'But how do you know you'd be sick if you didn't take it?' Healthy people never understood, lucky for them.)

The windows were grey. She couldn't tell whether it was still raining or not. Alka-Seltzers.

She ought to ring Laura but she might not be back from Brighton yet.

The blue case didn't look any different now than it had when she'd first started this morning; it was the last and that was always the worst. By midday it had been shut and locked – she always locked them – but then she'd remembered the time it had turned chilly down there so it all had to come out again to make room for the two sweaters and now she'd realized that the pink one with the gold thread in it was still at the cleaner's anyway; that meant the white chunky but it made her look so big at the hips, not that she was, which made it worse.

She wished Laura would call round but there wasn't a

hope of that because her mother was coming up to London. Laura would have the thing packed in five minutes and there'd be room to spare.

Sacchs. You couldn't get them down there, or she'd never seen them.

She tried at four o'clock and again at half past.

'What's up, darling?'

Everything was all right suddenly.

'Nothing. Did you get back all right?'

'Of course.'

'Is your mother all right?'

'She's fine.'

'I'll see you at the Terminal, then.'

'Of course. Is Mike taking your bags there earlier?'

'As far as I know. He might not be there himself, at the time.'

'He might not *what*?'

'Oh, he's coming all right but he might be going straight to the Airport in the car, or Stan's car, I forget which he said.'

There was a pause and she heard Laura more faintly saying something about 'the usual place'.

'I see,' Laura said into the phone.

'I expect she's excited to be in town again, isn't she?'

'Yes,' said Laura with a short laugh.

Her mother was never excited about anything.

'Well it's 11.20, isn't it?' There was a sure feeling, holding the phone, and she was reluctant to put it down.

'Why's Mike going direct to the Airport, darling?'

'He only said he might be. It's a contract for a house or something.' Laughing a little she said: 'He won't miss the plane, I know that much.' Mike enjoyed it down there, even more than Stan, though he didn't show it like Stan did. Last year he'd redesigned the whole of the Villa

Mimosa on paper, wandering about with a foot-rule, happy as anything.

'Look,' said Laura briskly, 'Alec's got some last-minute things to see to at the Club, and he says *he* might be going direct to the Airport too, so the best thing we can do is let them make their own way.' With slow emphasis she said: 'You and I and Chris will meet at the Terminal *anyway* at twenty minutes past eleven and take the coach, just as we've arranged – all right? And for God's sake don't forget your passport. *I've* got your plane-ticket with all the others, so that's the only thing you have to remember – the *passport*. Okay?' Then she said: 'Fay?'

'Yes, I'm just trying to think where I put it —'

'Oh, *Fay*!'

'I put it somewhere safe, I know that.' Even with the sure feeling of the phone in her hand the time seemed to be rushing on her. 'I'll find it.'

'Look, if you *don't* find it in half an hour, ring me back.'

'Yes. But I'll find it.'

'Of course you will.'

Then she couldn't think of anything more to say, so she had to put the phone down.

Under Taurus today it had said: *This is a quiet period and nothing out of the ordinary is foreseen, though small problems may arise and will be dealt with successfully*. That obviously meant she would find the passport, because it always turned out true.

'I can just see you.'

Chris laughed softly. 'Can you?'

'*Just*.'

'Well that's better than last week, but I hope you're going to like what you see.'

'I expect I will,' Ben said reflectively.

He wasn't playing with the others in his group today; the specialist said he should be left on his own under 'distant observation' to search for bright objects. But Friday was when Chris came, and Ben had threatened hellfire on them all if they didn't let him talk to her: 'bust things up', had been his actual words. They gave him more rope than the others because he'd been a burn case, the same accident.

'You've got shiny eyes,' he said. They were both kneeling on the floor, their noses almost touching. 'In a lot of dark hairy eyelashes.'

Her knees had begun aching; they'd been like this for minutes.

'You've been eating peppermints,' she said.

'Yes. They're like di'monds in soot, your eyes are.'

'Thank you very much! So you'll be calling me Sooty from now on?'

'No. Christine. It's nice for a name. Like Christmas.'

She hoped she would be here the first time they let him look into a mirror; it would be cowardly not to be here then, not to make a point of being here. It had been a gas-oven.

'Well I've got to go now, Ben.' Her knees really wouldn't take it any longer, and there was Mary to see, she'd promised.

'You're always having to go.'

'Because I'm always coming. That's a better way of looking at it.'

'Stay till it gets dark, till I can't see things any more. I'm special.'

She struggled up and felt a nylon go. She helped him stand. 'No, Ben, you're not special. You're lucky to be here with shiny things to look at and Mrs Joseph to tuck you up at night and peppermints and everything. If you start thinking you're special I shan't come and show you my sooty eyes every week.'

He was looking up at her and his face was not quite turned to her own because at this distance it wasn't bright enough for him to see.

'Don't *squeeze*,' he said patiently.

She let go of his hands.

'I was feeling how strong you are.'

'Will you come next Friday?'

'No. I'm going on holiday. But as soon as I'm back I'll come and see you.'

'I'll be here,' he said.

'I know.' She touched the side of his face, the healed side. 'I won't be long away.'

Towards evening the day telescoped on them all.

Fay had found her passport and rang Laura to tell her in case she'd worry. She'd just managed to catch the chemist open for some phenos: you couldn't get them down there and after the plane journey she wouldn't be able to sleep properly. All these last-minute details got in the way of what she should have been thinking: of how wonderful it was going to be tomorrow, waking up in the Villa Mimosa; perhaps that was why she couldn't think about it, because it would be so wonderful.

Mike came home for their cases and took them along to the Terminal so that she could just pick up her bag and get on a bus. He said she wasn't to worry if he didn't show up there: he'd be at the Airport, maybe even before the coach got there – 'If the Jag overtakes you we'll give a toot and you'll know it's us.'

Ron was home from work when Chris rang to say she was 'grabbing a bun' and going straight on to Mr and Mrs Bramford – they were the old couple she'd promised to cook a meal for and help work out the new pension forms. Ron told her that he was going to give Alec a hand at the Club anyway, and that if his brother George didn't arrive till late they'd skip the coach and go in Stan's car. She asked if he was all right and he said his foot still hurt a bit. Tomorrow he'd be 'dipping his tootsies in the Med' so she wasn't to worry. She said she'd almost forgotten about the holiday with so much to do, and he sounded disappointed so she told him she'd never looked forward so much to the 'Old Firm's Outing' in all her life before, and he perked up and said, 'This year it'll beat all the others – this is a vintage year!' It was one of Alec's phrases.

Stan worked on at the salon till gone eight o'clock, with three of the girls staying overtime because of a big do at the Palais; Mrs Riley was in to have a tiara fixed so that it wouldn't wobble; it was only a bit of alloy and paste but it sparkled like the real thing and they all stood back admiring it when she got up. Then he finally couldn't keep his mind on anything so he rang Dolly and she said she was dead-beat after a 'really ghastly day' at the modelling school and she was flying down tomorrow in any case so 'let's leave it till then'. He wasn't sorry because he privately didn't know if he'd be able to keep his mind even on *that* tonight and Dolly wasn't a girl to tolerate a handful of slack especially with what he called his 'Ronson reputation' (*first* time *every* time). In the end he popped into the Bullfinch for a double and then went to get the Jag filled up. It was a clear night and not very cold but he was wearing his camel-hair coat.

Laura spent the early evening being patient with her mother, who kept asking where things were; and every time Laura said 'the usual place' her mother went straight to it, which she could have done to begin with. But Mandy and Toops were delighted to see her and there was The Gap to discuss (Laura couldn't quite see why Mandy was *proud* of it and hoped she wasn't going to grow up into a tom-boy) and Mother opened the huge casket of crystallized fruit that Alec had brought and 'Rupert' was given first go. (The first time they'd told him his name the best he could say was 'Tooper', which had naturally developed into 'Toops', but Mother never used it.)

Alec said goodnight to them in bed before he went back to the Club. His brother George had arrived in town during the afternoon but Alec said there was still a 'bit to do' there. (George's wife had sent her 'love' to Laura through Alec, satisfying the proprieties.) He was looking privately impatient about something, Laura thought, but she didn't ask him why; it was probably Henry the barman, who became a bit of an old woman when there was a crisis on, such as George taking over for a fortnight.

'Don't let it get you down, darling.' He really did work bloody hard to keep the Club going. 'Tomorrow I'll feed you Neapolitans on the beach and oil your back and do you a monster *Salade Niçoise* for the evening.'

He smiled nicely and gave Mother a slightly exaggerated son-in-law hug and then had to say goodnight to Mandy all over again because she'd crept down the stairs to wish him a 'nithe time and a lot of lovely thwimming'. He'd got as far as the door when Laura said:

'Darling. The cases.'

He gave a slow blink and ruefully picked two of them up. 'What would I do without you?'

'Leave them behind.'

He came back for the other two and stowed them in the Cortina, taking them along to the Air Terminal and then going on to the Club.

That was the last detail seen to. The day had kept them all on the go and they hadn't had a minute to spare, but now everything was ready and they didn't have to be at the Terminal for another three hours. It was the time when everyone, just going on holiday, wondered what the rush had been all about.

CHAPTER 7

The sky over London was hazy. The lights made a glow between the dark buildings.

Ron had been keeping an eye on the car for twenty minutes. It was an old Austin, well kept, a four-door saloon, and he had chosen it because it was black and had the right door-handles. He knew it was safe because he had followed them as far as the Odeon and seen them buy their tickets and go in. It was standing in a mews opposite a private No Parking sign. He had looked several times at his watch. He had a coat on and string gloves.

Now it was time, and he walked into the mews and slipped the piping out of his sleeve and pushed it over the door-handle and broke the lock and got in. The ignition-key was there so he didn't have to join the wires. Most people left the key in and he'd expected it. The engine was warm and the petrol-gauge was at half. That was enough because they weren't going far. He started the engine and saw that the oil warning light had gone off. He drove out of the mews.

He reached the place in ten minutes. At this hour there was not much traffic. There would be more later.

Alec was standing at the corner and Ron stopped for him and he got in. They went down to the next corner and parked in an easy gap between two other cars.

Ron took his gloves off and lit a cigarette. Alec didn't smoke. They were silent for a while; there was nothing to say. The lights of a restaurant made a pink glow above the roofs.

Ron's breath sounded a bit shaky and he wound the window down and tried breathing more slowly. His hands weren't quite steady and the ash soon dropped from his cigarette. It gave him something to do, brushing the ash off his coat. His foot was still painful.

'What time,' Alec asked, 'did he say?'

He knew what time Mike had said but he wanted to hear Ron's voice to see how nervous he was. That was the only risk: Ron's nerves. Alec had lain awake last night trying to decide what was best. The obvious thing was to have a go at talking Ron out of it but if he didn't succeed the risk would be bigger because Ron's nerves would be worse; and he didn't think he could succeed. Ron resented being the youngest of them, being the 'kid', and he'd resent advice – he could look after himself, thank you, he was quite old enough to know what he was doing. Alec had lain awake arguing both sides, knowing Ron well enough to know how he'd react; and in the end he'd made up his mind. The bigger chance was that Ron would dig his heels in – I can't let the boys down, Alec, we're in this together, you know how it is . . . Ron would see himself as he always did, up there on the screen, this time as the Guy that Turned Yellow and Let Down the Gang.

He was nervy now but that was natural; he was keyed up, having to wait; it wouldn't affect his driving, once there was something to do. It would be more dangerous for them all if Ron were sitting here agonizing about what he'd told him: that he should think of Chris and what it would mean to her, that he'd be smashing up her life as well as his if they ran into trouble, that he wouldn't be 'letting the boys down' because they didn't really need a getaway car, it was just to give him some fun (Ron would resent that deeply: the 'kid' was just being given a ride).

It was safer to let him do what he had to do and hope it would get it out of his system.

'He told me half past,' Ron said.

His voice didn't sound too bad. It had been the right decision. The best thing Alec could do was to be here with him and look after him if there were trouble.

Ron looked through the windscreen at the street. The cigarette had a bitter taste, the saliva was coming quick. He felt clear in the head as if he'd taken a pep-pill. The street looked magnified and he could see everything sharp; noises were clearer and he could hear things a long way off. That was because he was ready for action.

This was the getaway car. He was sitting here quiet, just smoking a cigarette like they did, a vital part of the plan, waiting for the first stroke of the chime that would be his signal. He was the getaway man.

But underneath the excitement his common sense was making a decision for him. This was the real thing, a big-time operation, the kind of thing he'd seen so many times at the pictures and on the telly, and he was in it. He shouldn't be here but he was. He'd started it for devilment and then couldn't back out because a thing like this meant nothing to Mike, nothing at all, and Mike would have laughed at him if he'd tried to back out after showing so keen. So it was too late now. But when it was over he was going to make a change. He was twenty-four years old and had a wife and a home and there'd be kids coming along as soon as they could afford it. It was time he finished playing about. Sitting in the pictures watching them show off their guns, sitting there in the dark for week after week watching the same thing – it made you sick in the end. And nicking motors – what was the point in doing that? He didn't even flog them, never tried to make a penny out of it. He'd pack that in, nicking motors.

This was the real thing and he was in it. This was what he'd wanted to do ever since he was a kid and now he was doing it. And he didn't like it.

Some more ash dropped and it gave him a start because his eyes were everywhere and he was keyed up, and he brushed it off his coat impatiently, feeling silly about being startled like that. He wasn't cut out for this sort of thing, hadn't got Mike's calm-and-collected kind of brain, he could see that all right now.

'It won't be long.'

He started again because he'd clean forgotten Alec was here with him.

'I know,' he said sharply. Alec should know better than to talk very sudden like that to the getaway man on the job.

'Then we'll be meeting the girls,' Alec told him slowly, 'and getting on the plane, and then it's sunshine all the way.'

Ron saw Alec's face suddenly, his reflection on the windscreen. It was a well-kept motor but there was a film of dirt on the screen after the rain earlier and Alec's face was quite clear, watching him.

'It'll be great. Great.'

That was it. Think about the sunshine, the girls, Chris.

It was time he thought a bit more about Chris. Suppose anything happened to him? She'd have to come there and see him but they wouldn't let her see him for the first two months and then they'd only let her come every four weeks for twenty minutes a time and that was all he'd see of her, *see of Chris*, twenty minutes a month.

He threw the dog-end out of the window. He did it so quickly that he caught his wrist on the window-ledge and the pain went right up into his scalp.

There was one thing about it. They'd never get him inside again. Ever.

Sweat ran down him.

Suddenly Alec said: 'I had a little talk with Mike, you know, about this job.'

The strain of waiting had got on his own nerves now and the terrible possibility struck him with more force than it had before: maybe it hadn't been the right decision after all. But maybe it wasn't too late.

'You did?' Ron said with a grunt. He didn't want Alec to talk. It was close on half past and he had to stay calm, not let Mike down whatever happened, breathe slow, stay calm, not panic.

'Yes,' Alec said quietly. 'And you know, Ron, there's no actual need for us to hang about here if you think it's smarter to leave them a clear field. Mike told me himself that —'

'That's it.'

'What?'

'Listen.'

The half-hour was chiming.

Ron started the engine. Alec said something but he didn't hear it. A car was coming up and he waited and then pulled out after it had gone by.

'We're on our way,' he heard himself saying like he'd heard them saying so many times but it sounded different the way he said it, sort of scared.

Fay got to the Air Terminal a good fifteen minutes early, even though she'd left the bus two stops down the road, not wanting to stand about with nothing to do.

It was busy and there were a lot of people in the main hall, which surprised her until she remembered that they weren't all flying to Nice; they were going everywhere you could think of, Paris and Rome and Cairo and even farther than that. She saw an Indian woman in a sari and two men in long black silk coats and white baggy trousers and a very tall man who looked American because he just stood leaning at his ease near some baggage while everyone milled past him calling to one another.

Fay had never done much travelling and this excited her and she took one extra Marzine to make sure.

'Hello, darling.'

Laura was looking perfectly calm, frowning slightly as a whole herd of people went barging past waving travel forms at a harassed man with a smile fixed on his face to reassure them.

'I came early,' Fay said, thinking that if Laura had got here a minute sooner she wouldn't have taken the extra pill.

'Have you got your passport?'

'Oh yes.' She opened her bag and there was a rattle of tubes and boxes. 'Yes, it's here.' Looking up she said, 'This is fun, isn't it?'

'It's like a cattle-show. Have you seen Chris anywhere, or any of the boys?'

'Not yet.'

Diesel gas blew through the swing-doors as more people came in.

Laura looked at the big clock.

'We might as well get on.'

'Which one is it?'

'That one.'

There was a whole line of coaches but they all looked alike.

'How do you know it's that one?'

'By the number.'

'You know the *number*?'

Laura laughed and took her arm. 'Look, if we lose touch with each other just stay *exactly* where you are and *I* will come to find *you*, all right?'

Mike had made himself a pot of tea in one of the upstairs offices and now he sat drinking the first cup, looking around him in the faint glow from the windows. He still had his thin gloves on.

It was a nice office, very comfortable. There was a framed photograph of a rather lovely woman on the desk, not young but very handsome. She would be Mrs Metcalfe: that was the name on the door, I. E. W. Metcalfe. He turned the photograph to the window and admired it, then put it back on to the desk exactly where it had been before.

Mr I. E. W. Metcalfe knew his teas. This was Earl Grey.

There was still half an hour to wait. He'd allowed for anti-blowing bars, which would have meant drilling and a second pair of charges, but it was an old model of 1930 or thereabouts and the jelly had worked the first time: a discreet cough under the carpets and it was all his. About half of it was in ones and he was glad Stan would be coming; it was a shocking waste to leave so much behind.

It wasn't often you found an out-of-date peter in a place where the executive offices were as comfortable as this, but it was clear now that nobody had been here before; there were still a few places in the City with a virgin crib and this was one of them. You'd see a big difference here tomorrow; there'd be more gossip than work and there'd be visitors: dicks, insurance people, reporters, a man from Chubb's; by this time next week you wouldn't blow your nose within a mile of this building without making it sound like a church steeple on a bell-ringers' benefit night.

After a third cup he stretched his legs and from one of the windows saw the copper go past on his beat. That couldn't be much of a job, mooching up and down night after night with no one to talk to, worrying over the wife's arthritis or the moult setting in among the birds – quite a few of them bred canaries, quite a few. But not much of a job, that.

There was pink in the glow of the sky on the left, where the restaurant was.

When he looked at his watch again it was a quarter past so he put the cup on the tray and took the tray downstairs to the little tea-making place and washed up the things, leaving them to dry on the rack; it wasn't worth using the tea-cloth, it would only leave fluff and they'd be perfectly dry by the morning. Then he went into the accounts department and divided the bundles, one into each trouser pocket, one into each hip pocket, the doubles into his jacket and three each into his coat. He arranged the same-sized bundles on the floor near the door and stood waiting again.

They were sitting right at the back and Chris didn't see them until Laura waved a white-gloved hand. The coach was already on the move as she found an empty seat just in front of them. She was laughing and out of breath —

'I didn't think I'd catch it!'

'I didn't think you would either,' Laura said, and began relaxing. It was absurd really, this business of travelling: there were plenty of other coaches and plenty of other planes but you dashed about with one eye on the damned clock as if your life depended on it. There must be some explanation to do with primitive memory-traces: they'd probably started it when everyone had gone rushing into the Ark.

'Have you seen anything of the boys?' asked Chris.

'They'll be at the Airport, darling. Incidentally you look marvellous.'

It wasn't the outfit Chris had on; it was her young excitement making her glow. Fay envied Laura her confident flair for organizing things; Laura envied Chris for bright spirits; whom did Chris envy and for what? No one and for nothing; she looked like a girl in love, and probably – Laura thought – she was.

'I must look like a dish-mop!' She shook out her dark hair, running her fingers through it. 'You didn't see Ron?'

'He'll be there,' Fay said. She was half-waiting for the first stirring in her stomach, but so far she felt all right.

Chris took out a lipstick and made useless efforts in the coach window, putting it back into her bag. They cleared the first traffic-lights and gathered speed along Cromwell Road.

'Well,' she said, spreading her arms along the back of the seat so that she could talk to them, 'we're on our way!'

After he'd filled up the Jag, Stan went back to his flat to change his camel-hair for a smart black businessman's coat that went better with his Homburg. He'd look more the part in the City, and the pockets were almost as big – say five-hundred-pound-size instead of six.

This tickled him and he thought: Mike you old bastard what've you done to a good honest citizen, giving him ideas like that?

There was time for one more Scotch, a single, and he looked at Dolly's picture again that he kept in his wallet.

Dolly, my girl, you won't know what's happening to you tomorrow night, I'll have you up there on the bloody chandelier before we're finished.

He sprayed some Old Spice underneath his lapels to get rid of the stink of the setting-lotion and then locked up and went down the stairs.

'That's it then, Harry, I'm off!'

The caretaker put down his newspaper. 'Well I hope you have a good time, Mr Sedgeman, an' give my love to the Madamerselles.'

You couldn't say a thing like that to some of the other residents but Mr Sedgeman was a real gent despite he was a hairdresser, treated you like a human being instead of a bleedin' lackey, not mean, either.

'Bring you one back, Harry, if I can get past the Customs!'

He was into the Jag and off.

At the time Mike had worked out for him he was at the top end of the alley – Cooper's Lane – standing well back where he could see everything. He'd left the Jag in High Holborn and taken a taxi from there, walking the last half-mile and enjoying the air and the way the girls looked at the cut of his coat – it was Savile Row, no messing about – real smashers, some of them were, it made you wish you'd got nothing else to do.

It was only five minutes before the copper came round, passing him some distance away; there was no chance of being seen because of the shadows but he turned to face the other way and tilted his head back so that the brim of his hat covered his neck as Mike had told him.

When the copper had gone he crossed the road and went down the alley counting the doors, stopping at the seventh and giving a light rippling tap with his fingertips.

The door opened right away.

95

Mike was there, his big round face a blur.

'Just called on the off chance,' whispered Stan. 'Can I borrow your lawn-mower?'

'*Tch!* This is the third time, you know.'

Stan came farther into the office. 'My God, this place smells like November the Fifth!'

Mike let out a wheezy laugh. 'Open up that coat, now.' He bent down. 'Trouser pocket, right?' A car went past the end of the alley and he waited to make sure it wasn't slowing. 'Other trouser pocket.'

Stan stuffed the bundles in.

'This is old stuff, isn't it?'

'It's just as good and it makes less noise. Jacket pockets next.'

When the fourth bundle was stowed away Stan buttoned his coat and took the fifth.

'That's not your camel-hair you've got on, is it?' Mike murmured.

'No. City slicker job, I thought it'd look better.' He put the last bundle away.

'Very smart. Must be worth a lot of money, that coat.'

'It is now.'

Mike left his bag of tools where it was, in the corner. Some bright young copper was going to have a better-looking work-bench at home before long; it was a brand-new drill and they could never keep their hands off anything like that.

'Shut the door after you, Stan.'

'Eh? Is that all?'

'It's the lot. I filled mine up while I was waiting.'

Stan came after him into the alley and shut the door quietly. They set off together, the opposite way from which Stan had come because Mike had worked out the beats. In a minute Stan said: 'It's awkward, isn't it?'

'What is?'

'Walking.'

'You'll have to do better than that. You look as if your truss has slipped or something.'

Stan stopped altogether and slowly began shaking with laughter. They were in the main street now so Mike said:

'Go on, don't bottle it up, let yourself go.'

Stan's laugh was deep, like his voice, and it echoed among the dark locked buildings as they walked on.

'I really don't know,' he said, getting his breath, 'I really don't know what my dear old mother would have said if she could see me now . . .'

'She'd recognize you all right. You used to walk like this in your nappies.' There was a copper coming up from the intersection, hands behind his back. A taxi went past.

'For God's sake,' Stan said with the laughter still in his voice, 'how much've we got between us?'

'*Shhh* – you do say the most dreadful things. Eight or nine, better than I thought. Just give a bit of a lurch, will you?'

'A what?' He saw the copper now and said: 'Oh Jesus.'

'Just give a lurch – not too much.' Mike took his arm. 'And go on laughing.' But Stan had gone quiet suddenly so he said again, 'Just go on laughing, but mind you don't have an accident because the best place to change your trousers would be in a bank, if you see what I mean, and they're all shut for the night.' That got Stan going again and while he was enjoying himself Mike talked to him. 'Then of course Mary came down the stairs – most of them had gone by this time – and she came down the stairs and just looked at them, you know how Mary can look daggers when she's riled – give a bit of a lurch, now, not too much – and she said, "All I want to know is who

97

left a pair of knickers over the lampshade in Charlie's room?" And of course that did it – the rest of them were out of the place before they'd even got the door open.'

Stan was doing all right now, lurching a bit, and Mike kept hold of his arm. Fortunately old Stan was one of those people who couldn't stop laughing once they'd got into the rhythm, and it wasn't too loud; it was just right.

'But you haven't heard the *best* part of it,' Mike went on as they passed the copper, 'the *best* part of it was when *Charlie* went up and saw what was in the bedroom. You know how he tries to make out he'd never look at another woman when Mary's about – well *then* he sees what's over the lampshade!'

Mike kept it up for a while and Stan went on laughing but not too loudly and then they crossed the intersection and a car came down the street behind them and they didn't take any notice till it began slowing. Then Mike took a look and saw it was the black Austin that Ron had described. The copper was out of sight now and they got in.

Stan sat in the back, out of breath.

'How'd it go?' asked Alec.

'No trouble,' Mike said. Then the car gave a jerk and he looked at Ron. 'What's up, then?'

Ron's face had gone white and he didn't answer, just kept his foot down.

'We're in no hurry,' Mike said, and turned to look through the rear window.

They had a coffee while they were waiting and Fay went across to buy the *Telegraph* because she liked the colour supplement. Chris was finally managing to put some lipstick on.

'How long have we got?'

'Ten minutes.'

'*Ten?*' Chris swung round to look at the clock.

'They'll be here,' Laura said. She watched Fay coming back from the bookstall. Fay looked marvellous too this evening but in a different way from Chris; she had the knack of looking elegant and helpless at the same time: even now she was looking around her as if she'd lost her way.

'But they all know what time we take off,' Chris said, not wanting to panic in front of Laura but having to say it.

'That's why they'll be here.'

Fay had bought a *Vogue* and a *Harper's* for them.

'That's sweet of you, darling.' Laura chose the *Harper's*. It had a marvellous cover – mustard-yellow for Ascot this year.

Chris didn't open her *Vogue*. She said to Fay:

'We've only got ten minutes, did you know?'

'Have we? What happens then?'

Laura would have smiled but she didn't believe it this time. 'We get on the *aeroplane*.'

Fay laughed softly. 'I know *that*, but I mean where do we have to go?'

'Channel 5. Don't worry, Auntie Laura has it all worked out.'

Chris was looking down the length of the hall. 'It's the boys I'm worried about.'

'You don't really think they'd miss the plane, do you?'

'I suppose not.'

'Well, then.'

The Austin was in third gear and going fast.

'Slow up,' said Mike. He laid a hand on Ron's shoulder. 'Slow up.'

'I can't.'

They didn't recognize Ron's voice.

Mike felt Stan moving and said: 'Don't look back.'

The lights were green.

'They're on to us.' He didn't slow.

'No they're not. Ease your foot up. Don't turn anywhere.'

Their exhaust echoed in the dark stone street.

'Still there. I tell you they're still there.' He was watching the mirror more than the road.

Stan grunted something but they didn't hear what it was.

Ron said: 'Mike. What do I do? *Mike.*'

Alec worried only about Ron.

'You just keep on driving. But slower. Slower.'

There were some more lights coming up. They were green.

'We're all right,' Alec said.

'Of course we are,' Mike said.

They were still some way from the lights when they went amber.

Alec heard Ron make a sound in his throat.

'Mind the lights,' Mike said.

'*But they're still after us —*'

'Mind the lights. You won't get through on the amber. Stop at the lights.' He laid his hand on Ron's shoulder again.

The lights went red.

'Pull up gently. Gently now.'

Ron jerked his head back in a rasping breath but he was slowing.

'That's right. Keep in your proper lane.'

They stopped.

There was a short tinkle on the bell as the police-car drew out from directly behind them and pulled up alongside. The observer's window was down and he had turned his head. The driver was leaning forward to look at them past his colleague.

The observer reached over and tapped at the driving-window of the Austin.

Mike said: 'Ron. Wind it down.'

Alec thought that Ron wasn't going to. It looked as if he hadn't the strength.

Traffic was flowing across in front of them.

Ron was moving. The window came down.

The observer's eyes were in the shadow of his peaked cap. He said:

'When the lights go green, just pull up over there on the other side, will you please?'

Ron's head was turned to look at the observer.

'Over there?'

Alec could hear that his voice had lost any feeling now.

The observer nodded and pointed.

'Just on the other side.'

'Yes. Yes.'

The engines of the two cars throbbed together, idling.

The cross-traffic was still flowing. Under the noise Mike said with his hand on Ron's shoulder: 'When the lights go green, take this turning to the left. Are you listening, Ron?'

The cross-traffic was clearing. A mini-cab stopped. The red light was reflected in its windscreen. A grey Bentley had stopped on the other side. An Aston-Martin was revving up impatiently.

'Yes,' Ron said. 'Yes.'

'Take this turning to the left, and go as fast as you can till I tap your shoulder. Then get out and run clear.'

The middle of the crossing was deserted. Everyone was stationary.

The engines idled.

Mike sat back so that Stan could hear what he was saying, as well as the two in front.

'We're all going to run clear. Meet up where we said.'

Alec nodded.

In the back, Stan felt for the door-handle.

The lights went green and Ron banged the clutch in and swung the wheel and kept his foot down and dragged the lever into second and straightened up and kept on going and they all sat with their backs pressed hard against the seats and their fingers hooked on the door-handles and when Mike reached forward and tapped Ron's shoulder he stood on the brakes and they all lurched off the seats and kicked the doors open and started running.

CHAPTER 8

They were only a small group and they looked lonely, cut off from the life they had left on the other side of the glass doors, shut in here with each other unwillingly, strangers with nothing in common except that they stood here with their reflection in the big windows.

'Will you have your boarding-cards ready, please?'

A parson and three schoolboys. A man with a deaf-aid, staring up at the ceiling. Two businessmen with black briefcases, looking sideways at the girl in the mini-mink. A young man with sideboards and a bandage on his wrist.

The swing-doors opened again and a man and a woman came in with a child just about to cry; the man hoisted it on to his shoulder.

Chris said: 'Well that's it then.'

Fay looked at her with slow brown eyes. She'd be glad when they were on the plane instead of hanging about like this. But if the boys didn't come they might not get on the plane. Then she could sit down somewhere. Coffee was a mistake.

'They've got a few more minutes,' said Laura.

'Of course.' Chris stood facing the doors. 'But I'm not going on the plane without Ron.'

'That's up to you, darling.'

Chris swung her head. 'Will you go without Alec?'

'Oh no, I didn't mean that.'

'What did you mean?'

'I'm not absolutely sure; I just said it.'

103

'You think they've had an accident, don't you?'

'Good Lord no.' But that was what she did think. 'How many times have people been late – without having accidents?'

'Stan drives fast.' She looked at the doors again.

The group was thinning into a file and moving off. The hostess was taking their boarding-cards.

Will passengers on BEA Flight 205 for Nice please go to Gate No. 5 immediately.

Fay said: 'That's us, isn't it?'

'We're already here, darling. They mean late arrivals.'

The three of them were standing alone now; the end of the queue reached the hostess. She looked across at them.

'Is there some difficulty?'

The swing-doors thumped open and Mike came through first with Stan. Alec and Ron followed.

'No,' Laura told the hostess. She had the three boarding-cards ready and gave them to the girl.

'Sorry we're late,' Mike said.

They were all out of breath.

'Have you checked in?' Laura asked them.

'That's what kept us,' Alec nodded. He was helping Ron, who didn't seem to know what was happening.

'Are you all right?' Chris asked him.

'Yes. Yes.'

'Look, darling, let's go through.' Laura took Fay with her. One of her pet loathings was what she called 'travel-panic'.

Chris followed them and stood waiting for them to come through. She didn't like the look of Ronnie and she wanted to know what was the matter with him.

Fay said: 'Is it imagination —'

'No,' Laura said. 'It isn't.' As Alec came up she asked: 'Are the children all right?'

'Sure. It's nothing to do with them.' He did his best to smile.

Stan's face was waxy under his Sunless-tan. He let out a low whistling breath. 'We didn't think we'd make it.'

The hostess was hurrying them across to the boarding-coach.

'He's all right,' Mike told her. 'We saw an accident on the way up. Bad smash. We had to stop – the road was blocked.'

'All we want,' Stan said as he helped Chris into the coach, 'is a drink.' He was beginning to feel better. They'd got here and they were in the clear and that was all that mattered.

Chris sat next to Ron and held his hand. It was cold. When she spoke to him he turned his head and smiled, but it was worse than if he hadn't. She didn't say anything more. The trouble with people who had a lot of imagination was that they felt things more deeply than others; not that she'd want Ronnie any different. She rubbed his hands in hers.

'Poor darling,' Laura said. She'd never seen Alec so shaken.

'We're all right now,' he said, and closed his eyes as the coach swung past the aircraft bays. The flying area was on one side, a field of coloured lights. Laura watched them slowly swinging, their pattern changing.

Alec wasn't religious but as he sat beside her he was aware of gratitude towards something, towards whatever cosmic order it was that had let them off the hook tonight. It could have gone badly for them all. Ron was the only one he'd been worried about and now he was here with them, so he was satisfied; but as well as that, they were all safe – the girls as well – from something they'd all come close to, something that didn't bear thinking about. Later he'd have to think about it so that he could appreciate what it amounted to, and try to learn from it. Not now. He could only feel gratitude.

Crossing from the coach to the plane the sharp wind blew dust against their faces, stinging their eyes. There was the spit of rain in the wind.

Alec thought it seemed impossible that tomorrow they'd be in the sunshine. That was extra. It was almost too much.

People crowded down the aisle, edging sideways, a hostess helping them stow their coats and cameras along the racks. There hadn't seemed many of them in the waiting-room but the plane was more than half full.

The luggage was going in from the truck; the whole aircraft flexed as it took on the load. A mobile generator pulsed. Blue lights filled the windows along one side.

Ron sat against a window; Chris had let him through first; he always liked looking out at things; everything was a treat to Ron. But tonight he sat with his head against the seat with his eyes half closed. It was how Chris had seen people in the hospital when they were conscious again and been told that the worst was over. If the others weren't looking so shaken up she would have thought Ronnie was ill and she wouldn't have let him get on the plane at all.

Alec sat opposite Ron with Laura next to him. Mike and Fay were by the aisle and Stan had a seat on the other side, the odd man out. He still had his coat on.

It must have been a bad one, Fay was thinking. It was a pity they'd had to tell them about it just before getting on; it wasn't the time to have to think about accidents. But then that was selfish of her: they'd seen it and it was worse for them, and besides they couldn't have turned up looking like this without saying why.

'All right, darling?'

Laura was looking across at her, smiling to reassure her.

'Fine.' One of the officers was standing in the doorway, nodding about something a hostess was telling him. He had a lot of gold rings on his sleeve so he was probably the pilot. He looked very calm and efficient, but then of course they all were on BEA, you could feel perfectly safe in their hands.

The baggage truck was taking a wide circle away from the plane, bumping on its unloaded springs, the driver shielding his face with one hand against the increasing rain.

People were clicking their seat-belts.

Mike hadn't spoken. He didn't look so bad as the others because his face hadn't lost its colour; but he sat without talking, still in his overcoat.

He looked at Ron now and then, sorry for the poor little beggar. He'd been very angry with Ron at the time, but hadn't shown it because they'd all had quite enough to think about. All the same, the police-car wouldn't have taken any notice of them if Ron hadn't panicked and put his foot down – it was a dead give-away. He'd learned one thing: never take an amateur on a job. This time they'd been lucky.

The mobile generator had stopped and through the window Chris saw it moving away, keeping well clear of the wing. Another plane was sliding among the lights, and somewhere there was one taking off with a long-drawn-out roaring that unsettled her. They were safe enough, safer than cars, but they were so enormous and made such a noise, all that power. Life was too fast these days; you couldn't go anywhere without huge powerful machines and even when people just went shopping they had to strap themselves round with belts or risk getting killed. It wasn't sense – pop into the town for a pound of butter and you could finish up dead. Life was too fast.

She wished Ronnie would get his colour back. It must have been a bad one, terrible, with people screaming perhaps, trapped inside. As a first-year junior she and her group had gone to a police lecture where they'd been shown pictures of wrecks and told how to get people out if you were first on the spot. It wasn't the sort of sight to give you much colour, even in pictures. Poor Ronnie.

'Would you like something to drink, sir?'

'A brandy, my love. A double.'

Chris didn't ask Ron what he'd like: Stan knew the right medicine and she asked for the same, and a ginger-ale for herself.

'Don't you want your coat off?' asked Fay.

'I think I'll stay as I am. Feeling all right, are you?'

'Fine.'

'Full of Marzine?' His eyebrows flicked up in a smile.

'It works.'

'Well that's the main thing.'

The engines were running.

Stan sat thinking of his double that was coming. He'd been sobered up tonight in a big way and as soon as he could he was going to get drunk in a big way. Down there in the sun. With Dolly.

The ventilation came on and people reached up to adjust the draught. A man with a creased waistcoat got up and fished about on the rack trying to find something in his coat. There was always someone like him on every flight; as soon as the *Fasten Seat-belts* panel lit up they'd find something to do just to show they'd done enough trips to know how to break the rules. His wife told him to sit down.

A load of booze, the sunshine, and Dolly. All it was

worth thinking about. Forget the other thing. But by Jesus Christ it was a close one, that. And what made it worse was that it'd been luck, or they'd never have made it. Luck was a terrible thing, what it could do with you. If that young tear-arse, God bless him, hadn't been so eager with his split-new Aston-Martin the patrol-car would've had a clear run. It had given them what – thirty seconds? You could go a long way in thirty seconds with your feet wound up and the fear of Christ pushing you from behind.

A hostess, the one with the gorgeous eyes, was shifting a parcel on the rack to make it safer. She shouldn't stretch up like that with her long legs apart, it made you think of highly reprehensible bloody conduct.

Dolly, my girl, you'll never be the same again.

He'd seen Mike – Mike had been ahead of him all the way, a fantastic performance for a bloke his size with a padded overcoat on. Alec had been somewhere behind, and one of them had called out for him to stop: *there* was a silly thing to tell him to do. He'd never seen Ron; he must have nipped up the alleyway they'd passed. He'd thought of going up there himself but it was dark and it could have been a cul-de-sac, though obviously it wasn't or Ron wouldn't be here.

The plane was rolling.

But it made you sweat and that was a fact. It was best not to think about it. Just remember one thing, that was all. The next time Mike says he's got something lined up, tell him to put it where the monkey put the nuts.

The Terminal buildings swung across the window, all lit up. It looked like a town on the end of a string.

Then they stopped again. There was nothing but a sea of blue lamps. Raindrops hit the windows.

Fay looked out at the dark and the lamps. They seemed a long way from anywhere now; they might be in mid-ocean or somewhere. But the pilot had looked very calm and efficient, and Marzine had never failed her before, and there was the Villa Mimosa waiting down there for them. It was silly to worry.

She looked across at Alec. He wasn't worrying. He was watching the lights through the window, interested in them; they were really very pretty and she ought to be enjoying them, like Alec.

The hair of the girl across the aisle was blowing gently in the draught from a ventilator.

The man in the creased waistcoat was looking at everyone, his eyes trying to catch their attention so that they could see how bored he was by this flying business.

Alec watched the lights, a sensation of peace in him. Later down at the Villa he'd have a few sleepless nights realizing how close they'd all come to tragedy; but it was too soon yet to feel anything except gratitude. This reaction seemed natural and he gave himself to it and was glad of it; the strain of the last couple of hours had been greater than he'd realized: in the series of taxis (he had changed three times for the sake of caution) on the way to the Airport he'd sat worrying, not being sure that Ron had got clear. Mike and Stan were all right – they'd been ahead of him because he'd slowed, hoping to draw the patrol-crew away from Ron. But he couldn't have gone back at any time to see if Ron had made it; they'd all had to keep going; that was what Mike had told them in the café next door to Alvin's Garage: if there were trouble it was every man for himself and they'd make for the Airport separately.

Ron had got there a few minutes after him, white with nerves and bewildered-looking, and it was only then that Alec had known he'd got clear. It had been a revelation to see him walking into the building, and from that moment the feeling of peace and gratitude had come into him: because he knew them all so well and he knew that in any kind of crisis Mike and Stan would fall on their feet and that Ron might not, because his own over-sensitive nerves would be against him. Seeing him come into the building, he had thought of a word, could still remember seeing it written across his mind in pale orange letters: *deliverance.*

The hostess with the lovely eyes was passing down the aisle, glancing at their seat-belts.

The sound of the engines pitched up and they all sat with a feeling of sudden helplessness, strapped in and unable to do anything even if it weren't too late to do anything. The brakes came off and the lights began drawing past them faster and faster until they made a stream of blue with the white haze of the Terminal buildings tilting against the night and the rain as the ground fell away below.

Life's too fast.

Dolly tomorrow.

Eight or nine grand, more than I thought.

Silly to worry, safe in his hands.

Better ring Mother, say we've arrived.

Deliverance.

The power was eased off and plastic surfaces creaked. London appeared below and was slowly blotted out by the rain.

'Would you mind waiting a moment, sir?'

The man with the creased waistcoat put away his lighter.

The little panel was still illuminated. *Fasten Seat-belts – No Smoking.*

Fay was watching it when it went dark, and in her relief made a joke to herself. They ought to light it up again saying: *Well Nothing Happened, Did It?*

People were clicking the buckles.

'Brandy, sir, was that right?'

'Dead right, my love.'

It was going to be bloody hot in here with an overcoat on. Old Mike looked done to a turn already, served him right, he should learn to keep respectable things in his pockets like handkerchiefs and French letters, then he could take off his coat like a law-abiding citizen.

Laura found a cigarette and Alec flicked his lighter for her.

'Happy landings,' he said with his slow smile.

'Better now, darling?'

'Sure.'

'Rotten shame.'

'Oh, these things happen.'

The rows of soft lamps tilted level at last.

Their drinks were in front of them on the tables.

'Well here's to us all, my loves!'

Stan's colour had come back and he looked Sunless-tanned again, his grin whiter than ever.

Mike's eyebrows flicked up and he made a *'phew'* with his mouth in Stan's direction, meaning it would be nice when they could get these coats off.

Chris moved Ron's double brandy an inch towards him on the table. 'Knock a hole in it, Ronnie, it'll do you good.'

The hostess was taking an empty tray back, saying something to her colleague as they passed; one of them laughed, the sound thin against the rush of the engines.

Then Ron began leaning forward little by little across the table, his hands meeting and becoming slowly locked in a clasp so tight they trembled as if in desperate prayer, his face squeezing into lines of agony until his eyes looked out from slits at Alec, opposite.

He was trying to say something, and Alec leaned towards him with his head slightly turned to listen, and Ron's lips went on moving painfully, saying it over and over again until Alec heard what it was.

'I've killed a copper...'

His lapel was touching the brandy glass now and it tilted over, spilling.

'Alec... *I've killed a copper...*'

CHAPTER 9

Looking from the window Chris thought that the lights of the coast really did remind you of a string of pearls, just like the travel-brochures said.

A faint thump was felt through the plane.

'What was that?' asked Fay.

'The wheels going down,' Alec told her. 'Now we shan't be long.'

He gave her his nice slow smile and she thought that only Alec would have that much patience with her; she was probably the only person on the plane who hadn't realized what the thump was.

The voice was distorted, coming from nowhere.

'Ladies and gentlemen, in a few minutes we shall be landing at Nice-Côte d'Azur, so will you please fasten your seat-belts and refrain from smoking until the aircraft has come to a stop. The weather in Nice is fine and the outside temperature is 21 degrees Centigrade, 70 degrees Fahrenheit. We hope you have enjoyed your flight with BEA and that we shall have the pleasure of welcoming you on board again.'

As the plane turned above the Isles des Lerins some of them could see the airport in the distance like a field of bright flowers at the edge of the sea.

'You must be baking,' Fay said to Stan across the aisle. She had talked to him now and then so that he wouldn't feel odd man out.

'Done to a turn, my love, but you've got a treat in store because all you'll see me in tomorrow is a Mark IV

Water-Babies jock-strap fully guaranteed not to pinch under the armpits.'

He cocked a roguish eyebrow at the old dear sitting opposite, whose blue-rinsed head had turned at his remark. She'd be travelling first-class in future to get away from the riff-raff, you could see that much.

Laura was putting her cigarette out and shutting the ashtray. There was still a glint of brandy along the edge of the table where the metal lip had stopped the dishcloth getting. The hostess had been sweet about it but Laura thought it was a shame to wring out Courvoisier into the sink. Ronnie was looking better now; whatever he'd said to Alec had got it off his mind, and Alec's answer had obviously been exactly right, and they'd brought another brandy anyway and some of Ronnie's colour was back. She thought it was sensible of Chris not to go on fussing over him – but then Chris was actually trained to cope with people who got upset.

She'd chipped her nail-varnish again; this Gayglow stuff was absolutely useless.

When the bump came Fay didn't ask Alec what it was. Even she knew when a plane was touching down. The lights swung past the windows and made her feel dizzy; she shut her eyes until they'd turned round and stopped. She listened to the engines moaning to silence and thought what a fool she was, worrying all the way.

'Wasn't it a wonderful flight?' she said.

'It was *now*,' Laura laughed, 'wasn't it?' She thought that when Fay was happy – or at least not worrying – she looked really beautiful. She must have been like this when Mike had met her.

Alec and Ron were in the end seats by the windows, so they came away last. Chris, just in front of them going down the steps, heard Alec saying something to Ron but didn't catch what it was.

Stan gave Fay his hand at the bottom of the steps and her apple-green shoes flashed under the lights.

'But it's *warm*!'

'Well we didn't come here to feed the polar-bears.'

Waiting in Customs for their luggage to come through, Laura asked Alec quietly: 'Is everything all right, darling?'

'Sure.'

Once the luggage was on the counters it didn't take five minutes because it was a night-tourist flight and Stan said loudly: 'Well we could've come here loaded with roast beef or whatever it is that England's got and France hasn't! What's England got anyway?'

The man with the creased waistcoat standing next to him said: 'Mr Wilson.'

'They wouldn't've let him through and that's a fact. Never mind, they've got Charlie de Gaulle here, nose and all, so it's a fair swop. You on holiday, are you?'

'That's right.'

'So are we, and I hope you enjoy yourself, and if I happen to see you on the beach with Brigitte Bardot I won't let on to the missus – oh, excuse me, madam.'

Stan was on form again. He watched the man with the creased waistcoat being led firmly away.

'Poor old sod, he should've jumped out and got it over with.'

Going through the big glass doors into the main hall Mike breathed normally again. They were night-tourists and the only risk of a search would have been through a tip-off and there wasn't one; but Stan's life-of-the-party sense of humour had got him worried while they were in Customs. It was just another reminder *never* to bring anyone else in on a job, even if it meant coming away with only half the poppy.

'Where do we go?' asked Fay. She had her cigarettes out.

'I don't know. Light one up for me, will you?'

It had been impossible in the plane to get a hand anywhere near his own and he hadn't bought any from the trolley because he couldn't get near his lighter either, and if he'd borrowed Fay's every time she might have asked if he'd lost his own. It had been bad enough making excuses for not taking his coat off, and Fay might seem the helpless type but she had her head screwed on.

But now he had to feel some smoke in his lungs: they were through and past the post.

'We take the coach, darling.'

Last year they'd hired two taxis because there were eight of them and one wasn't big enough (Stan's girlfriend had been with them) and afterwards Ronnie had said they could have had a five-course dinner for that much money (Ronnie had to watch things more than the others), so she had written to the transport people this year and arranged for the correspondence coach to Cannes to drop them off at the Villa Mimosa on its way through Antibes, as it was making a stop at the Hotel de la Reine in any case, close by.

It was waiting for them.

'Oh, look...' Chris said softly, reaching for Ron's hand. She didn't mean the coach but the scene beyond, with the floodlit palm trees and the flags hanging motionless against the hazy sky. 'Doesn't that make you feel better already?'

'Yes,' he said. 'Yes.'

Stan was gallantly handing the girls into the coach and as Mike got on with him, the last of the passengers, Stan said, 'It really is a terrible shame, this fifty-quid travelling limit, isn't it? Makes it so difficult buying postcards.'

Mike would have worried about that because Stan had a voice like a bass-drum and the coach was full of people but there was no risk now and he let his quick wheezy laugh break out as he squeezed his overcoat through the doorway.

When the coach started off and made a U-turn, coming back towards the bridge, Fay looked from the window and in her slow brown eyes was the reflection of the glowing palm trees, their fronds quiet in the warm air of the night, and she thought: This is really beautiful, beautiful, you could call those trees the gates of Paradise, they're so beautiful.

They went by the road along the sea towards Antibes, where the half-moon sent dazzling light from the waves, so that a camper's tent on the beach stood black, a cardboard cut-out at the edge of a silver dish, and beyond it the square fort on the peninsular and the lighthouse flashing.

'What was that wonderful place,' she asked dreamily, 'where we went last year, just over there?'

'Les Remparts,' said Mike.

He never made any attempt at the proper accent, and she smiled, watching the sea.

'It's "lay",' she murmured, 'not "lez".'

'Is that a fact?'

She could actually feel the smile on her mouth, the softness of it. He would never say it properly and she'd never want him to. His bad French was a part of all this, and nothing must ever change.

Ron sat stiffly with his hands on the rail of the seat in front of him.

'What am I doing here?'

'You're all right,' Alec said again.

'I've got to go back.' The coach bumped over a patch of

road where it had been repaired and he bobbed up and down, gripping the rail.

'We'll have a talk about it first, Ron.'

'I shouldn't have come.' The light from the sea hurt his eyes and he lowered his head. 'Why did you let me come?'

'I didn't know about it till we were on the plane.'

'Is that when I told you? On the plane? I don't remember when it was.' He spoke against his chest, his head turned a little towards Alec. 'It was all mixed up, see.'

'Sure. That's why we want to have a talk about everything.'

Alec had got on to the coach before Chris, as if he hadn't noticed her behind him, so that he could sit next to Ron and help him bear with it until they reached the Villa; then he could break down if he wanted to; it would be a good thing if he did.

'I tell you I've got to go back. Soon as we stop anywhere.' His head lifted with a jerk and Alec thought he was going to get up and tell the driver to let him off the coach.

'You're all right. There's no hurry.' He put one hand on the rail in front so that if Ron tried to leave his seat he could stop him. He'd been all right on the plane, after he'd said what he had to say; the brandy had pulled him together a bit and he'd just sat letting the whole thing ride over him. It was getting off the plane and hanging about in Customs that had upset him again and Alec hadn't moved an inch from him. *You're all right.* He must have said it fifty times. At every minute he'd expected Ron to start breaking out, going wild.

Chris had been fine, not fussing Ron, letting him find his own way back to normal. It was almost as if she knew.

Alec shut his eyes suddenly as if the pain were physical.
'What am I doing here?'
He'd lost it again.
'You're all right,' Alec said.

The driver helped them get their cases off.
'*Celle-ci?*'
'The blue one. Er – *bleu*, yes. *Oui.*'
'*Après?*'
'Er – those two white ones. *Blancs* —'
'*Les blanches?*'
Laura came up and Stan left it to her.
'*Il n'y a qu'une seule qui reste – la grise, là-bas.*'
'*Mais vous parlez comme une française, madame!*'
'*Vous me flattez, m'sieur.*'
They must get so sick of it, nobody ever knowing a word.
His brown arms swung in the light from the coach and the last valise was put with the others on the porch.
'*C'est tout?*'
'*C'est tout. Je vous remercie infiniment.*'
She made it twenty francs.
'*C'est moi qui vous remercie, madame – et bon séjour!*'
He started the engine and turned, backing against the dark stem of the mimosa tree; the exhaust gas was sharp in the air. Then the coach had gone and they stood in a group, looking up at the house. In the moonlight the peeling paint of the shutters didn't show and they could see only the Italian balustrade edging the roof against the milky sky, the balconies where geraniums spilled their blooms – pink, violet and crimson, as they remembered, but dark now – and the single palm tree with the moonlight on its leaves.
'It could be a palace . . .' Fay said in the silence.

Stan said: 'Well as long as Madame Dupont doesn't hear you. We pay enough rent as it is.'

But even Stan didn't move yet. The warm air was on their faces and there was no sound anywhere, even from the sea.

Then Ron was going towards the porch suddenly and Alec went with him, picking up two of the cases. 'Keys, Laura?'

As the lights came on inside the villa they remembered the rooms as if it were only last week and not a year ago. The mosaic floors smelt of Javel cleanser but they didn't mind, didn't notice, because the ancient guitar still hung on the wall where Madame Dupont always left it for them, and a basket of pink apricots was on the bottom stair with a note pinned on it – *Soyez le bienvenu, tout est en ordre!*

The cases were taken up, the girls leading the way to the same rooms they always had; they had never changed about since the first time they had come here: there was a garden all round and the view was lovely from everywhere.

While the girls were busy with the cases Mike and Stan went along to the little spare room at the end of the passage and came out again without their overcoats, even taking their jackets off, the night was so warm.

Alec had put two of the lights on in the salon below, to make sure Madame Dupont had stocked up the bar as usual. It was all there.

His hands were shaking as he broke the seal of a Remy Martin bottle and gave the cork a twist to loosen it; then he got out the glasses and stood them ready. Now there was nothing more to do and he stood alone in the big high-ceilinged room for a minute rehearsing it again in silence. The room was all the quieter for the sound of their voices upstairs, the light tone of the girls' as they unpacked, and Stan's much deeper one, making a joke about something; then laughter.

He went across the hall to the bottom of the stairs and called to them.

'Doesn't anyone want a drink?'

CHAPTER 10

When they had first seen this room they had been enchanted. The Villa Mimosa had been built around 1900 and like many others along the coast it was in the Italian style, a good copy of the Florentine villa of earlier times, with balustrades and stone cupolas and deep fenestration. The main salon, opening on one side through double doors to the staircase and on the other side to the terrace, was in the middle of the villa; it had originally been decorated in the same style, with walls expertly painted to resemble silk, the floor a *grand motif* mosaic of stone-blue and sand-white tiles, the ceiling encrusted with plaster reliefs in flower-pattern and carrying four gilded cherubs, one in each corner.

Three changes of ownership and two world wars had left their mark on the Villa Mimosa: a Marseilles industrialist had thought to have the doors repainted in the style of Louis XVI; an Austrian composer had inserted a panel of carved teak showing a stag at bay with leaping hounds, fortunately near the windows and therefore against the light; and Madame Dupont's late husband had brought in a bit of baroque. In both world wars there had been soldiery billeted here, first Italian then German, changing the whole appearance in small ways by rough usage; and this had led to further repainting and general touching-up.

But here and there were the remains of elegance and even beauty of a sort, and on first opening the double doors one had the impression of half-forgotten grandeur and more sumptuous times.

Four years ago when Madame Dupont's tenants – her *'très gentils anglais'* – had first opened these doors their immediate impression had lingered indelibly.

'Angels!' Fay had said, pointing upwards.

'And silk walls!' Chris had said, touching them and finding they weren't and saying nothing.

'It's a cut above Early Purley,' Stan had nodded.

So that the ornate salon of the Villa Mimosa had taken on an added beauty for a short time every year, and though it was in the eye of the beholders it was real to them. This was where they had passed so many evenings, lingering over a meal and talking afterwards until suddenly it was dusk and then as suddenly dark before they realized; this was where the candle had dripped on to the *petit-point* cloth (they'd drawn lots to decide who should tell Madame Dupont when they left); where Stan's particular style of *flamenco* on the warped guitar had finally snapped the A-string and he'd never missed it; and where one night a great gold moth had come through the shutters and they'd fetched honey from the kitchen and watched it delicately sup it from the cardboard lid while they held their breath.

Tonight Alec came back into the room and stood alone for a moment, remembering none of these things.

Stan was first down, his *espadrilles* flapping on the marble stairs – he always made them flap deliberately – and his gold watch and signet-ring flashing in the light as he came through the double doors and cocked a look at Alec.

'Stuff's in the spare room for now, don't let the girls go in there yet for God's sake, now what are we going to drink? Should've picked up some champagne.' His energy carried him on towards the french windows.

Alec heard the others coming down and said:

'Don't open the shutters, Stan.'

'Why not?'

'It's three in the morning. We don't want to disturb people.'

Stan turned back from the tall windows. His jacket was off and the sleeves of his white shirt were rolled up and he stood with his hands on his hips looking at Alec.

'Well it's only a nightcap, not a piss-up!'

Although Alec remembered none of those things that had happened in this room in the past he realized that from now on there were new things, happening in the present, that he would remember one day: Stan framed against the windows with his hands on his hips and his head slightly tilted, trying to make out what it was in Alec's voice.

'What'll it be, Scotch?'

With his head still slightly on one side Stan said:

'Everything okay, is it?'

Chris and Ron came in before Alec could answer, Chris leading Ron by the hand – 'Brandy for my boy-friend, give me what you like.' She tried the wall-switches. 'Are these all the lights we've got?'

'I only put two of them on,' Alec said, and pulled the cork of the Remy Martin. Chris looked at him and then at Stan, who gave an absent-minded wolf-whistle because she'd unpacked a pretty little number and slipped it on.

The room was silent when Mike came down.

'Where's the funeral?'

High heels clicked on the stairs.

'It's a wonderful colour —'

'But absolutely useless, chips as soon as it dries —'

'I didn't mean I wanted to try —'

'Darling, you can *have* it —'

And Stan gave another whistle as Fay and Laura made their entrance hand in hand, both beautiful.

'Name it,' said Alec. He was at the baroque console that served as the bar, his back to them.

'Gin and lime, darling, I'm a different girl on holiday.'

'Fruit juice,' said Fay.

Stan helped Alec with the drinks and Ron sat in the Louis XVI chair and Chris perched on the arm, her hand resting lightly on his shoulder. His face was stiff and he was looking up at Alec.

'Cheers,' Alec said. He was drinking brandy. He didn't sit down.

'Here's to us,' said Chris. 'All of us.'

Laura looked at Alec and said: 'And now you'd better break it, hadn't you?'

They all looked at her.

'Break what?' asked Chris, and felt relieved in a way because she'd been trying all the time to believe nothing was wrong.

Alec looked into his glass. Maybe this wasn't after all the best way to do it; it was just the best way he could think of. Maybe it wouldn't matter, after a time, how it had been done.

'We've struck a bit of trouble,' he said.

They waited and he tried to remember the careful sequence of facts he'd rehearsed, the sequence in which they would sound less terrible. On the plane and at the airport and in the coach here he'd got it all worked out; but he hadn't realized how much courage it would need, or how little he had.

Ron spoke.

'I've killed a policeman.'

Alec remembered seeing a shiver cross the surface of the drink in his hand, remembered for a long time afterwards.

'He thinks he has. We're not sure.'

Ron said out of his white pinched face: 'You know when you've done a thing like that. You know.' He spoke clearly but like a machine.

'It's not true,' said Chris flatly. The room had seemed to give a lurch and when someone else began speaking she couldn't hear them properly and she looked at her drink in case it was that; you always tried to think of a reason for things. She had begun to feel cold and it reminded her of something Ronnie had told her once, about how cold it was in a prison.

'That was the accident, was it?' Fay was asking. 'The one you told us about?' Her head felt light and there was a thumping in her chest.

'You ran him down?' Laura asked. 'And didn't stop?' She wished Ron would drink his brandy. He looked dead.

Then Mike was coming slowly across the room, big and light on his feet; he squatted in front of Ron and put a hand on his knee and asked him with a blank face:

'*Did you have a gun?*'

'Yes. Yes.'

Mike nodded. 'I see.' He got up and put away his drink untouched.

The silence settled like dust.

Far away through the slats of the shutters a cricket whistled.

Stan's low voice came, startling them. 'Why aren't we sure, Alec? You said we weren't sure.'

Ron said mechanically, 'You know when you've done a thing like that.'

'Get that drink down you, boy, you look terrible.'

Suddenly it hit Chris, a reeling disbelief in all reality. Mike was nearest and she didn't fall. He led her to one of the bamboo chairs that Madame Dupont had left locked up in here for them to use on the terrace when they arrived. The blue cushions had long ago been faded by the sun and they were nearly white.

'I'm not going to faint.'

Alec took the glass from her and put it back on the gilt console; that kind of comfort was the last thing she'd want.

Ron hadn't moved. Fay thought it was odd to see him just sitting there, not even looking at Chris or at any of them. Normally he'd have been the first to help her but he just sat with his head back looking upwards with narrowed eyes at nothing: she could see his eyes weren't even focusing. She wondered if Dr Giraud would mind if they went to fetch him at this time of night, if they had to go and fetch him.

Chris sat with her legs drawn up. She was ashamed of nearly passing out. *You can go to your room, Nurse. I'm all right, but – You will go to your room at once.* Sister Romford had been wrong: she wouldn't have passed out if she'd been allowed to stay. You had to stick it and think things out, in this life.

She'd said at first that it wasn't true but of course it was, or it could be. If you went to prison before you were twenty-one you'd go there again. Prison didn't cure you of what you had.

'Why aren't we sure, Alec?' Stan was at the bar, pouring himself another. His voice left a faint hum on the strings of the guitar that hung near the doors.

'I've not been told much, Stan.'

Laura had waited until she felt less angry. They'd taken so much bloody trouble, hadn't they: Alec had to 'go back to the Club' and Ron was going to 'help him' and Mike had to 'complete a contract for a house', so they 'might' have to go direct to the Airport in Stan's car.

Their poor little idiot wives had to be left to their packing because they wouldn't understand – this was a *man's* game. But they hadn't taken enough trouble to play it properly, so their poor little idiot wives were now in the most hellish mess imaginable.

'I don't care how much or how little you've been told, Alec. I want to know the lot. Who's got enough guts to tell me?'

She took her slim leather bag and lit a cigarette.

The cricket whistled, far away.

'What happened, Ronnie?' Chris could only just manage not to go to him and hold him. He didn't answer.

Mike had sat down on one of the Arab *pouffes* and his big arms were across his knees, his fingers interlocked. He said:

'I had a job lined up. I always do them on my own but this time we were all in it, for a bit of fun. A patrol-car got on to us and we had to scatter. That's as much as I can tell you.' He looked at the girls in turn. He didn't look at Ron.

'That's what happened,' Stan said. 'I don't know anything more than that.'

Laura looked up at Alec. Maybe the Boy Scout could explain how they'd got into this kind of jam. It wasn't in Alec's line to go around killing – she couldn't finish the thought; her mind had blanked off and she half-realized that the good red-blooded anger was only a cover for cold fear; and this was new and shocking in itself; she'd never been afraid of anything in all her life.

Alec was leaning against the false-silk wall; the light from the gilt bracket above him made pools of shadow across his eyes; and Laura thought how little it took to change a face you'd known for so long. That too was frightening.

'When we scattered,' he said slowly, 'Ron had a gun on him.' He wasn't sure how to go on, because he didn't have the facts; he hadn't been there when it had happened. Even Ron didn't have the *facts*; things done in panic weren't clearly remembered; it always sounded a bit phoney when people in the dock said something 'just came over them' and they 'didn't remember what happened after that', but most times it was probably the truth.

Ron hadn't told him anything on the plane except that he'd 'killed a copper'. Alec hadn't disbelieved him: it wasn't a thing you'd say for a joke. It could only have been with a gun; Ron was too small to do anything with his hands. There'd been nothing to do on the plane except shut him up and make out nothing was wrong until they could all reach somewhere they could talk together in private.

He looked down at Ron now. No, you couldn't ask him. He wasn't in a fit state to be asked anything.

They were still waiting so he said: 'One of the policemen was chasing Ron, and he thinks he fired on him. We're not sure.'

'Ronnie.' Chris was leaning forward, making herself do it. 'Tell us what you did.'

'Yes.' He didn't look at her or any of them. 'I went up an alley. To get away.' He had his hands together loosely and his head lay against the embroidered cushion. The stiffness had gone out of him in the last few minutes but he didn't look relaxed; he looked as if he'd been thrown into the big Louis XVI chair like a rag-doll.

'Then what happened, Ronnie?'

'Yes. It didn't lead anywhere. There was a wall at the end of the alley. With a gate in it. But he was coming nearer me and so I knew I couldn't get through the gate in time. My foot was hurting. So I got out the gun. It was in my pocket. He saw the gun but he didn't stop.'

He broke off again as if he thought he had told them it all now.

One by one they were looking away from him. They couldn't look away from his voice, though. It was quite clear, every word was quite clear but it was dreadful because it wasn't his voice, the one they thought they knew. It reminded Fay of the voice on the plane that said it hoped you'd enjoyed the flight; you knew it sounded like that because of the microphone making it sort of metallic; but Ronnie wasn't speaking into a microphone; it just sounded as though he was.

'Go on,' Chris said.

You can't ask him to, Alec thought.

'Yes.'

'Does it matter?' It was Stan. He didn't want any more of this. There'd been a game at school – he'd never played it but he'd seen the little bastards at it, making a frog jump over a stick, every time the poor little bleeder stopped they gave it another poke with the penknife to make it hop again.

'Yes, it does matter.' Laura's voice had cut across the room. 'If we can't find out exactly what happened how can we hope to get out of this damned mess your "bit of fun" has got us into?'

She and Stan faced each other and in a moment he looked down. They had never heard her so angry before; her cigarette had gone out, flattened by her fingers in the middle.

'What happened then, Ronnie?' Chris said. She felt very cold now, right through.

'He didn't stop. He looked down at my hand instead of my face and said put that away it won't get you anywhere, and then when I fired he looked at my face again with his mouth in a sort of oh. Then he fell down. Then he fell down.'

After a while Stan looked at Laura and said: 'Are you satisfied?'

She got up and threw the flattened cigarette into the hearth through the gap at the edge of the embroidered screen that was always there; they'd never been here in the winter; they came for the sun.

'Yes. Are you?'

'I wasn't there,' Stan said sharply. 'Not in the alley. Don't forget that.'

She walked away from them through the double doors and said without turning: 'You're there now. We all are.'

When Ron broke down they left it to Chris.

Stan closed the tall windows. He knew now why Alec had told him not to open the shutters.

Fay went upstairs; Mike didn't follow her. He hadn't spoken for a long time. Now he said: 'We'd better share that stuff out.'

Stan and Alec were each side of him; they stood at the gilt console with their backs to the room and Stan was pouring himself another brandy. Alec wasn't drinking. He looked at Mike with no expression.

'I don't want any of it,' he said.

Mike said softly and impatiently: 'I know all about that but you've got to be practical.' He broke off because Ron sounded bad now and you couldn't talk through it; he was sobbing and trying to tell Chris *but it's what I've done to you, it's what I've done to you*, and she spoke to him all the time saying they weren't sure he'd done anything to anybody yet.

When Ron was quieter Mike went on: 'You've got to be practical. You may need that. We don't know what's going to —'

'It's not a question of scruples,' Alec said. 'You offered me a share before we began and I told you I didn't want any. I was there to look after Ron, that was all.' His tone went flat. 'I didn't do much good, did I?'

Ron sounded wilder again and Alec was ready to go and help Chris because she wouldn't have the strength if he tried to damage himself. She talked to him all the time and it wasn't easy to listen to because there was an intimacy between the two of them deeper than if they'd been making love.

Stan felt this too. 'We ought to get out of here, oughtn't we?'

'She might want help,' Alec said.

'All right,' Mike said, 'if that's the way you want to look at it. The offer's closed.'

Stan stood with the drink in his hand, one bunched fist at his hip, staring at Mike under heavy lids. 'You surprise me, you know.'

'Is that a fact?'

Alec knew that Mike didn't worry what people thought of him; if people got wrong ideas about him that was too bad: they'd have to think a bit straighter and they'd have to do it for themselves.

'Take your share, Stan,' said Alec quietly. 'You may need it.'

'No thanks.'

Alec said no more. He'd had longer than the others to think, a full hour in the plane with no interruptions. Mike was way ahead of him already and he'd cope on his own but the others would take time to realize what had happened; most people under shock reacted in the same way in the early stages: they pretended nothing had happened at all; that was why Chris had said at once: '*It's not true.*'

She was still talking to Ron and he was quieter at last and drank some brandy. The crisis was over and Alec said: 'We all need some sleep.'

'We're going up now,' Chris said in a whisper, suddenly exhausted.

'Fay's got some tablets,' Mike told her. 'Ask her for some.'

'Yes.'

Then they heard someone on the staircase and saw it was Laura, bringing her two valises down. She put them on the floor below the basket of apricots Madame Dupont had left.

'Where are you going?' Alec asked.

'Home.'

He went up to her. 'You can't.'

Her eyes were hostile. 'Yes,' she said, 'I can.'

'You don't understand. None of us can. None of us.'

CHAPTER 11

The light came through the shutters in thin lines and she could smell coffee and her head moved, making the lines of light tilt one way and then the other. The hostess with the lovely eyes said coffee, was that right, and Stan said we could have brought roast beef.

Ron was asleep. She could hear him breathing. That was all right then.

The lines of light tilted and she watched them and he said, they're like di'monds in soot, your eyes are, and she brushed her cheek and felt it was wet. Yes, I'd like a cup, please, she said, and Ronnie took down the guitar and looked at her with narrowed eyes and said it's cold in there, it's always cold, and as he touched the strings it exploded and she saw it was a gun and she screamed.

Her heart was pounding and she looked across at his young sharp face but he was still sleeping and there was no sound in the house; she couldn't have screamed at all. Propped against the bedhead she watched his closed eyes and quiet mouth and wished they could both stay like this for always, lying peacefully in the first light of the day. *I love you,* she said silently with her lips.

The ornate room was empty. The stubs of three Stuyvesants were in the ashtray and Mike's drink stood on the edge of the console, a midge drowning in it. The dark spots on the arm of the Louis XVI chair were already drying.

They had gone into the kitchen together and she made

some coffee and they talked for almost an hour there, not wanting to go back into the salon.

'He told you on the plane, didn't he?'

'Yes.'

'Then why did you have to bring us all the way here?' Her eyes were still hostile. 'We could have gone straight home on the next flight.'

'I couldn't tell you on the plane because of the other passengers – it would've led to scenes —'

'How embarrassing.'

'I wasn't worried about that, but it would've been dangerous.'

She looked full into his eyes. 'Why?'

'We couldn't have hung about Nice Airport either, because people would have noticed. We had to come here, where we could talk in private.'

'Why did you say dangerous, Alec?'

He was fear in her eyes, something he'd never seen before. He thought to touch her hand but he knew she would only draw it away. She hated the idea of being protected.

'Because it's a dangerous situation we're all in.'

'My God, don't I know that? But there's nothing we can do about it now and I don't see what earthly difference it would have made if you'd told us on the plane. Or was it that you didn't have the – didn't feel up to it?'

She looked away from him, getting another cigarette and lighting it. 'But I suppose it took more guts to keep it to yourself all that time. All I want to know is *why*.'

She was perched on the stool near the sink and he was on the edge of the table. Some of her coffee had slopped into the saucer when she had opened her bag for the cigarettes and now as she lifted her cup he said:

'There's a drip. You'll spoil your dress.'

She gave a grim little smile. 'Thank you.' Using the tea-cloth she thought that only Alec could be as considerate as that at a time like this. But it was more than considerateness; to be able to think about a drip of coffee on a dress at all he must have a stability in him that even she had never discovered in all their years of marriage.

'All right, Alec, you've got it all worked out.' Her head ached like hell but she was damned if she were going to take aspirins. 'Just let me in on it, will you?'

'It won't matter what I've got worked out unless we can all agree.' There was pale light showing among the slats of the shutters and it made the light from the bulb look yellower on the peeling walls. 'We don't know yet if he was killed, or only wounded.' In his mind the word had lost some of its ugliness over the past hours, but it still sounded odd in the kitchen of the Villa Mimosa, as if everything had slipped out of focus. 'We'll have to wait till we know that.'

She said with surprise: 'Does it matter? I mean ... to us.' It was the first time she'd thought about the policeman. But then she'd never known him, didn't even know his name. In the ordinary way you'd see it in the paper and think 'how shocking' and look for the fashion page; just because Ronnie was responsible it didn't make you think more about the policeman. 'Even if he recovers it'll be called attempted murder and they'll still do everything they can to find who it was.'

'Sure. It won't affect the hunt.' It was another word they'd all have to get used to. 'But it'll make *us* feel different.'

'All right, but I still don't see —'

'Come on, Laurry ...'

'I know, but I've got such a swine of a headache.'

'Have an aspirin.'

'No. If I begin on aspirins now I'll want knock-out drops before we've finished.'

He drew a breath. 'It'll be a bit of a strain for the next week or two and the point is that if he *isn't* dead we shall cope much easier.'

'And if he is?'

'We've still got to cope.'

'Anyway,' she said wearily, 'I'm going home.'

'You can't. I've told you that.'

She was off the stool – 'You've got a *bloody* nerve, Alec! *I* can't go home where my own children are? Christ, you try and stop me! For how long exactly – for just how many *years* have you given me the holier-than-thou routine while all the time you've been living as a professional crook? I'll say one thing – you took me in completely!' Laughter came suddenly in her voice and it had the same roughness as the rage. 'When I think I used to call you a Boy Scout, for God's sake! And all the time I've been living with what they call "a member of the criminal classes" – that sounds worse than calling you a crook, doesn't it, more sordid somehow, people with big ears and stubble and a shifty look, a rotten enough bunch at the best of times but dangerous when they're cornered . . .' She stared into his face with her green eyes blazing and he didn't recognize her any more than she recognized him. It was a moment before she could go on and when she did her voice was deathly soft. 'And *you* tell me I can't go home to my children. I'd kill you if you tried to stop me. It's going to be "a bit of a strain" for the next few weeks – how right you are – and what I've got to do is try shielding *them* from the worst of it, and try to explain why you won't be coming home – because they'll get you, Alec, you know that, they won't rest, they never do, they'll turn London upside down and it won't matter where you go – they'll get you.'

Slowly she put her hands to her face because all the time the rage was coming out she'd been thinking of other things with half her mind, Alec as she had once known him, sitting on Mandy's bed with the comic and saying, 'All I can see here is people hitting and shooting each other – can't we be happy without smashing things?' and bringing home crystallized fruit because Mother loved it more than anything, and helping the girls on with their coats after one of their wonderful evenings, and coming to see her three times a day at the nursing-home when there'd been complications with Rupert, always bringing something and giving it to her solemnly as a gift and not a gesture. Those things had been Alec, and a thousand more, and they were always done with gentleness and with an underlying protectiveness that had sometimes brought her to the point of open irritation because she was too independent to want it, even to appreciate it for what it was without accepting it.

And now he'd blown it all up, all and everyone – Mandy and Toops and her mother and herself, as effectively as if he'd come home one day with a bomb and thrown it against the wall.

'I don't understand anything,' she said, drawing her fingers slowly down her face and looking at him again.

'It's been a shock,' he said quietly.

'Yes. It's been a shock.' Her head throbbed with an almost pleasurable pain. 'It was a shock for you too, I suppose.'

'Yes.'

'I mean you didn't know he was carrying a gun.'

'No.'

'I don't understand that either. But then I didn't know him as well as I knew —' she broke off with a rueful little breath through her nose.

'Laura,' he said, 'we've got to start thinking straight. If we don't we're sunk.'

She got out the packet but it was empty and she slung it into the sink. 'We're not sunk already?'

'No. Not till they find out who did it. And there's a chance they'll never find out.' He spoke slowly, watching her face to see whether she was taking it in. 'That's the chance we've got to use for all it's worth. We've got to improve on it.'

'In the hope they won't find out?'

'It's more than just a hope. We've got a chance to *stop* them finding out.' She was watching him rationally now, exhausted but attentive. 'And if you go home, Laura, we'll lose that chance, and it's the only one we've got.'

Chris found them still there in the kitchen.

'I could smell coffee,' she smiled.

Her eyes were pink under dark wet lashes and her hair was tumbled. She stood in the doorway beside the glass-covered bell-indicator that never worked any more, looking from one to the other with her small hands linked loosely in front of her.

'There's some left,' said Laura and felt a rush of pity that surprised her; she'd believed anger was the only thing she would ever feel again. She found a cup from the shelf.

'I don't want any. It's just a nice smell.'

Alec had got off the edge of the table. Chris looked smaller than ever in the high doorway; even her shadow was bigger than she was, cast by the single bulb against the wall outside. 'I'll make some tea,' he said.

'No, thank you.' She smoothed her dress. 'I slept in my things. Am I interrupting?'

'We were just talking,' Laura said.

The daylight in the shutters was stronger.

'He's still asleep,' Chris told them. 'I made him take something Fay let me have from her dispensary.' She smiled again.

'Did you sleep?' Laura put one arm round her and they leaned together in the doorway.

Alec had often seen Laura and Mandy like that.

'Yes. I remember dreaming.' She was looking steadily at Alec. 'Will you please tell me something? Why did he have a gun with him?'

'I don't know.'

'Did you know he had one?'

'No.'

'Did Mike know? Or Stan?'

'No. They couldn't have known. They're not the sort of people who have guns.'

'Nor was Ronnie.' He didn't answer. 'I've got to find out what I can because I'm his wife and I want to look after him as much as they'll –' her voice tripped but she went on like a child correcting herself with a poem she was reciting – 'as much as they'll let me.'

Alec said gently, 'We're all going to look after him. We're all together in this.'

'The Old Firm.' She nodded, but it sounded empty.

'Sure.' There didn't seem anything he could say to give her comfort. 'You must wonder why I didn't talk to him, Chris.'

'Talk to him?'

'Try to make him back out in time.'

141

She shook her head. 'He wouldn't have listened.'

'Don't you think so?' He hadn't meant to seek comfort for himself.

'I wish I knew how he got it.' She was thinking again of the gun. Alec said:

'I don't suppose he realized he had it with him.'

'He must have.'

'Yes, but I mean he didn't have any intention —' and he shivered because it was a word they'd hear again one day, if it came to it, in court. 'I mean it was just a toy, with him. You know Ron better than I do – he got a big kick out of crime pictures, fancied himself as James Bond, people like that. Let's face it, there's always a gun in someone's fist on all the posters – it's a natural part of our lives these days, though I can't see why.'

'You mean he was sort of playing.'

'Sure. And a lot of people are fascinated by guns – we give them to kids and put them in the petrol ads and take pictures of fashion-models with them, you can see guns made of chocolate in any sweetshop and we don't think a thing about it. Maybe one day we'll all grow up and get it out of our system but just now it's with us in a big way.' Chris had her eyes closed and he didn't know if she was listening or if he was doing any good.

'I know,' she said, and he knew she hadn't been listening. 'He says he's got to go back.' She opened her eyes. 'And he's right, isn't he?'

Laura was watching him.

'We shall all be going back soon, at the end of the – at the end of our stay here.' There were bars of sunshine on the wall now and he switched off the light. 'That'll be time enough.'

.   .   .

The music came again and Stan twiddled the knob and got nothing but atmospherics.

'How d'you get England on this bloody thing?'

He looked up when Mike came back but Mike said: 'They won't be in for another two hours.' He gave Laura two packets of cigarettes and a copy of *Nice-Matin*.

'It might be in here,' she said.

Stan got up from his haunches and the music went on in the background, half tuned in. Alec was watching Laura's face; they all were.

'No.' It was like a reprieve.

'What about inside?'

'It'd be on the front page.' Her hand was shaking as she ripped the Cellophane from one of the packets and tugged out a cigarette, her long nails tearing the paper at the end.

Stan went back to the radio, crouching in front of it. It was an old model; the veneer along the top was rippled and the station-finding panel had warped at one side, so that the exposed bulb cast a wedge of light upwards against his face. The radio was on the floor because there was no room for it anywhere else unless some of the ornaments were shifted; and Madame Dupont liked them left where they were. The aerial wire ran slackly upwards to a hole in the corner of the ceiling, grey with dust.

... *In the House of Commons yesterday Mr Ernest Welsh, replying to a question* ...

'That's it!'

'I know, but it's bloody well fading —'

... *Conservative Member for West Hartlepool* ... *that in the public interest he must confine himself to* ...

They came closer to listen. Their shadows darkened the corner of the room; the shutters had been left closed and the sun was already too high to reach through the slats and there was a kind of twilight in the room.

... Unless, as Mr Welsh put it, there were 'greater pressure brought to bear'. His reply, according to ...

The voice was very faint now. Stan's darkly-veined hand moved the knob a degree to the left and right but the atmospherics got worse and the voice grew fainter still.

... Manchester yesterday ... a meeting of ...

The smoke from Laura's cigarette drifted across the wedge of light.

... Dockyard situation ... a measure of ... said Mr Hawthorne, but ...

The static blotted out the last of the voice.

Mike's breathing was heavy. 'Leave it there, Stan.'

'What?'

'Leave it tuned in where you've got it.'

Stan straightened up and they moved back to give him room. 'One o'clock isn't it, the next lot?'

'We'll have the papers before then,' said Alec.

'It might not be in them yet.' Laura dropped into one of the bamboo chairs, leaning her head on the cushion. 'It's not important anyway. We'll know some time or other.'

'I'd like to know now,' said Stan. 'Now.' He was restless, kicking at one of the leather *pouffes*. They didn't know whether he'd slept during the early hours; his usual energy was still with him but it didn't come easily any more; it was forced.

When Chris came down Fay was with her, pale but managing a smile; her slow brown eyes focused badly and they could see that she had doped herself to sleep last night.

Mike asked: 'Where's Ron?'

'He hasn't woken up yet.' Chris had made up and changed her dress.

Mike said: 'We'll have to decide without him.' His

voice was no louder than normal but there was a terseness in it they hadn't noticed before.

Stan said suddenly: 'I'm going back anyway.'

Mike threw a glance at him and said to the girls: 'I should sit down if I were you.'

'Why don't we open these bloody shutters?' Stan said.

'It'd make it hotter.'

'We could do with a fan in here.'

They had never sat in this room during the day; it had always been the beach as soon as they were up.

Fay thought: I feel like this because we were dumped down in a foreign country and that made it worse; the Villa Mimosa's not strange but we're doing strange things in it; *I want to go home.*

Mike was still standing, his arms folded across his crumpled shirt. He looked at Alec. 'You'd better do it.'

Alec shook his head slowly.

Mike said: 'You'll do it better than me. I've not got the knack.'

Stan swung on him – 'Let's have it out straight for Christ's sake. We can take it.'

'I was thinking of the girls,' said Mike.

Laura said past her cigarette: 'The "girls" are tougher than you are, don't worry.'

Mike's red eyebrows jerked up and it looked odd without the quick smile that normally went with it. 'Fair enough.'

A bee came in through the shutters and droned somewhere above them.

Mike looked at Laura. 'Has Alec told you what we were doing last night, the four of us?'

'No.'

'We were on a job, you know that much. It was my job – I planned it and did the breaking-in and did the work on the safe. It was finished before the others came in.

Stan helped me bring away the stuff, that's all. Ron had a car lined up for us; we didn't want one but I let him do it for a bit of fun.' He looked at Chris. 'Ron never touched the stuff. He tell you that?'

'No, Mike.'

'I don't suppose he remembers much. Alec didn't touch the stuff either. He was there to look after Ron if anything happened.' Laura was watching him with narrowed green eyes. 'He didn't say so but I knew that's what he was there for, to look after Ron.'

Laura turned her head. 'Is that true, Alec?'

'More or less.'

She drew on her cigarette. 'That was big of you. And while you were so busy looking after people it didn't occur to you that your own children would suffer if "anything happened"?'

'No. Any more than it occurs to you when you drive too fast.'

Mike looked at his feet. She didn't say anything more.

'So that's how it was,' he said, looking up again. 'As far as the job itself goes they wouldn't be too tough on Alec and Ron. Stan's deeper in it because he handled the stuff. But if that policeman's dead they're going to be tough on the lot of us and we shall get thirty years each.'

In the silence the bee went on hitting the drops of the chandelier because they were reflecting the light from the shutters and it was looking for escape. Dust came down.

Fay was leaning forward trying to focus on Mike's face and on what he was saying.

'That's if they find us,' Mike said.

Stan gave a grunt. 'They won't find me.'

His face had gone grey and Alec could see that he hadn't spent any time in thinking, the past few hours; he'd been dodging it, relying on his energy and his own confidence

146

in himself to get him out of this; but his energy wasn't going to be enough when the pressure came on: he'd be taking blind swipes without letting himself think straight. *I wasn't there, in the alley.* That was the prop he'd been depending on but now Mike had knocked it from under him.

'They'll try, Stan.'

'Let them try.'

'They won't have to if you go back to London —'

'I know where I am in London.'

'In the dock.'

'I've got my wits.' He was raising his voice, not looking at Mike. 'I can look after myself.'

'You're on your own, is that it?'

'What other way can we get out of this?'

'By sticking together till the crunch comes. Then it might not come.'

'Look, I know all about the "Old Firm" and all that but this is different, don't you know that?'

'Don't I *know* it?'

Alec had seen a smile like this on Mike's face before, when he'd come quietly into the Club that night and looked at the protection boys who thought they were going to zip the place up.

Stan was facing him now, hearing the tone in his voice.

'Yes,' Mike said, 'I know it's different now. And I know a few other things you've not troubled to think about, for all your "wits".' His head was lowered and his bright eyes looked up at Stan. 'If any of us go back to London they'll give themselves away, you know that? It's getting too much for you already and you're showing it. You think you can keep a poker-face over there in the thick of a full-scale police hunt when you've only got to make one small mistake in front of your staff at the salon or your pals at the pub and you'll go down for thirty years, never set eyes on another woman for thirty years, come out a queer with grey hair? I'll tell you the kind of "wits" you've got. You ever hear of a fox walking straight out of cover to meet the pack?'

He turned away and took a step, light on his feet.

'You can put it that way if you —'

'I've not finished yet.' Mike was back facing him, his massive arms still folded. 'That's only as far as it concerns *you*. But you'd give me away too, and Alec, and Ron, because once they'd got you under interrogation you'd break. You'd break.' Slowly he shook his head. 'Listen to me. *I'm* not going inside for thirty years because *you* can't stand the strain. So you'd better find what it takes, Stan, because it's not started yet.'

Watching him Fay was beginning to understand what this meant. Mike was forty-two and as strong as an ox and the business was just getting on its feet and when they let him go again he'd be an old man out of work.

'So you think I'd break.' Stan hadn't liked that.

'You'd break all right. You don't know those boys like I do. They want to know who killed their chum and once they'd got you inside four walls you'd not come out till you'd told them.' Softly he said: 'Even *I* wouldn't.'

Not even an old man out of work: she knew him better than that. He wasn't the kind to behave himself and suck up to the warders for the sake of the remission; it'd be a series of escapes and attempted escapes and each time he'd go back for longer. Put it another way. She'd never see him again.

'What I've told Stan goes for the rest of us. Who else wants to go home?'

'I shall be going,' Laura said. 'There's an Air France plane about three.'

Mike came across the room and dragged up a *pouffe* and sat on it in front of her and said: 'Because of Mandy and Toops.'

'That's right.'

'I can't stop you.'

'But you'll try.'

He shook his head. 'That'll be up to Alec.'

Through her teeth she said: 'You think I'll listen to him?'

'He's the best man you've ever met. I don't care how good the others are. He's the best.'

Her eyes were narrowed to green slits. 'He really is the original shining Jesus Christ, isn't he, Mike? All his friends say so and they must be right. But I'm still going home because someone's got the job of making sure that his children don't find out that he's wanted by the police on a murder charge.'

'Alec had nothing to do with it —'

'Will that be the charge or won't it?'

'Technically, but —'

'They put people away for thirty years for technical reasons? You know what Alec did. He said goodnight to Mandy and Toops and tucked them up in bed and then went out on what the prosecution's going to call a "criminal enterprise" during the course of which a poor damned policeman got shot to death – a man with a wife and kids of his own most likely.' Her voice started shaking. 'My God, I'd rather be *her* telling *them* what happened to Daddy than go home and lie to my own kids and hide the paper and warn my friends till I can think of a way to break it to them before they find out at school – or do I keep them away from school like a couple of lepers and shut them up in the flat?' She flicked her cigarette past him into the hearth. 'And he's the best man I've ever met?'

Alec was standing near the doors with his hands in his pockets and his head down listening; suddenly aware of movement he saw that Fay had turned her head and was smiling shakily up at him.

'He went out,' Mike said patiently, 'to help Ron if there was trouble. That's why he went out.'

A terrible thought came into her mind: she wished he'd gone out saying, 'We're doing a job tonight that Mike's got lined up but we'll be on the plane so don't worry.' It was the Boy Scout act that she couldn't stomach.

'So he knew there might be trouble?'

'Nothing's certain in this life, Laura.'

'So he took the risk. They won't thank him for that when they're old enough to understand.'

'It wasn't a conscious risk. He tried to explain that to you, remember? When you're tearing up the miles in the Cortina and getting a big kick out of it for your own pleasure you never think of Alec having to hide the paper from them one day so they don't see the picture of the wreckage, but it happens to an awful lot of people.'

'There's a difference between driving fast and committing a crime —'

'It's not what we're talking about, is it? We're talking about consciously exposing the children to a risk, it doesn't make any odds what kind.' His voice grew quiet. 'But since you've brought up the subject we might as well admit there *is* a difference. You drive fast for your own pleasure but last night Alec was trying to help someone else.'

She didn't look at him; her hands were restless. The opened packet of cigarettes was on the little Florentine table, the one with the wonky leg; it was the table Stan had once used for showing them a conjuring trick with a walnut and a glass of wine, giving them a wonderful line of patter but sending the glass over just the same; it had been red wine and he'd whipped off his white yachting-slacks before he'd reached the staircase to go up and put them in the bath and they'd declared it an all-time record in striptease. That seemed a long time ago now; they'd been different people.

Mike passed her the packet from the table, seeing how restless her hands were.

'So you're flying home today. What are you going to tell the children?'

'The sun was too hot down here and I missed them.'

'That's easy, then. What about your mother?'

'I've had a row with Alec.' She got the lighter from her bag.

'I see. Will she go back to Brighton?'

'Not until Alec comes home.'

'So you'll be with her in the flat for the next ten days, telling her everything that's wrong between you and Alec —'

'Not necessarily.' She drew the first smoke into her lungs.

'If you've bust up a holiday – the kind we've always had here – and flown home on the first day, she'll expect you to be full of it, the row with Alec; it'd have to be a real rip-snorter, wouldn't it? But you'll think of something. It'll be quite a strain for ten days, keeping up the act, but —'

'Why don't you leave me alone, Mike?' He could see the pain across her eyes. 'I've got a headache.'

He got up from the *pouffe* and took a pace or two. 'You see, you'll have more to do than just act the injured wife who's run home to mother. Your mother knows Alec and she knows he'd be the first to make the effort to patch things up; it wouldn't be like Alec to go on with his holiday as if nothing was wrong: he'd follow you home in a day or two because his marriage comes first. So your mother's going to start worrying when he doesn't show up – she likes Alec, she's fond of him – and she'll say he must be ill or had an accident because he's not even phoned.' He stood still for a moment, looking down at her. 'Or maybe you think he'd phone, do you? He's got into trouble helping a chum and we know what you think of him – you've just told us; and now you're off home full of righteousness and you don't give a damn whether it gets him a thirty-year stretch or not. But maybe you think he'll phone? I don't.'

She said in a rough whisper: 'Leave me alone.' She had closed her eyes. There were rings under them and her skin was sallow. She looked older than yesterday, years older.

'Mike,' Alec said. 'We don't want to hear any more.' His face was hard.

Mike's head swung. 'There's not so much more but you'll have to hear it. You think I'd have the impudence to talk to *your* wife like this in front of *you* if there wasn't a good reason? I wouldn't dare!' Slowly he moved up to face Alec. 'You know my reason. I'm trying to stop a tragedy happening.'

'All right, Mike. But talk to me if you've got to, not to Laura.'

Mike took a pace away and swung round again. 'That's fair enough. So her mother's started worrying, right? And by the end of the week she'll be sending a telegram here, asking you to phone; and by that time Laura's going to be screaming with nerves because she can't tell her mother the truth and make her stop agitating. And every day there'll be the front-page stuff in the papers about the hunt the police have started, with her mother talking about it and saying how shocking it is and saying she hopes they'll find who they're looking for – and Laura knowing you're one of them, Alec. You think she won't let her mother suspect anything? You think she can carry on as if she didn't *care* what the police are doing all over London, all over the country? And what about the postman and the tradespeople and her friends – the neighbours in the other flats? It'd take a professional actress to keep up that kind of pretence, but Laura's the most honest person I know – that's why she can't stand this.'

He heard Laura say bitterly: 'Don't let's get sentimental, Mike.' She had opened her eyes and was ready for anything more he was going to tell her, to her face or through Alec. She resented Alec's attempt at protection.

Mike turned and looked down at her.

'You'll be okay, Laura, if they don't get on to us. Your mother and the rest of them won't connect you with a murder-hunt just because your nerves are all to hell – you've had a row with your husband, that's fair enough. But if they get on to us there'll be a lot of questions asked – they'll talk to your mother and the neighbours and the tradespeople and the lid's going to come right off, and your story about a row with Alec won't be worth another breath. They'll see the obvious, fast enough – the police aren't stupid. They'll know you went back home because you knew who they were looking for – and didn't tell them.' He put his head on one side and his tone was deliberately casual. 'For obstructing the course of justice on a police-killing case I reckon you'd get five years. Is that going to help Mandy and Toops?'

Her eyes had widened; her lips parted but she said nothing.

His tone was still casual. 'But there's a choice you can make, so it's okay. You can stay down here with us, and

153

your mother and the rest won't suspect a thing – give her a call to say we've arrived safely, send her a few postcards. If the time ever comes when they get on to us you can say you didn't know about it – we've only just told you, seeing it's all up.' He glanced around him – 'That goes for Fay and Chris as well. You've not been told yet: that's our story and we shan't let you down.' He swung his head back to Laura. 'So you're safe enough if you stay here – *they're* safe, the children. Or you can go home now, by the next plane – it's your choice, as I say. They'd still be safe providing you phoned the police the minute you got there and turned us in. They wouldn't have a thing on you then and you'd be in the clear.'

CHAPTER 12

They went down the short drive together, not speaking till they reached the road.

Fay walked on Alec's side, not between him and Stan as she would normally do, there being one girl and two men; but they didn't notice; it seemed to have happened by chance. The drive was made of small grey pebbles brought from the beach on the other side of the peninsula towards Nice, years ago when the Villa Mimosa was built. Marcel, the French boy who lived near, was often in the drive here looking for extra good pebbles for his catapult, 'picking about like a blue-tit', as Mike had told him once; Marcel always wore blue.

'Remember the mimosa tree, Alec?'

'Sure.'

The tree was leaning across the wall from the garden, a cascade of yellow-gold above their heads. There was a photo of it in the album at home, with Chris standing below it and reaching up to touch the blooms. Alec was glad that Fay had room in her thoughts for the mimosa tree.

Stan had gone off to the left and had to turn and catch them up when he realized. 'I've forgotten where the bloody place is.' He meant the post office.

They heard by his voice that he was still bitter about what Mike had said to him in front of them all: *'You'll break.'*

Fay wondered if it was true. Mike could judge people, especially men; he looked right through what they said and what they did and saw what they were. Normally he wouldn't let people know what he thought of them but today he'd said more than she'd ever heard him say before, getting at Stan like that and telling Laura that Alec was the best man she'd ever met.

Mike hadn't come with them because he said he wanted to talk to Ron as soon as he woke up; he hadn't said what about. Chris had stayed behind in case Ronnie needed her. Laura had gone to bed with ice from the fridge wrapped in a scarf on her forehead: she wouldn't take any Aspros.

'She didn't mean it, Alec.'

She'd felt physically sick for a moment when Laura had said that, about Alec being 'the original shining Jesus Christ' – and with Alec there listening; there'd been an actual pain in her stomach, not exactly a pain but a sort of cold grey feeling as if she'd swallowed something bad. Plenty of people had rows, it was a part of most marriages; but Alec and Laura had never shown anything – there'd never been one of those atmospheres in the flat at Carlton Mansions. It had been dreadful just now, actually hearing her say such a thing to other people, with him there.

'I don't suppose so,' said Alec. He took her hand as they crossed the road. The tar had begun melting under the sun's heat, and the yellow line had gone wobbly – last year when they'd crossed the road here it was just the same and Ronnie had said: 'Oh dear, oh dear, that bloke had sunk a good few glasses of Pastis when he painted that!' And they'd all laughed.

'It was just the shock of it all,' she said.

'Sure. I'd rather she said it than kept it on her mind. Besides, what's wrong with being an original shining Jesus Christ? Think of all the things she *could* have called me.'

So Fay knew it had hurt him, because he'd remembered

the exact words too. They'd been worse than hateful or angry: they'd been contemptuous; that was why she'd felt the sick feeling in her stomach. The two names 'Alec and Laura' had always meant something abiding to her, a whole small world that would always be there; and just now it had been like seeing a rock beginning to crumble. It had frightened her and she'd come out with Alec to be near him because his part of the rock would never grow weak and there was nobody else to help her: Mike had shut himself in with his angers and forebodings (she knew he'd been dreadfully angry with Ron though he'd said nothing), and Laura hated the boys for what they'd done; Stan couldn't help her: he was going to look after himself from now on, since nobody trusted him – that was his attitude, you could hear it in his voice; poor little Chris had enough to do, looking after Ronnie. So there was only Alec now.

'She'll apologize when she's got over the shock. She didn't mean it.'

'I don't suppose so,' he said again.

She could tell he was only humouring her; there was nothing she could do for Alec in return for being near him.

Outside the post office she opened her pink purse and gave a franc piece to the Spaniard with the guitar and one leg; he was always here at this time of the year. *'Vous êtes de retour!'* He smiled up at them from the pavement, his brown fingers idle for a moment across the strings, his neck twisting so that he could greet Stan as well; but Stan hadn't stopped; he was going up the steps of the post office and Fay tried quickly to explain to the brown crumpled man that her friend hadn't seen him, and he nodded that he understood; his hand stroked a chord as they went away.

The first year they'd seen the man sitting here Stan had asked him to show him a new chord every time they passed, and afterwards he'd tried it out on Madame Dupont's guitar. Stan called him 'Señor Corona-Corona, my private tutor from Barcelona'.

It was cooler inside the post office because of the marble floor.

'You didn't see Señor Corona-Corona,' Fay said.

'What?'

The way Stan looked at her she could see he thought she was barmy. It didn't mean anything any more to Stan, the mimosa or the musician, things like that. It was as if they'd died, and the thought frightened her.

She said: 'What are you going to tell her?'

'I've got tonsillitis. Alec's going to ring.'

'Suppose she still decides to come down to nurse you?'

'Dolly?' It was the first time he'd laughed since Ronnie had told them what he had done. It wasn't his normal kind of laugh: it was ugly.

He gave Alec the slip of paper with the number and it took fifteen minutes to get through and then there was no answer.

'Christ,' said Stan. The sweat was trickling down the sides of his face. He was paler today because he'd forgotten to put on his Sunless-tan cream. 'What do we do?'

'Send a wire,' Alec told him. They worked out the best wording: DON'T COME STOP HAVE CONTRACTED ACUTE TONSILLITIS STOP TRIED TO RING YOU STOP LOVE – STAN. They had to sign a form assuring the French postal authorities that the telegram contained nothing obscene, because it was in English, and when Alec told Stan what it was all about he gave another laugh and the sweat got worse because the thing Fay had said – about Dolly wanting to come down to nurse him – had started him thinking and now he couldn't get it off his mind.

All the time they'd been waiting for the connection he'd been picturing the phone ringing in Dolly's flat with the blue nude on the wall and the black cushions on the white hide settee – Christ, it'd looked as if they'd played football with those cushions the first time she'd invited him round there – and those panties of hers everywhere, you could put them in an egg-cup and leave room for the egg. *Dolly* come down and nurse him? She'd be off with that tall thin bastard with the bow tie and the Buick – it'd been a toss-up whether she'd go to Majorca or fly down here and he'd nearly bust a gut the last night they'd spent at her flat, proving he'd got the edge.

But that wasn't what was putting the fear of Christ in him. He could just about manage for ten days with cold showers and pure thoughts so long as he didn't look at Laura; it was what bloody Mike had said – *you'll never set eyes on a woman for thirty years, you'll come out a queer with grey hair*. It hadn't sounded bad at the time, or it'd sounded so bad that it didn't make any sense – it couldn't ever happen. But now he was standing here in this marble morgue desperate to stop Dolly catching the plane – to stop *Dolly* coming down here – and it was going to last for ten days. This time yesterday he'd have said it could never happen, so nothing was impossible, ten days or thirty years. The sweat ran down him.

'. . . can try, to get her a message?'

'What?' There was a girl at the counter with legs right up to her arse and little white shorts on, tapping her foot with impatience so that her bare thigh quivered. 'Look at that *bitch*,' he said to Alec. 'What was that?'

'I said isn't there anyone else we can try? Someone who could ring Dolly at intervals?'

'Intervals?'

'In case the telegram doesn't reach her in time,' said Alec quietly.

'Christ. Yes. Harry. Ring Harry.'

'Who's he?'

'The caretaker at my place.'

He gave Alec the number and they waited for the connection and he watched the girl in the little white shorts going out and knew it was no good thinking, *Never mind, there'll be Dolly tonight,* because there wouldn't be Dolly tonight. Face it, then. Suppose that copper was dead and the Yard picked up a clue right away: it could mean that when they flew back in ten days they'd go straight into a blue van and that'd be the last anyone would see of them except in the dock. There'd never be another chance of a woman. It'd mean this wasn't the first day of ten days; it'd be the first day of thirty years. Today.

'*Vous avez demandé Londres, m'sieur?*'

'Go on, Alec. Name's Johnson.'

Alec went into Box No. 3 and shut the door.

Go on, Alec. Make sure she doesn't come. Make sure I don't have her. Dolly. Ever again.

Standing here in his canvas slacks and sports shirt among the other people buying stamps and sending coloured postcards, a man on holiday and dressed as they were, he made up his mind about something. If things took a turn for the worse he'd get out so fast that no one'd see him go – South America, Africa, anywhere. And if it looked all right to go back to London and he was wrong and they tried to pick him up he'd fight with everything he'd got, in the van, in the dock, in the cell, fight them all the way along the line. If they wanted to put him in clink then they'd have to kill him first and drag him there.

· · ·

Chris sat alone in the ornate room listening to their voices. Ronnie had spoken a few minutes ago and Mike had gone up, saying again that he wanted to talk to him, 'ask him a few things'.

'Don't upset him, Mike.'

'Upset him?' He stood with his arms folded. He always stood like that now. He'd withdrawn from them all as if he'd been among friends and suddenly realized he was among strangers, and now he looked out at them from behind his folded arms. 'We're all upset.'

'But you think it was his fault.' She watched him steadily and knew what he felt like about them all; she felt it herself: this wasn't Mike, it was a stranger.

'I've not said anything.'

'No. But that's what you think.'

She'd never realized how big he was. His head almost touched the chandelier: the red of his hair coloured the glass drops. He stood with his feet planted apart; the enormous strength in him wasn't in his size alone or in the shadowed muscles of his arms; it was in the firm planting of his feet and the set of his head and the steadiness of his eyes.

'It was an accident,' he said. 'We had good luck and bad luck in turns. Like on a pin-table, you hit and you miss.'

She said: 'It'd be better perhaps if you blamed him out loud. Not that I'd let you. But it might make you feel better about him. I don't want you thinking things you can't tell him out loud. So you can tell me, if you like. I'd listen. It wouldn't do me any harm and it might do you some good, and it'd be good for Ronnie.'

He looked surprised. 'I would've thought it was the other way round. You've not blamed me, yet, for getting him into this.'

'Did you?'

His head tilted and the colour flowed among the glass drops. 'I think so. I told him he could come along.'

'But he wanted to go, didn't he? If he hadn't wanted to go you couldn't have made him. You didn't get him into this. He did it himself and he's got to get out of it himself, with me helping, because he and I are the same person. I've got to get him strong again and that's why I won't let you upset him. So if you feel like shouting at him you can shout at me instead, that's all I want you to know. You can go up and see him now.'

She realized how small she must look in the chair, saying he could go up now. But size didn't matter; if necessary she would have to show him she wasn't small at all, nor was Ronnie; they would show everyone. Mike said:

'You've got the feeling you're on your own now, have you? You and him?'

'Yes. We all are. We've got to stick together – you've said that yourself and you've convinced even Laura – but it's going to get harder and harder. This is only the beginning and we don't know how it's going to end, but all I know is that when the end comes we'll all be thinking of ourselves. So I'm starting now. I'm thinking of Ronnie and me.'

The shutters were still closed and the small bedroom was stifling. Mike sat on the bed waiting for Ron, who was still in the bathroom. It had been the sound of water running, downstairs, that had told Mike he was awake.

When he came into the room he seemed surprised to see Mike there, or anyone at all. His stare was so blank that Mike could see he didn't even recognize him for a moment. He didn't speak but gave a quick surface-smile, the kind you gave someone in the street when they seemed to know you but you don't remember them.

Drips fell from his toilet-bag where he'd splashed it; he hung it from the window-fastener. He had a pair of shorts on and Mike thought absently: ten-eight, ten-nine. Mike had boxed for Streatham Athletic once and was a good judge of weight.

The smell of toothpaste and shaving-soap was in the room. They began talking, and neither of them thought of opening the shutters even though the window faced north and had no sun against it. There had been no shutters opened anywhere in the house since they'd arrived.

'Is Chris all right?'

'She's fine, Ron.'

'Where is she?'

'Downstairs.'

'She's all right, is she?'

'She's fine.'

In the half-light of the shuttered room Mike could see he'd had a good shave and washed his hair, which was still dark and wet and combed close to his scalp. Ron had clean habits and down here at the Villa when someone asked where Ron was someone else would say he was probably in the bathroom.

Mike had expected to find him half-doped still from sleep and the pills they'd got him to take; his eyes were drained-looking but his movements weren't slow. He took a comb and began loosening his hair to dry it.

'You can't go home,' Mike said.

'I've got to.'

'No, Ron.'

'I've got to go. I shouldn't have come. I don't know what I'm doing here still.'

Water flicked from the comb.

'Either we all go home or none of us do.' Ron said nothing. 'Are you listening, Ron?'

'Yes.'

'We could let the girls go home but they'd have to explain why we were staying down here without them, and there's no story to fit that one.' He spoke slowly, watching Ron's face in the bamboo-framed mirror to make sure he was listening; but Ron's face was blank; he looked like a wax dummy combing its hair.

'Chris is going home with me. I've got to tell them she didn't have anything to do with it.'

Mike got off the bed and stood beside the window with his arms folded. 'Are you going to tell them the rest of us didn't have anything to do with it?'

'Of course I am.' He looked directly at Mike for the first time since he'd come into the room. 'You don't think I'd let you down, do you? Try putting the blame on you?' He looked bewildered, and Mike was relieved to see some sort of life in his face.

'The blame's on us already, Ron.' He remembered that Ron hadn't been downstairs when they'd all talked about this. 'We're all for the high jump – you, me, Alec and Stan. So it'll make no odds what you tell them.'

'But you didn't – you didn't have the gun.'

Even having put it into words had drained the colour from his face and for a moment the energy that was forcing him along was cut off as if by a switch.

'We all had the gun. That's the law.'

'It can't be.'

'There were a couple of kids, once, named Craig and Bentley —'

'I don't know anything about —'

'Listen, Ron. They were on a job and got chased, and Craig shot a copper dead. They couldn't hang him because he was under age, but they hung his chum Bentley because he was old enough – he was nineteen. Even though he didn't have a gun. That's the law in England.'

'It can't be.' Ron's mouth sounded numbed.

'You'll just have to believe me; the others'll tell you the same thing. It's like this, you see: if we'd known you'd got a gun on you last night we'd have taken it off you, quick. I've never touched such a thing in my life and I don't suppose Alec has, or Stan. But it's no good telling anyone that; they don't want to know. We were there. And when a copper gets killed they'll take who they can get.'

Ron put the comb down without looking at what he was doing; it slid off the edge of the dressing-table and hit the floor. Water from his wet hair trickled down from one of his sideboards and he didn't feel it.

'So I can't go home?'

'No.'

'But I can't do anything else.'

'You can stay here.'

'Stay here.' It wasn't a question, he just repeated it as if it were a number he had to remember. Then he jerked a look at the dressing-table and down at the floor and picked up the comb and wiped it on his shorts and started using it again, all in a quick series of movements. 'Yes,' he said. 'Yes.'

Mike felt his mouth drying and he wanted to look away. Something had happened to Ron. The heart had gone out of his body and left only the nerves: he was a dummy, a robot; the switch had cut in and he was energized again.

'You'll stay here?' Mike asked. He had to try getting through to him.

'Yes.'

He'd been washing and shaving to get ready for the trip home and now he wasn't going home so he was drying his hair because it was wet and he couldn't stay here with wet hair. A feeling of slow dread was coming into Mike; he thought that if he took Ron by the shoulders and turned him to face the door he'd start walking.

'You'll be all right with us.'

'Yes.'

Mike turned away and looked down through the slats of the shutters and saw with a shock the bright red of the geraniums and poinsettias in the garden below and the sun sparking on stones. It didn't look real out there. He heard Ron saying:

'I didn't want them to put me in Brixton again.'

That made sense. His memory was okay. His memory was too good.

When he turned round he saw Ron standing stiffly at the dressing-table staring into the glass, his hair sticking from his head in spikes. He was only just keeping his balance; the muscles in his feet were having to correct all the time as he swayed an inch forward and an inch back. Mike knew what he was doing: he was staring through the glass and his face and the puff of smoke at the other face with its mouth 'in a sort of oh'.

Jerkily he said: 'I swore they'd never get me inside again but that wasn't why I took the gun with me. If I'd thought there was going to be trouble I wouldn't have gone at all. I took the gun because it looked nice and I liked the feel of it. It was heavy, not like the tin one my Mum found tucked down inside of my gum-boots and threw away. This one was nice and heavy. Soon after I bought it I went along to the amusement park. I knew the boy at the gallery there and I asked him to set up the target and then I pulled out the gun while he was getting the rifle ready and I put two in the bull and the rest not far away, you should have seen his face. That's what I wanted it for. I'd thought about it for a long time, all right Johnnie set it up for me will you, putting 'em in and seeing his face. It happened just like I'd thought. Then he said for Christ sake you'd better get out of here and I just walked away, taking my time, walking slow, with him watching.'

There was a smile touching his mouth; he had been talking to himself and his voice had trailed off and he wasn't swaying any more. It may have been a slight sound Mike had made that brought him back to the present; the smile vanished as if it had been hit away by the back of a hand.

'I went into the alley because my foot hurt. I thought I could hide up. But he came in after me and I didn't know what to do. All I knew was that they mustn't put me inside again.'

Mike lowered his head and looked at his folded arms, the black hairs on them, the second-hand of his watch circling, the beat of his pulse under the strap.

'Where did you get the gun?'
'A pawnbroker's.'
'When?'
'About a month ago.'
'Do they know you there?'
'Where?'
'The pawnbroker's.'
'I only went in there once.'
'Did you sign anything?'
'What like?'
'Did you sign anything at all in there?'
'No.'
'Where is it now?'
'I threw it away.'
'Where?'

'I don't know.'
'Don't *know*?'
'I can't remember.'
'Try and remember.'
'I can't.'
'You've got to.'
'What difference does it make?'
'You've been inside, so they've got your dabs on file in Criminal records. Once they find that gun we're done for, the lot of us. So try and remember.'

CHAPTER 13

Stan had gone into a bar near the post office and was less silent on the way back to the Villa. As soon as they came in he poured himself a double.

Mike was in the salon with Ron and Chris. He asked straight away – 'Did you get the papers?'

'They're not in yet.' Alec opened a bottle of mineral water for Fay and himself.

Fay said lightly: 'You think it's hot in here – you should feel what it's like in the town!'

'They said ten o'clock.' Mike was watching them, thinking they might have got the papers and didn't want to say anything because Ron and Chris were here. He could see Stan had had a drink but Alec looked okay and Fay was almost cheerful.

'They'll be in about five this evening. They said if they hadn't arrived this morning they'd be there about five.' Alec sat down and drank half the glass in one go. 'Have you heard Laura?'

'I think she's got off to sleep,' Chris said.

Alec thought of going up quietly but he might wake her and if she was awake anyway they'd only talk and it would be better if they didn't, at least for a while. Her mother had sounded surprised that Laura hadn't been on the phone herself, but he'd said it had been a bumpy trip and she was in bed with a couple of aspirins. It hadn't been easy because Mother probably knew Laura wouldn't take aspirins unless she felt really bad, but then she'd have to feel really bad not to ring her mother personally. He'd said they were all dead-beat because they hadn't arrived until two in the morning and it was so hot down here that you couldn't breathe, so it wasn't surprising. He'd only half succeeded: Mother hadn't actually asked them to ring again but her tone meant she hoped they would, so that she could be sure Laura was all right.

He was trying to watch things like that. There was a chance – he believed there was a chance – and they had to make everything seem normal, especially to people in London: Laura's mother, his brother George, Ron's sisters, everyone. They were down here on holiday, enjoying themselves.

He'd made a mistake already. It had come to him too late, just when he was putting the phone down: he should have told Mother that Stan had got tonsillitis. She wasn't likely to be in touch with Dolly or Johnson the caretaker; she didn't know either of them, didn't know they existed; so it was almost impossible – but not *quite* impossible. He didn't know the exact relations between Dolly and Stan, but Stan had brought her to the Club one evening to introduce her, since she was to join them on the holiday. Suppose she was the jealous type and didn't believe the cable, or at least wanted to check up and make sure Stan hadn't got another woman down here? She might ring the Club and George would say he'd not heard anything but he could give her the number at the flat: she might then ring Mother. No, Alec didn't say anything about acute tonsillitis... So Dolly would suspect Stan was here with someone else and might even fly down to take him by surprise: jealousy was never passive; it drove people to self-hurt. She wouldn't find a woman with Stan but she'd see them as they were now, tormented and unnerved in the half-dark of a shuttered house.

Almost impossible, but not quite. It had been a mistake

and he mustn't make another one. He'd made it because he hadn't slept since the night before last. He would have to get some sleep, or try.

Mike began searching for a clear programme in English on the radio and Stan said: 'You won't get it till one o'clock.'

'Is that a fact?' He was trying to pick up the American Forces Network or one of the pirate stations in the North Sea. The trouble was that when there was music you couldn't tell what nationality the station was. The static was so bad that it got on everyone's nerves.

'For Christ's sake,' Stan said, 'we can't spend the day listening to that bloody din. The papers'll be in at five and then we'll know.' He banged his empty glass down on to the console and put his hands on his hips. 'I'll lay ten to one it only winged him anyway. All Ron saw was that he fell down – that's what you said, isn't it, Ron? That doesn't mean he's been shot dead. You know what I think? I think he was taking avoiding-action, throwing himself flat in case there was more to come. Wouldn't you? They're not daft, they don't fancy running straight on into a hail of bullets. Work it out for yourself.'

He picked up the bottle of Scotch and thought better of it and put the cork back.

'It could be true,' Fay said.

'I'll give you ten to one.'

'I killed him,' Ron said mechanically.

'You thought you did,' Stan said. 'I'd have thought so too if I'd been you. Shoot at a bloke and down he goes, what else can you think? But you've got to reason it out afterwards. If we'd been —'

'Stan.'

'Eh?'

'Just a minute.'

Alec got out of the chair.

Mike was still at the radio but he'd heard Alec above the static and looked round.

Alec was going to the french doors and they saw the shadow on the slats just before he opened the shutters.

'Christ,' Stan murmured.

The sunlight was blinding and all Alec could see at first was a shiver of blue moving away. Stan saw the boy more clearly because he was farther inside the room and the light wasn't directly against his eyes.

'We've been hoping you'd come,' Alec said.

Marcel had backed away and stood ready to run, the fright still on his face. Alec held out his hand and he came towards him hesitantly.

'I did not know if you are arrived, *m'sieur*.'

'Sure we are. How are you, Marcel?'

He was a thin boy with dark hair cut in a fringe and bright olive-black eyes; he walked with his feet splayed as if already outgrowing his twelve-year-old strength; and he always smelt of garlic. His hand came up on its brown skinny arm and rested in Alec's for an instant.

'I am very well, thank you.'

He darted a look behind Alec into the dark room. His eyes, their irises almost as black as the pupils, showed nothing; his fright was in the way he stood, still half-ready to run, and in the quick withdrawing of his hand.

Alec heard the radio being turned off; then Chris came on to the terrace smiling and Marcel went to her with a laugh of relief and she stood holding him in her arms.

'We gave you a scare,' she said, 'opening the shutters like that.' She threw Alec a questioning glance above the boy's head but saw no answer. 'We didn't know it was you.'

Every year they left some of their things in the little spare room, mostly the things they didn't use except down here:

snorkels and masks and flippers and the two Li-lo's and the growing assortment of sun-hats they could never resist buying from the shops on the promenade each time they came. It was all mixed up with Madame Dupont's broken bamboo screens and warped silk lampshades and cracked pictures of the Madonna and Child.

Looking for his gear, Stan saw that someone had moved the croquet set, wedging the long box on end behind the pile of chairs. He noticed it because it was usually near the door and he usually barked his shins on it.

They were as quiet as they could be so as not to wake Laura, but Alec had looked in on her and they heard them talking.

'We're taking Marcel on the beach.'

'All right, Alec.'

She was lying down and kept her eyes closed.

'It'll look odd if we stay in the house all day.'

The ice had melted inside the Jacqmar scarf and the pillow was darkening.

'Naturally,' she said.

'I'll get you some more ice before we go.'

'Don't worry.'

'You can't sleep on a wet pillow.' He remembered giving her the scarf for her birthday a month ago, the morning when Mandy had said she had another tooth 'going wobbly'.

'I'd rather you didn't worry about me, Alec.'

Every time he thought of Mandy it brought a knifing pain through his head. Toops was younger and explanations would be easier for a while. It was when he was reminded of the children, in spite of his effort not to think of them and to keep them apart from all this, that he stopped believing there was a chance for them all; and he knew this wasn't because the children could affect whatever chance there was, but because it would be so terrible if they lost it.

'We'll be at the usual place,' he said, 'the Midi Plage.'

It was no use asking her if she minded being left; she had a cat-like independence and when injured she would look for a remote corner and heal herself.

Most of the others had gone downstairs and he followed them.

Chris was still helping Ron in their room at the back of the house. When they had said they were all going on the beach he had accepted it without a word and gone up to get ready, but now he didn't know how to go about it.

'I should put on your striped trunks, Ronnie.'

'Yes.' He looked around him and she saw it wasn't so much that he didn't know where they were but that he'd forgotten what they were like, how to recognize them.

'Here they are,' she said.

He put them on and couldn't find the drawstring because they were back to front.

'They're the wrong way round,' she said.

He took them off again. 'Why are we going on the beach?'

'That's what we came here for.' She pretended to look for the sun-lotion. 'We don't have to think about anything while we're on holiday.'

She got a towel for him and folded it narrow so that he could put it round his neck and hold the two ends in front of him; he always carried it like that, the way sporty-looking men did it in advertisements for cigarettes.

'We ought not to be going on the beach.' He was looking down at his striped trunks trying to understand what he was doing in them, as if they were fancy-dress. 'I don't want to go. People will see me.'

She didn't know what he meant. Later she realized.

'Come on, Ronnie.'

'Yes.'

Going to the stairs she took his hand and made the joke they always did when they were leaving the house for the beach: 'Have you got your bucket and spade?'

'No.' He stopped, as if he must go back for them.

She tightened her hand on his. 'It was only a joke,' she said, and they went downstairs.

They took the lane through the eucalyptus trees and Fay remembered the smell of them and breathed it in, unable to believe that a whole year had gone by since they were here last. Everything seemed the same now and she was the first of them to forget, just for a moment, that it was not the same.

Marcel, for whom nothing had changed except the passing of a single year (and at twelve a year meant nothing because there were so many thousands left), talked most to Fay, perhaps sensing she was the only one of them who seemed the same. He took her hand sometimes, darting on and coming back to her, explaining in his quite good English that his mother had told him he mustn't go to the Villa Mimosa until they called for him, but that he had been so impatient to see them that he had disobeyed. He had heard them arrive in the night and had lain awake listening, and in the morning he had stayed in his room to keep watch on the Villa from his window; then when the shutters stayed closed for so long he became 'unquiet' and disobeyed his mother ('You will not give me up, please, because she will be strict with me?') and came to see what had happened to them all.

'We were tired,' Fay told him, 'and Laura isn't very well.'

'She has the *grippe*?'

'I expect that's what it is, yes.'

He darted ahead of them again, splay-footed and with his thin arms outstretched to touch the green-and-yellow trunks of the eucalyptus trees on each side of him as he always did here in the lane to the sea; but for Fay the scene slipped out of focus – she was looking at the past even though it was happening now in front of her eyes, because Laura wasn't here this time, walking with them in one of her gay floppy hats.

'Then she must be made a visit from Docteur Giraud,' said Marcel, coming back. He had taken his time to consider what had been said, in the way he had; sometimes there would be long silences from him while he thought things out.

'It's not serious,' Fay said.

'*La grippe* is serious, yes.'

She told him that Laura would be all right tomorrow and would be coming on the beach with them, and he either went off into further consideration or decided that there was nothing more to consider. They watched him flitting between the trees in his blue shorts, and Alec tried all the time to think of the best way of asking him how long he had been there outside the shutters.

Only two things happened during the afternoon.

The Midi Plage was almost deserted when they reached there; it was too early in the season for the Dutch and Belgians and Italians and too late in the day for the French, most of whom had left promptly at noon to eat at home.

The *maître nageur* and his wife were delighted to see *les anglais* and remembered them well enough to inquire at once after '*la dame elegante aux jolies chapeaux*', and Alec told them she was tired from the night-flight and would be down here tomorrow. Yes, they would like to make a reservation for the week: four parasols and seven mattresses in the row nearest the water's edge.

Nobody wanted anything to eat but Stan ordered a cognac and Fay asked Alec if he would buy her an Orangina, since she had lost her purse.

A breeze sent the fringes of the blue parasols swinging and brought miniature waves bubbling in from the sea; farther out in the bay the water was deep indigo.

'You really mean you've lost it?'

'Somewhere in the town – I missed it when we got back.'

The beach-boy straightened their mattresses and lowered the parasols an inch, settling the little square tables more securely in the sand and fussing over them to show how glad he was to see them, his white teeth gleaming as he ruffled Marcel's head – '*Tu es content maintenant, toi, avec tes amis!*'

The sand was already hot under their bare feet.

'We'll go and look for it this evening,' Alec said.

'There wasn't much in it.'

'It was a nice purse. You must have left it in the shop by the post office.'

'I'm always leaving it somewhere.' She had taken the mattress next to Alec's. The nearer she was to him the easier it was to believe that everything was still the same. She'd tried talking to Mike on their way through the lane but it was no good; he was still shut in with his worries. It had happened before and she'd grown used to it over the years; when he was worried he'd never talk about it and at first she'd been miserable because she would have liked to help, if only by talking; then she had decided that he couldn't expect much sense from someone who kept missing buses and burning the potatoes and losing her purse, and she had just settled for it and left him in peace till he got over it. At those times she felt the distance between them widening and she was back in the days before she'd met him, lonely again.

She had never known what his worries were or whether they were big or little; but now she knew, and the distance was as wide as the sea out there, and as empty. That was why she must stay close to Alec; otherwise the loneliness would be too much for her this time and she would drown in it.

'You could get some sleep now,' she said, 'if you wanted to.' He was already stretched out on the mattress with his eyes closed. 'I won't let anyone disturb you.'

She didn't know if he'd heard; it didn't matter. She would keep Marcel quiet if he came near. Sitting beside Alec and sipping at the ice-cold Orangina the boy had brought, she gave herself to the feeling, headily strange, of helping him, however little, in return for all he meant to her now that there was no one else.

Marcel was standing alone in the sea, gazing down, his thin reflection broken by the waves and forming again. He was waiting for someone to swim with him but no one came. At this time of the year they were his only friends; his mother had told them that when he was nine he had shown so much intelligence at the *lycée* that his *professeurs* had called him an infant prodigy; the breakdown had been what Docteur Giraud had termed the 'inevitable result' of his having been forced beyond his limits, which were lower than they seemed. He was now allowed a tutor for short and carefully regulated periods and between times was encouraged to play, sleep and eat as much as he liked, in the hope of his gaining weight. Freed now from the pressures of serious study he was exposed to new dangers: an invitation to regard himself as a freak, being set apart from children of his own age, and the lack of company during the school terms. His only friends were the people who came to stay at the Villa Mimosa from time to time, and there were not many who wanted the responsibility of a stray French boy on their hands.

He stood knee-deep in the waves, scooping up water and watching it glitter as it fell. He stood with his back to the beach.

Stan sat with his glass of cognac.

'How much d'you reckon he heard?'

'It's too late to worry,' said Mike.

Stan fell silent again. Whatever you said to Mike now, you'd get no useful bloody answer. He finished his drink and put the glass on the little table and stretched out on the mattress, shutting his eyes against the glare.

In the next hour three of them slept: Alec, Stan and Chris. When Chris woke the first thing she missed was the feel of Ronnie's hand; her own had been curled in it when she had dropped off. Until then her waking had been slow, a gradual merging of dream and reality: the waves had fallen sighing against the high leaves of the eucalyptus trees and Marcel was breathing peppermint over her, saying 'I'm special', but she said 'no, you're not special, you're always eating garlic'; and Laura was there with the big blue parasol spinning slowly on her head while Stan had tried to undress her and the judge counted the apricots in the basket, his wig blood-red; then her hands began moving, brushing across the sand to and fro and touching nothing; the waves fell but her hand was still dry and the fringe of the parasol swung in the breeze immediately above her with the long white stem running up; and her hand brushed faster at the sand, faster and faster because the other one was gone and she had to find it –

'Ronnie?'

The sunshine burst against her eyes and she sat up so quickly that her elbow hit the stem of the parasol – 'Ronnie?'

She could only see their legs; they were all lying down; the shadow of the parasols hid their faces until her eyes got used to the glare; then she was on her feet with sand falling from her and it was difficult to run properly through its softness – 'Marcel! Where did he go? Where did he go?'

He pointed at once to the sea and she stood shielding her eyes but could make out nothing at all.

'He is a long way,' Marcel said.

'Can you see him? Please, can you?'

'Sometimes, when the waves are not making. He is very far.'

She plunged and surfaced, throwing off the shock and striking out much too fast, getting nowhere and trying to steady the stroke; then water went churning past her and Mike's red hair showed among the spray as his great arms settled into a rhythmic crawl. She called out to him and he answered, telling her to go back, everything was okay. She kept up her feeble breast-stroke until light and dark fluttered behind her eyes and she turned, dragging her way back and falling on the warm dry sand, lying there with Marcel speaking to her from high above, fright in his voice.

'It's all right, Marcel.' The blue and gold of the sky and sand swirled against her but she put more effort into it and got to her feet, annoyed with her own feebleness. 'You must never ... go in ... when you've got too hot in the sun ...' She was smiling to him stupidly, trying to make the fright go from his crumpled face.

'*C'est très dangereux, vous savez.*' He nodded, forgetting to speak English. '*Ça va mieux maintenant?*'

Fay was coming down the sand and they went back together, Marcel trailing with them. The *maître nageur* came across looking concerned – he had been helping the delivery-man bring crates down from the van on the road, and wanted to know what had happened, and when Marcel told him the English gentleman had swum out very far he nodded and went into the surf and splashed his neck and stomach, diving in.

Alec and Stan were still sleeping, their limbs at odd angles as if they were drugged. Fay asked Marcel to go up to the bar and bring a cognac, and he ran with the sand flying from his feet.

'I don't want anything, Fay.'

'It'll warm you.'

'I was still half-asleep when I went in, that's all.'

'He's all right; he's a wonderful swimmer. He only wanted to be on his own for a while.'

'I know.'

Chris sat hunched with a towel that Fay had put round her shoulders. The chill gripped the whole of her body and the sun felt cold on her skin. She answered Fay and said yes, it was a silly thing to do, panicking like that, but she knew nothing was important except what was happening far away from her on the deep blue water where she couldn't go. Fay said things to her and she answered, but nothing here had any meaning except the minutes going by; time was something you couldn't see or hear or touch but it could hold you like this and you couldn't move because you knew that moving would make no difference to anything: only time could make any difference now, and you had to wait to know what had been decided.

Sand scattered near her legs.

'Here we are,' Fay said, her voice a long way off. 'Drink a little of it, for my sake.'

'All right.'

The sun was cold on her skin. The spirit was cold in her throat. But time had gone by; she was nearer to knowing.

He was out there somewhere. All her life was out there, everything she knew and loved and wanted back again. Her hand, this hand, this one with the chilled fingers, would be empty from now on and for always, if he made up his mind that it was the only thing he could do now that he knew that whatever happened he could never be again what he had been before, that neither of them could be the same again to themselves or to each other.

The breeze was cold on her legs, blowing grains of sand against her; the fringe of the parasol rippled above her head; another small wave came in and melted away. It meant that time was going; she was nearer still to knowing.

'Ils reviennent!'

Marcel was darting down to the water's edge, waving his spidery arms.

Fay went down to ask him what he was saying. They stood together watching the sea. He began waving again and Fay left him and was smiling when she reached the parasol.

'They're coming back, all three.'

Chris lowered her head to her knees and felt warmth at last as the tears fell against her skin.

Ron lay sleeping, covered with dry towels. The *maître nageur* had given him neat rum and fifteen minutes' massage, lecturing them all as he worked: the sea was not warm enough yet for people who were not habituated; they must remember that although it was nearly June on the beach it was still April in the water because there was a time-lag in the temperatures; also they should not swim alone as far as that; every year there were accidents here along the coast because people did not respect the sea.

Marcel translated for him, adopting the same stern tone. Alec and Stan had been wakened by all their voices and were still trying to understand what had happened.

The Midi Plage was busier now; women whose husbands were working brought their children down for the afternoon. A man with a tray threw sugared peanuts into their laps to tempt them and Stan bought three packets to share. The shiny paper crackled and flashed in the sun and for a moment they were all as young as Marcel and knew that a bag of sweets could make everything come right again. Then they smelt coffee and got up and stretched and went up to the bar, all except Chris who stayed with Ron; they brought her a cup and a doughnut to go with it, a doughnut for each of them and two for Marcel to help him put on weight; and afterwards they rinsed their sticky fingers in the sea. Then a man came past selling English papers and they bought a *Daily Express,* and the headline said LONDON POLICEMAN SHOT DEAD.

CHAPTER 14

The beach-things were in a heap on the porch, the masks and flippers and snorkels and the two Li-lo's; it was where they were always left at the end of a day by the sea, so that sand shouldn't be brought into the house; but today there were no white stains on the rubber where the salt had dried, because nothing had been used; and no dead crabs left by Marcel as presents.

It was only six o'clock and the sun was still on the higher leaves of the palm tree, and the geraniums at the back of the house glowed red as if left on fire by the long day's heat; but inside the house it was already twilight because of the shutters, and in the ornate salon it was quiet, with nobody there. One of the glass drops of the chandelier was trembling, finely suspended on its wire link, as someone walked across the room directly above.

The first cool air of the evening crept through the shutters, so that one string of the guitar on the wall was slackened by the smallest degree and eased across the bridge, its faint note picking at the silence and dying away. A moth, falling at some hour of the day into a used tumbler that someone had left on the console, floated on the dregs, the gold powder spreading across the surface, shed by the struggle for life that had now ceased.

The newspaper lay untidily on one of the bamboo chairs where someone had dropped it on their way through They had all read it except for Ron, who had told them he had known anyway.

. . .

A London policeman was shot dead last night in an alley off Courier St near the heart of the City when the crew of a patrol-car gave chase on foot to four men they wished to question. He was Police-constable James Henry Goddard.

According to witnesses the officers in the patrol-car at first gave chase to another car – since found abandoned – and continued on foot after the men wanted for questioning got out and ran along Courier St. One of the men took to the alley, which is a cul-de-sac, and P.C. Goddard followed him, calling on him to stop. He was fired on at a range of some five yards and police reports say that he died instantly.

Meanwhile P.C. Mark Edward Bolter, the driver of the patrol-car, followed the other three men but was unable to catch them.

It is the first time a policeman has been killed in a shooting incident since the triple murder near Wormwood Scrubs on August 12 1966, for which Duddy, Roberts and Witney received life sentences.

Det.-Supt. J. M. Braithwaite, aged 51, of the Yard's Murder Squad, has taken charge of the investigation. Mr Tomliss, Home Secretary, has been informed. Senior officers, among them Deputy Commander Charles Fenwick, Deputy Head of London C.I.D., Cmdr Bill Logan and Cmdr Norman Straker, held a conference at the Yard last night, and it has been decided to bring in every available policeman from all London divisions. Rest days and leave have been cancelled immediately for hundreds of officers and many are expected to return to duty before their leave expires. All Scotland Yard Flying Squad officers not at present engaged in priority investigations have been ordered to join in the hunt for the killer of P.C. Goddard and a countrywide alert has been put out to all police forces. A signal has been sent to the headquarters of Interpol in Paris in case the wanted man has succeeded or succeeds in leaving the country. Scotland Yard has appealed to anyone who was in the immediate vicinity of Courier St between 10 and 11 o'clock last night to come forward. Sir Clive Avery, Director and Principal

Librarian of the British Museum, who witnessed part of the chase from his Bentley on his way past the top of Courier St, has already reported to the police in the hope of helping them in their inquiries.

P.C. Bolter, the driver of the patrol-car, has reported that when he and Goddard were on routine duty in the City area they came up behind a black Austin saloon with the number AFJ 6364 and had no reason to take special notice of the car until it suddenly put on speed, arousing their suspicion. Pulling up alongside at some traffic-lights, the crew of the patrol-car requested the driver of the Austin to draw into the kerb on the other side of the crossroads as soon as the lights went green. The driver, a neatly-dressed man of between 20 and 25, agreed to do this, but instead swung left and accelerated. Halfway down Courier St the car halted suddenly and the four men inside it got out and began running. There is no clue, as yet, to their reason for avoiding questioning.

A preliminary examination of the bullet taken from the body of P.C. Goddard has revealed that the gun was of light calibre. Dr John Hennison-Jones, the pathologist, was working late last night to give detectives a lead. It has been unofficially disclosed that because of the extreme accuracy required for a weapon of such small calibre to kill a running man even at five yards' range it is believed that the gunman 'brought off a lucky shot in panic'. An exhaustive search for the murder weapon has already begun, on the chance that the killer decided to get rid of it as soon as he could.

P.C. Goddard, 41, of Acton, was married and the father of three children, a girl of 16, a boy of 10, and a baby girl of 2. He had received three commendations since joining the Metropolitan Police in July 1951, and only two weeks ago he was recommended for a special award for having rescued a child of 6 – Elizabeth Prescott – from a reservoir. His hobby was growing roses, for which he won several prizes locally.

The cooler air of the evening crept between the slats of the shutters. Their shadows made faint stripes across the blue-and-white tiles of the floor, moving immeasurably slowly as the sun lowered behind the house. A few grains of sand had fallen from the paper on to the faded blue canvas cushions on the bamboo chair. The glass drop trembled on its wire link, turning a little to the vibration of feet upstairs and sending a miniature ray of reflected light across the face of a cherub high in a shadowed corner of the room.

Someone spoke, upstairs, and was answered with a single word. They were not calling to each other from room to room through the open doors as they always had before; someone was using the shower in the bathroom with the glazed mauve columbines on the wall but there was no whistling, and no one laughed. A drawer slid shut; a door opened and closed.

They were changing for the evening, though no one had suggested where they should go, or that they should go out at all. Many things they did now were from habit.

Mike came down and Alec soon afterwards; they were talking quietly in the salon when Stan followed them. They had put on casual clothes; they never bothered with jackets and ties on holiday, except Ron, sometimes, who liked to be neat. Stan was wearing a peacock-blue sports-shirt and a silk scarf drawn into folds by a gold ring; his face had caught the sun today and the smell of Old Spice came into the room with him.

'Anyone join me?'

The cork squeaked.

'Not just now,' Alec said.

'Bit of bad luck, wasn't it?' There was the old energy in his tone, and a new defiance.

'A bit of bad,' Mike said, 'and a bit of good. That's the way it goes.'

Stan tilted his glass ironically. 'Cheers.'

'Cheers, Stan.'

'It's a shame you won't join me. It's the only answer, you know. Stops you thinking.'

Mike leaned at the doors, his heavy arms folded. 'You been thinking, have you, Stan?'

'Who me? Oh no. I was down there in my fucking waders making fucking sand-castles, didn't you see me? Lovely day on the beach it's been.'

Mike looked away from him. 'There'll be a few worse days than this one before we're finished.'

'All right – you dole out the doom an' despondency and I'll stick to the Scotch.'

Alec said: 'We were just talking about the policeman. Goddard.'

'You were?'

'We're only in a spot, but he's dead.'

He had been trying to get it out of his mind ever since they'd read the front page. Elizabeth Prescott, the kid in the reservoir, just about Mandy's age.

'Dead, is he?' Stan came slowly up to him, one hand on his hip. 'Well so he is, now you remind me. You know I'd clean forgot. It's something quite alarming, you know, my memory.' He looked at them both in turn. 'But it's all coming back to me now – young Ron had to put his foot down at the wrong time an' drop us all in the shit, that's right, isn't it. Wasn't enough though, was it, had to kill some poor fucking copper to show how big he was. Now fancy me forgettin' a thing like that —'

Mike's hand came down edge-on and the tumbler exploded on the blue-and-white tiles. Stan slowly doubled up with his wrist held into his stomach; the pain was squeezed into his face but he made no sound but for the grunt of his breath shutting off.

Mike turned away. His tone was conversational.

'Don't say anything like that again. Don't say it to me, or Alec, or anyone.'

The sweat had started on Stan's face, springing from the whitened skin. He was breathing again, the sound hissing through his clenched teeth. The spilt whisky was creeping along the cracks between the tiles.

Mike turned back, flicking away the broken glass with his toe. He stood over Stan. 'You can say *I* dropped you all in it if you like. That'd be fair enough. It was my job we were on; I planned everything. But don't say it was Ron.'

A door opened upstairs.

'What's happened?'

It sounded like Chris but they couldn't be sure.

'I dropped a glass,' Alec called up. 'Sorry.'

He moved through the doors and stood at the bottom of the staircase.

'Is everything all right?' Half in relief, half in doubt.

'Sure. I dropped a glass.'

There was no answer but in a moment a door closed. He came back, looking at Stan. He still hadn't straightened up. Mike was still standing over him, saying softly:

'Just remember. Don't ever say it was Ron. He's got enough on his back without you as well.'

Stan's breath went on hissing through his teeth.

Alec said: 'Come in the kitchen, Stan. We'll put some cold water on it.'

Mike swung his head up and looked at Alec. 'You won't do much good with cold water. It'll be broken. Take him round to that doctor chap, d'you mind? I'll clear up this glass before the girls come down.'

Chris shut the door quietly but the handle was loose; someone had put a nail through the hole where the screw had come out and it was the wrong fit; most of the handles were like that all over the house, except in the salon because that was Madame Dupont's pride.

'They dropped a glass,' she said.
'D'you think it woke her up?'
'I'll go and look in on her in a minute.'
'Has she got a temperature?'
'A slight one.'

He must have seen her taking one of the thermometers out of the bathroom; there were about a dozen in the big white cupboard, stuffed in a cardboard box marked *Laboratoires Modernes S.A.*, most of them broken. She was glad he'd noticed; it meant he'd begun taking an interest in things again.

'It's the worry,' he said.
'I know.'

He was lying on the bed with his back propped against the pillow, smoking a cigarette; it was the first one he'd smoked since – since when? Not here and not on the plane last night; not after breakfast yesterday morning. Since the night before, when they'd gone for some supper at the Wimpy. It worried her to realize how much she'd left him on his own in the past week, so busy looking after other people – little Ben and Mr and Mrs Bramford and the girls at the store and everyone – that she'd never had time for Ronnie. And he'd never complained, and that made it worse.

'We'll be together from now on,' she said.

She was trying to make a ribbon stay in her hair, twisting her head about in the bamboo-framed mirror, so she didn't see his face.

'Will we?'

It was his tone that made her turn and look at him. It wasn't that he didn't know why she'd said it; he was thinking there wasn't much chance of them being together. His face was pinched-looking again.

'Yes, Ronnie. We will. Nothing's going to happen.'

'That's all right then.'

He almost meant it; his face had cleared and he drew at his cigarette again, moving the tip of his little finger across the ash to make it fall into the ashtray she'd put there for him. She couldn't have rallied him like that before they'd gone down to the beach this morning; it was the long swim, taking him away from everyone for a little while, that had done him so much good; she'd been stupid to think what she had.

Only once, when she'd been reading about it in the paper, had she felt a kind of faltering inside her, a kind of hesitancy; the whole of her world gave a lurch and there was nothing to grab at, no certainty anywhere; and for this half-minute she lived through an agonizing doubt and had to deal with it as best she could. It was because the hand that had been enfolding her own, the hand she had missed when she woke – missed with a greater sense of loss than she had ever known – was the hand that had held what they called the 'murder weapon'.

It hadn't, before, seemed possible or even to make sense. It had all been vague to her: the boys had got into a jam and an appalling accident had happened, but with luck it would blow over; her mind had refused to go into it more deeply than that; all she must concentrate on was Ronnie, on helping him and safeguarding him because whatever he had done she loved him and would always love him. Now the scene was clearer, and uglier than she had let herself imagine; and oddly enough it seemed more real now that it was in the paper – that made it official.

In that half-minute she faced the truth. Nobody should kill. Nobody should kill a policeman, not even Ronnie.

But that was what he had done, and she ought to go to the police and tell them she knew who they were looking for. The judge would one day say that it had been a terrible decision for her to make, but it was the right decision, even though it had meant giving up her own husband to the law, because P.C. James Henry Goddard had been a husband too and his life had been taken away when he was trying to protect people like herself.

But there was another truth. She loved him.

'It's pretty,' he said, watching her in the mirror. 'Your ribbon.'

'Is it, Ronnie?'

Suppose she could have done such a thing, what would have happened? They would have shut him away for a long time, for years, for half his life. That wouldn't bring James Henry Goddard back to his wife and his children and his roses. It would avenge him, that was all; and if you started to ask yourself what vengeance really was you wouldn't have to go far to find out: a baby in a rage would break things out of vengeance. Of course if they shut him up for a long time it would stop him shooting another policeman; there'd be people who would believe he'd do the same thing again, and that was natural enough; it was just because they didn't know Ronnie. The same person might do a thing twice, but he wasn't the same person now and he would never be, however long he lived.

'Are the others going out?'

'I don't know,' she said.

'Do you want to?'

'I don't think so.'

People would see them.

She knew what he'd meant now when he'd said that. There were English people down there on early holidays, sitting along the promenade reading the *Express;* they'd look up at them as they went by and then look down again at the paper, not knowing. In a strange way she felt it would be embarrassing for them even though they didn't know, like deliberately going into crowded places with a bad birthmark.

'Why are you putting your ribbon on, then?'

'For you to see.'

'It's pretty.'

She smiled to him in the mirror.

Something had happened to him, all that way out in the water. Perhaps he'd looked back and seen how small the beach was now, and the people; perhaps everything had seemed less important from right out there, and he'd brought the feeling back with him, and now he could look at her and talk to her again and even notice the ribbon she wore. He wasn't a stranger any more with Ronnie's face on.

She went over to him and sat on the bed, taking his hand, but he tried to pull it away and a nerve-spasm passed through him – she could feel it, like a slight electric shock. She held his fingers tightly and said:

'It's all right now, Ronnie.'

'Yes.' He got up, pressing his cigarette into the ashtray. 'It's my nails that's all. I can't seem to get the black out of them.'

Maybe that was it. Maybe he'd been born with them, born with black nails.

They met Mike coming out of the salon with the yellow plastic dustpan and the brush with curled bristles the fluff always stuck to. There was glass shining in the dustpan.

Not with actual black nails, of course. Black nails inside where people couldn't see. Maybe a lot of people had them but it didn't matter as long as it didn't show.

Chris asked: 'Where are the boys?'

Mike said: 'Popped round to the doctor's. Stan cut his hand.'

'I could have seen to that for him.'

'You're off duty.'

Mike went into the kitchen and the glass tinkled into the wastebin.

Maybe it wasn't only his nails. His hands had done it but there was more to it than that. Your hands did what you wanted them to. Where was the black, all the black, inside? In his blood, in his heart, in his brain? Maybe there were some sort of gods and when they stepped on you the black came out like out of a beetle and then it showed, then they started looking for you.

How could she bear to touch him?

'Mind, Ronnie, there's still some about.'

It scraped under their feet.

There was more to it than you'd ever think, more to it than just your nails or your hands because they did what you wanted them to. Once inside there and you'd go back sooner or later because it wasn't what you did, it was what you were.

'He should have brought the soft one.'

Chris went out to the kitchen and he was alone and the walls came in at him and the big chandelier swung down and the angels flew at him like gold bats and he knocked into something going through the doors. Then he was leaning at the bottom of the stairs with both hands round the newel-post and his head pressing against his knuckles but he couldn't hear anything. *What shall I do now, Mum?* But it was quiet up there.

It was a glass knob on top of the newel-post, not like the old one, the wooden one with the stain worn off where they'd swung on it. This was a different one, just like his hands were different.

The room was all right when he went back. The paper was on the chair. London Policeman Shot Dead. And there was an ad for gin: This isn't the Gin for Everyone, That's why it's for You.

He didn't care for gin. It was the ads for lighters and cameras and cars he went for, anything that worked when you pressed it. But he didn't want them. You could see through the ads all right – if you hadn't got a gold lighter or a zoom lens or a flash car you weren't really living, you weren't really a man at all, you were nobody. It must be awful for some people, not having all the things the ads said you ought to have. No wonder there was so much pinching.

'I'll do it, Mike. You stay there till I've got it all up.'

The glass shone. It was as if she was sweeping up stars.

He'd never wanted things like that, but the ads were nice, lovely colours and everything, good pictures of cars, smashers some of them. That wasn't why he'd used to nick them. If you went nicking everything you took a fancy to there'd be nothing left for anyone to buy. It was for the kick. The kick of doing something he shouldn't. Like banging on a door and running before they opened it, although he'd never done that, it was more fun doing things for Mum.

'It couldn't have bled much.'

'We wrapped it in a handkerchief.'

No, he'd nicked motors because he'd known it was wrong. It wasn't just to see Aunty Miriam having a fit when she saw him go twice round the square. She wouldn't have a fit at all, just think he was testing a motor for Alvin's, he often did it. He'd wanted to do wrong.

The light burst against his eyes but it was all right, Mike had switched them on so Chris could see where to brush.

195

It wasn't just to see Johnnie's face at the shooting-gallery when he pulled it out and let fly. He'd bought the gun because it was wrong to carry firearms without a licence and it had given him a tingly feeling all the time it was in his pocket, the same feeling as when he was pushing a nicked motor down the street.

'Okay, I'll take it.'

'Well leave the brush in the pan till you get to the bin.'

But there was more to it than that, because of the black stuff inside. He knew now why he'd bought the gun. The others hadn't bought one. It was only him. It was him who'd panicked and brought the coppers on to them and it was him who'd run up a blind alley instead of down the street. He wasn't trying to get away. It only looked like that. He'd got himself in a spot where he had to do what he'd wanted to do ever since he'd bought the gun. Kill someone.

CHAPTER 15

They didn't go out that night. Laura was feverish and Stan went to lie down as soon as Alec brought him back from the doctor's, and Chris said she'd stay in so as to be on call if they wanted anything.

There wasn't any question of anyone else going out; they'd always done things together.

Chris asked the boys what had happened exactly and Alec had to make something up because she could see Stan's wrist was in plaster and he couldn't have broken it dropping a glass. Alec said something about passing a bottle across to Mike from the console; it had slipped because of the sweat on his hand – it was very close in here tonight – and Stan happened to be sitting in the chair near the console with the glass in his hand; the bottle had caught him on the wrist and it was almost full and quite heavy. Dr Giraud said that sort of thing happened easily; it had been the angle of the bottle and the angle of the wrist-bone when they'd impacted that had done the damage.

'It was bad luck,' Chris said.

She didn't say anything more than that. When she'd swept up the last of the glass there hadn't been any near the console or the chair Alec was talking about; and it wasn't like Stan to go up to bed, even though it must have shaken him up because of the delayed shock. It would be unkind to ask Alec more questions because he'd done his best to make it sound plausible; but it worried her just the same. If the strain was getting on their nerves already they'd have a bad time all through next week.

Fay said nothing about it at all because she knew what must have happened. She'd seen Mike do it before once or twice. Some of the men who came to their place were the kind she could never make friends with; not that Mike expected her to. They didn't come often, perhaps three or four times in a whole year, and then she'd talk to them for ten minutes and excuse herself, going to bed and leaving Mike with them. They were men with hard faces and no conversation, always polite but very reserved. One of them had begun shouting, quite late, and she'd come back to see if Mike was all right. She needn't have worried, of course; it was just instinctive. It hadn't been the man's wrist, that time. He was on the floor and his friends took him away in their car; she could still remember the way his arms had dangled when they were carrying him.

'What happened?' she'd asked Mike.

'I didn't like him.'

And that was all there was to it. There'd been someone else, a huge man as big as Mike. It had been at a roadhouse very late but no one was drunk or anything. That time it was his wrist. All she knew was that they must have said something pretty bad to Mike; he'd take a lot before he got annoyed, but the moment he decided he 'didn't like them' he let them know it. She'd been frightened, those times. Frightened for herself. They'd never had rows; there wasn't enough between them for that; they didn't seem to mean enough to each other; but sometimes she'd ask him a lot of questions when he'd stayed away for the night without telling her why, and he'd keep silent and his face would go hard and although she knew it was no good keeping on at him she couldn't stop because it seemed unfair that he didn't let her share things, even his worries; all her life she'd wanted to share things with someone but he wouldn't let her, and it was worse in a marriage not to share things, worse than if you were on your own and couldn't expect to.

Perhaps she'd kept on at him at those times half-hoping he'd lose control and do what he'd done to those men; perhaps it was like saying to him: 'Hurt me, at least let's share that'.

Sitting in the Louis XVI chair with the fruit juice Alec had got for her she realized she'd been more lonely living with Mike than when she'd been on her own. It was only when they danced together that she was happy with him, really happy; that might be because they'd met like that, dancing, two strangers dancing, and it was all they had for each other because it was what they did best.

Someone had turned the radio on and there was some music, not too loud in case of waking Laura. She remembered the way Stan had crouched over the set with the light from it slanting across his face, trying to find London; it had only been this morning and now they'd turned it on for some music. But it wasn't that they'd forgotten. They knew the worst now and they were getting used to it.

'There are some eggs,' Chris told them, coming back from the kitchen. 'Shall I do some?'

Nobody said they were hungry but she said it was nearly twenty-four hours since they'd had anything except for a few doughnuts and they'd get depressed. Alec went with her to help.

Fay sat for another minute in the big embroidered chair and made herself face the thought that had come into her mind just now. She had been more lonely living with Mike than before, when she'd been alone. So if they had bad luck and he got a long sentence she wouldn't miss him – say it quickly – she wouldn't miss him.

There were so many things to get used to this year at the Villa Mimosa.

Ron was helping Chris in the kitchen now and Alec had left them on their own, Chris with the ribbon in her hair, Ron neat in the blue Airtex he'd bought specially for the holiday. They looked like a young married couple setting up house; maybe that was why he'd had to come away.

Mike was alone in the salon sorting out a pack of cards he'd found in the escritoire among all the out-of-date calendars and plastic ball-points and perished rubber bands.

'Where's Fay?' Alec asked him.

He had never missed her before, coming into a room, not so immediately.

'Gone up to see Laura.'

It was because they'd been close to each other all day in the town and on the beach; all day she had seemed to need his company, urgently but without saying anything, and he had noticed it because it was new and strange to be needed.

'Has she called out, then?'

'We heard her moving about.'

Their room was directly above the salon.

He thought of going up but Laura wouldn't want him to.

'Is it a full pack?'

'Three missing, all spades.' Mike was edging a porcelain-handled paper-knife into the back of the escritoire behind the divisions, where things had slipped down. 'Did he say anything?'

'Who?'

'Stan.'

'No.' They had talked sometimes on the way to Dr

Giraud's but Stan hadn't said what Mike meant by 'anything'. 'But I think you'll get an apology.'

Mike flicked a card out with a knife and caught it, twisting round to look up at Alec, his eyebrows jumping.

'From Stan?'

'Sure.'

'After what I did to him?'

'He knows you didn't mean it.'

'Then he's wrong.' He slid the knife in again, picking at the corner of another card. 'He doesn't know why I did it, that's all.'

'Of course he does.'

'We've got to look after young Ron.'

'Stan knows that. We upset him, though. He feels just as badly about Goddard as we do; that was only an act. You know Stan; it's the only way he can express himself, putting on an act.'

Mike got the Queen out and put it with the others.

'Let's have a drink.'

Alec poured some whisky, looking at the glasses against the light before he set them up, just as he used to do at the flat when the 'Old Firm' had one of their 'evenings' there.

Mike kept his voice low because the double doors were open and they could hear sounds from the kitchen. 'Ron tried to kill himself today.'

The neck of the bottle rang against the rim of the glass. Alec put the cork back. 'I've poured too much.'

'I'll have that one.'

Alec opened a new Perrier. Faintly he could hear Ron talking to Chris in the kitchen.

'When?'

'In the sea.'

'Are you sure?'

'I was there. He was half-spent when I got to him but

he wanted to keep on going, tried to fight me off, I had quite a job with him.' He drank the top off his Scotch and felt it hitting his empty stomach.

Alec said: 'Did that chap tumble to it?'

'We were turning back by the time he got there. I don't know. He might have. Ron was still in a mess. Why?'

'He's a registered life-guard.' He sat down slowly on one of the leather *pouffes* and put his drink on the floor and laced his fingers together and looked at them.

'I've told no one else, Alec.'

'No. Keep it to ourselves. Has he said anything to you?'

'I've said a hell of a lot to *him*. Told him if he thought he was going to run out on us like a bloody little welsher he'd got another think coming, went on like that a bit.'

Alec put his face in his hands to shut out the light for a minute. The smell of fried eggs was coming into the room. Two of them would be for Ron; he always liked two. They hadn't had to leave them in the fridge. He said:

'He wanted it to look like an accident, overtaxing his strength —'

'It doesn't make much odds if it was going to look like an accident or not.'

Alec said through his hands: 'It would have made a difference to the rest of us. With a suicide there'd be inquiries —'

'Fat lot of difference it would've made to Chris.'

'I know that. But there was nothing he could do about Chris once he'd made up his mind. He was thinking of the rest of us.'

'If he was thinking of anything at all. He'd be a bit mixed up if you ask me.'

'He would've done all the thinking before he went into the water. That's why he went in.'

Mike took a pace or two, standing under the chandelier

and listening to the sounds from the kitchen. 'Well we can skip the inquest, as it turns out.'

'Listen, Mike, didn't he say anything *at all* to you? Afterwards?' He drew his hands away from his face. There must have been something and it was important they found out. Ron hadn't tried to welsh on them all. That wasn't Ron.

'I've told you, I did all the talking.'

'But he must have said something. Even a word.'

They'd gone to sleep side by side, her hand in his. Ron couldn't have simply left her like that.

'He said yes and no, when I talked to him.'

'All right, but out there – didn't he say anything out there in the water?' He knew Mike didn't want to talk about that. But they had to know.

'All I remember him saying was that she mustn't touch him.'

'*She* mustn't touch him?'

'He kept saying it. "She mustn't touch me." It made no odds to me what he was saying. All I was trying to do was keep his head up.'

Alec nodded. 'So that's why he went out there. He meant Chris.'

Mike turned away from the chandelier and looked down at him. 'Oh, Jesus.'

'So he wasn't welshing on us.'

'No. Poor little devil.' He took a deep breath. 'What can it feel like, Alec, thinking of yourself that way, not wanting people to touch you . . .'

'The thing is, we'll have to look after him better from now on.'

Fay stood at the window.

Someone had opened the shutters, probably Chris. There was no light on in the room so the insects wouldn't come in. Below in the garden there were blobs of crimson slowly turning black as the half-moon rose. The night was full of sound outside the house. She could hear the traffic in the town, across the walls where the green-and-yellow ivy grew and across the mimosa trees two gardens away; the town was where the glow of light showed in the sky. There were voices in the lane where people were coming up from the beach; the night was heavy and they'd stayed on for a last swim in the moonlight.

She could hear frogs calling, very far away where there were reservoirs in the nurseries; they were the small emerald ones that could sing under water. And she could hear crickets whistling; they weren't the ones that rubbed their legs together; this was a definite whistling noise, pretty to listen to; they were Italian crickets. Marcel talked for hours about things like that, and brought specimens to show them.

A light came on among the trees; somewhere a door slammed. That would be Marcel's house, or Dr Giraud's; it wasn't easy to tell because of so many trees. It didn't matter whose house it was; it was part of the Villa Mimosa, like all the other things were: the glow in the sky and the voices in the lane and the crickets and frogs and the moon. She had never forgotten any of them since the first time they had come here, and now she must press them into her memory like wild flowers in a book because it didn't seem as if they'd be coming here again.

Laura stirred and she turned from the window.

'I'll go, if you like.'

She knew Laura didn't want people around her when she wasn't well, but Chris was busy in the kitchen and they'd heard her moving about and she might have wanted something.

'No, don't go yet.'

The light was faint in the room from the moon and the glow of the town. The little travelling-clock was ticking on the bed-table and Fay found she was looking at it without the usual feeling they always gave her, a sort of chill feeling in her chest as if she'd suddenly breathed snowy air. It looked a nice little clock.

Are you going on holiday?
No.
Then why did you want it?
I didn't want it.
Then why did you take it?
I don't know.

The ticking was sharp and soft at the same time, like the crickets, the ones that rubbed their legs together.

'It's a nice little clock,' she said.
'What darling?'
'This little clock.' She ran her finger round the edge, touched it with her finger. 'It's sweet.'
Laura's head moved on the pillow.
'Present from Alec.'
'I expect so.'
'You can have it.'
Fay smiled. Laura was always like that; if you admired something she wanted to give it to you.
'I had one, once. I don't want one again.'
It was such a long time ago now. Everything that had happened before last night was a long time ago.
'It's so hot,' Laura said, moving her head again.
'Yes.'
'It's not only me, is it?'
'No, everyone's feeling the heat. You'll be all right in the morning.'
'I intend to be. It's only the damned curse, a week early because of everything.'

She hadn't asked if they'd got an English paper yet and Fay was hoping it wouldn't occur to her; it would make her feel worse.

'Don't worry about anything, Laura.'

'The thing that maddens me is that there's no particular answer to this. I mean we're all in each other's hands.' With soft anger she said: 'It's the first time in my life I've come up against something I can't organize, Fay.'

'But there's no one as good as —'

'Oh my God, anyone can organize plane-tickets and passports.'

Fay said: 'I can't.'

Laura was watching her from the pillow, the shine of her eyes showing up in the shadow and the dark of her hair. 'I think you're organizing this thing better than I am, you know.'

'Me? But there's nothing I can do about anything.'

'You haven't fallen flat on your back. You've organized *yourself;* you've come to some kind of terms with it in your own mind. You seem to have found – I don't know – some kind of faith.'

Fay looked from the window. It had gone out again, the light among the trees; but it would always be there now; no one could ever put it out again.

'You've got more to lose,' she said, 'than I have.'

'You mean Alec?'

'Yes.'

'But you've got Mike.'

The moon had moved a very little and the edge of its light struck across the glass of water that Fay had put near the bed. Its reflection made a still pool on the ceiling.

'I must let you try and rest now,' said Fay.

'What are they doing?'

'Cooking something. You don't feel like anything, do you?'

'I feel like a bloody good howl.'

Fay came away from the window and took the folded handkerchief from Laura's hot forehead. 'You should try and stop thinking. Just leave it all to Alec.' She went across to the bathroom and soaked the handkerchief with fresh cold water. When she came back Laura said reflectively:

'I could have, once.'

'You can now.'

'No. It's too late now.' The cold against her forehead eased away the throbbing. 'But he was always ready to look after me from the very beginning. I didn't fancy a lifetime of wet-nursing, though.'

Fay held her fingers against her dress to dry them.

'I suppose you could call it that.'

'What would you call it?'

'Love.'

In a minute Laura said: 'You're more romantic than I am.'

'Do you think so?'

'Not cheaply – you know I didn't mean that. I mean you feel more deeply than I do. People really matter to you; you need to share things with them; it's not enough for you that they're just somewhere around. But it's been enough for me. That's where I went wrong, probably way back along the line.' Her head shifted restlessly. 'I've been too bloody independent, Fay. No one could do anything as well as I could do it, so I didn't need them.'

'It's not a bad thing, independence.'

'But there's a price-tag. People cast up on desert islands are independent – they've got to be. And the reverse is true. And that's where I've been all my life.'

Fay touched her hand. 'I shouldn't have let you talk. It's putting your temperature up.'

For a moment Laura's hot fingers were linked with Fay's. It didn't feel like Laura's hand at all; the cool sure touch had gone.

'You did a good thing, then. It's what I need, a bit of human warmth, even my own. Especially my own.'

Fay left her side. 'I'll go down now, so you can try and sleep.' She was at the door when Laura asked:

'I suppose you got an English paper at last, did you?'

'Yes.'

'I don't want to see it. Do I?'

'There's nothing new in it,' Fay answered warily. 'Nothing we didn't know.'

Laura watched the reflection on the ceiling the glass of water made. Mandy had her own name for them: 'fairy ponds'.

She said absently: 'He's a better person than I am.' Her head turned sideways as weariness came, and the pillow muffled the rest. 'I suppose there's always one parent better than the other in most families. So if the crunch comes they'll be taking the wrong one away ... but they won't know that, and it wouldn't make any difference if they did.'

CHAPTER 16

On Sunday morning they all went to the market in the old part of the town. It wasn't until they were there, standing in the midst of its noise and scents and colours, that they felt surprise at having come.

No one had suggested it as far as they could remember; they had woken early and Laura's fever was gone and they were glad to see her (Chris was seriously relieved, knowing that nervous depression could lead to almost anything); Alec had made some coffee and the smell had brought them all downstairs; and someone had thrown open the shutters and the clear early sun had streamed into the salon; then there was a basket in someone's hand and Laura fetched one of her floppy hats from the spare-room and they were walking down the drive in ones and twos, waiting for each other by the gold mass of the mimosa near the gates.

Perhaps it was because they had had a full night's sleep and had left some of their despair behind them in their dreams, and because their memories were stirred by the sights and sounds of other years when they had been here: the sun on the bright leaves of the palm tree and the voices of people in the lane. They had always gone to the market on Sunday mornings.

Stan's arm was in a sling but he turned it to good account, strutting ahead of them with Napoleonic gestures – 'Of course I normally spend my Sundays in bed with Josephine but occasionally I have to let the people see me – *noblesse oblige*, you know.'

They stood among spring flowers, nudged by women in black shawls and children who scampered past, and then wandered between the stalls buying Gruyère and Boursin *aux fines herbes*, golden apples and Belgian endives and long crisp loaves; and somewhere Alec found some pickles and gave them to Mike and Fay.

On their way back past the post office Alec was missing again and when he caught them up he had Fay's pink purse in his hand.

'It was where you thought?'

'The shop next door.'

'You're wonderful, Alec.' She lifted his hand and kissed it. 'I'll never leave it anywhere again.'

'I hope you will.'

They bought coloured postcards and sat on the terrace when they got back and 'filled them in', as Stan called it, borrowing each other's ball-points and finding a pen in Madame Dupont's escritoire, and a bottle of mauve ink.

They were silent, doing this; it had been a mistake, reminding them of home and the people there, Florry and Madge and Aunty Miriam and Laura's mother, Alec's brother George, Dolly and the girls at Crowning Glory; and Stan had to write with his left hand, giving it up after the first card.

'I'll send a couple for you,' Mike told him. 'You're down with tonsillitis anyway.'

'The state I'm in I'd make medical history, and not a pretty young nurse in sight.'

It was the first time they'd spoken to each other since the night before, and Fay was glad to hear them. She had been trying to think what Stan must have done to make Mike hurt him like that. It mustn't happen again. Their friendship was all they had now and if they lost it they would lose everything.

When the postcards were finished Alec got his camera and moved about with it, trying for natural shots instead of poses, and after a while he forgot that he was doing this in case proof were later needed that this year was no different, that they were having a wonderful time. It was easier to forget than he would have believed, because there was so much the same here still: Laura stretched languidly in the chaise-longue, a sun-hat tilted across her face; Chris with her quite unconscious child-at-the-party pose, hands linked in front of her; Fay looking a little lost as if she couldn't remember where she'd put her bag.

He took Stan from the left side with someone close to him on his right to hide the difference in this year's scene because, looking through the album in the years ahead, they wouldn't want to see it there. Ron had gone indoors when Alec fetched the camera.

Fay wanted to take one 'for herself' and he showed her what to press and went into the salon, where Mike was trying to fish the last card out of the escritoire with the paper-knife.

'Alec.'

He came out again.

'I want one of you,' Fay said.

'What for?'

'Under the mimosa tree.'

He stood there for her while she swung the camera around, trying to get him into the viewfinder.

'I'm over here, about south by south-east . . .'

She laughed and tried again and got some kind of a fix on him though the thing was tilted when she pressed the button.

'That's my Fay . . .' It didn't matter which side of the camera she was, you'd see her in the picture.

She gave it back to him. 'Will you let me have that one

when they're printed?' She was smiling but her slow brown eyes were serious, intent on his face.

'You think they'll print that one?'

'You must make them. It's for me.'

'Then I'll see they do.'

She didn't go back to her deck-chair but wandered off through the shade of the big palm to be alone for a while.

Just as no one had suggested going to the market, no one suggested that they stayed in the garden all day instead of walking down to the beach. Perhaps there were reasons: Laura didn't want to swim, and Fay knew this; it wasn't full summer yet and in the shade of the trees it was not so warm as to make them think of the sea. Chris had no wish to go down there: for a while the sea would mean nothing but anguish to her; and Stan found things awkward with his arm in a sling.

Or perhaps there was the one reason that was common to all of them except Laura: they couldn't think of the beach without seeing again the man selling papers there.

Soon after Alec had taken the roll out of his camera and put a new one in, Mike managed to find the last of the missing spades in the back of the escritoire and the men sat down to some poker at the Florentine table, Stan spreading his cards on his lap. Ron was quiet but played well enough, his mind on the game.

Laura stayed on the terrace and slept for an hour. Chris stood on a stool and fetched down the fruit-squeezer from the top of the cupboard in the kitchen that always smelt of garlic, and made juice from some of the apricots that Madame Dupont had left, the ones that were going off. Fay helped her and they talked a little though not about anything serious.

When the sun had moved round the house and the

terrace was in shadow they made some tea, and then Mike went off and was gone for twenty minutes. He said nothing when he came back but they knew now that all day they had been waiting.

Stan spoke first.

'Something bad?'

'They were shut.'

'They were open this morning,' Laura said. She lit a cigarette, her hand not quite steady.

'Well they're shut now.'

'Sunday.'

'Yes. They shut in the afternoons.'

'They've got to shut sometimes, haven't they?'

'Did you try knocking?'

All day they had tried to forget, telling themselves it didn't matter what was going on; the house and the trees had enclosed them, giving them shelter. They hadn't wanted to know.

Now they wanted to, because they were denied.

'What about the station?'

'Is there a bookstall there?'

'There's bound to be.'

'They might not have English papers.'

'On a station?'

'They would have opened up if you'd knocked.'

'Oh for Christ's sake!' Stan was on his feet. 'What do we want the bloody papers for? We know what's going on, don't we? They're trying to find us. Well they can try – there's nothing we can do about it. All we can do is stick together and keep smiling and wait till it all blows over. So what do we want with the papers?'

His deep voice vibrated under the canopy and Alec said: 'Not so loud, Stan.'

He jerked a glance around him and stifled the rest of

what he was saying, looking at them one at a time, his left hand gesturing. 'Look, you want to know what I think? I think we're making a bloody sight too much of all this. What's happened? We've got on the wrong side of the law and serves us bloody well right, we shouldn't go poncing around the place as if we were the Mafia. Some poor copper's had to suffer for it and we know what we think about that – there's not one of us who wouldn't have done *anything* rather than let that happen. But we got ourselves in a position where we scared easy and when you're in a panic you'll do things you'd never think of. All right, so it's done. But what do we do now? Go back and face it? What good's that going to do anyone, it won't help Goddard, will it? So if we're going to stick it out down here let's at least try to keep cheerful.' His voice had got louder and he realized it, and leaned nearer them. 'What have they got on us? Nothing. Nothing at all. So I've got better to do than hang about waiting for the papers so I can give myself another nasty turn. I'll tell you this much – if we don't pull ourselves up sharp and get this thing off our minds we're going to look a bit peculiar to the people round here, and the next thing we know is we've given ourselves away.' He looked at each of them in turn and then stepped over the lintel into the salon, swinging round on them – 'You know where I'm going? On the town. On the bloody town. Tonight's the night, that's me – kick off with caviar and a bottle o' bubbly to get me in the groove and then it's action stations and no mistake. Someone's got to come with me if only to help me home, so don't be bashful, one pace forward the volunteers!'

From the lane, where people came through the eucalyptus trees in the falling dusk, the Villa Mimosa stood radiant among the dark of the leaves, with every window glimmering. Girls' voices came through the open shutters and a man was singing, his voice much deeper, rich and somehow comical.

One of the children in the lane, hearing the voice was foreign and perhaps Italian, dragged at his mother's hand. *'Ecoutons! C'est sûrement un artiste de l'opéra, là-bas!'*

They stood listening, and his father stopped to wait for them. *'Pense-tu . . . c'est un amateur. Mais pas mal, pas mal du tout.'*

'Mais quand même, Papa, elle est jolie, cette villa. C'est sûrement un palais enchanté!'

'Bien sûre – et moi, je suis un éléphant volant. Allons-y! Il fait nuit déjà, allons!'

The child went with them, undismayed by grown-up answers. It really must be a famous opera-singer there in the enchanted palace.

The dusk lowered and stars came to cling at the tips of the eucalyptus leaves.

In the house beyond the walls where the green-and-yellow ivy grew, the boy, older by some years than the child in the lane, watched from his darkened window, his arms along the sill and his thin legs dangling. He knew that they were making ready to go out, perhaps into the town. He knew everything they did, because they were his friends and he watched over them. The little cold river began again, starting at the back of his neck and trickling down and spreading until he shivered, squeezing his eyes shut; then in a moment the warmth came back and he was able to look out again at the lights among the leaves.

They walked to the Hôtel de la Reine. It wasn't far.

Stan had been against it at first because it wasn't exactly what you could call 'going on the town', but the others said they'd have to walk farther than this to the nearest taxi-rank so what was the point? The bubbly would be just as good – the Hôtel de la Reine was very swish and the chef had a reputation. So that was where they went.

They had got out their 'soup-and-fish-kits' and the girls looked beautiful and the men resplendent. Stan had a white silk scarf as a sling outside his dinner-jacket, and sported his new evening shirt with the pale gold embroidery down the front. The lane was rough and the men helped the girls with their high heels until they reached the promenade and turned along by the sea.

'You can smell the ozone now it's cooler ...'

'Are you serious? That's Old Spice!'

The moon, a little more than half, was almost overhead and there was no reflection on the water except where sometimes a wave curled at the edge. Nobody was down there on the beach; the concessions were shuttered and the rows of parasols stood folded like dark flowers closed in the night. It must look like this in winter, Fay thought, the sea cold and the sand deserted. Chris walked with Ronnie, holding his hand, not looking at the sea at all.

The restaurant at the Hôtel de la Reine was half-empty or seemed so, because of its great size and the fluted columns that hid some of the tables. An orchestra was playing *Rose Marie* and the leader bowed slightly to them as they came in, and the girls smiled to him, flattered. They chose a table with a banquette where the fronds of potted palms curved down from illuminated niches.

'Well just look at the bloody weeds,' Stan said. 'We're back in Bournemouth, my loves, and that's a fact!'

Before they ordered Alec murmured: 'Ring your mother, why don't you? They'll book the call.'

'You think I should?'

'She'd appreciate it.'

'You rang her yesterday.' She took out a cigarette over-quickly.

'I know, but I had to tell her you were in bed. She'd like to hear your own voice; otherwise she'll worry.'

'All right, Alec.'

Holding his lighter ready he said: 'It's the wrong way round.'

'Stupid of me.'

'Everyone does it sometimes.' But he had never seen Laura do it before.

They booked the call.

Stan announced that since this was his idea he was their host. 'So if you don't ask for the most expensive things you can find on the menu I'll tell Toscanini to go on playing *Rose Marie* till you've learned to behave yourselves.' He turned to the waiter. 'Now then, *mon garçon, mes amis et moi, nous sommes mucho soif,* right? *Tout de suite,* we want – er – *nous aimons champagne, beaucoup,* in buckets – *bouquets, avant mangeons, vous savez?*'

'Thank you, sir, I'll fetch the wine-waiter at once.' He was a young, cheerful-looking boy with a slight North Country accent.

'That's the trouble with these Froggies,' Stan said despairingly. 'They've never learned to speak their own bloody lingo.' He winked at Chris and touched her hand across the table. 'You're looking superlative tonight, my little love, just out of a candy-box and still with the ribbon on. Now tell Uncle Stanley all your secrets – you fancy the caviar, the smoked salmon or the *pâté de foie gras* with truffles?'

'I'd really like some melon —'

'Oh blimey, then it's *Rose Marie* already, is it?'

'But I love iced melon, Stan.'

'Well I must say the crew's in an ugly mood tonight. What about you, Laura my love?'

They chose while they were waiting for the champagne, and then the call came through —

'You can receive it at the table, *madame,* if you —'

'I'd prefer not, thank you.'

'As *madame* wishes.'

Stan kept it up until she came back; it was a little forced even by his standards but Alec helped him out and Chris was laughing before long. She had been all right when they'd been getting ready at the Villa but the walk here had seemed to depress her. She was more herself now.

There were three bottles open by the time Laura joined them again.

'How's Mum?' Stan said right away.

'They're all fine.' She looked for a cigarette but Alec moved her glass an inch nearer.

'Then there's nothing else to worry about.'

'No.' She took up her champagne. 'She sends her love to you and – and says the crystallized fruit's all gone.'

'Surprise.'

'And Mandy left a special message for us both – she promises never to read *Bash!* any more.'

'Did she?'

Laura heard the note in his voice and didn't know how to save him. Mandy and Toops always turned over a new leaf when they left them. 'It's because she misses us.'

'Yes. But it won't be for long.'

'Of course not.' She touched his hand for the first time, and realized how strong it still was. 'We're all right, Alec.'

'Sure.'

The girl in blue saved the evening for them, quite by chance. She came in with her mother and they took the next table but one.

Stan didn't move his head; only his eyes moved, to rest under hooded lids on the girl in blue.

'I regret, my loves,' he said solemnly, 'that I must leave you. Duty calls.'

Mike's eyebrows jerked up in one of his quick smiles. Stan's basic urge had suddenly surfaced and he was into the act without even trying. The others glanced briefly at the next table but one and then at Stan; and Fay was already smiling.

Exceptionally handsome tonight in his dinner-jacket, with the white silk sling lending elegance and drama at the same time, he was slouched in the pose of a decadent potentate assessing the worth of a slave-princess his captains had dragged before him for his idle pleasures.

'If you make it,' Mike said, 'the bill's on me.'

Stan's bass tone rumbled below the orchestra. 'Make it? How vulgar a way to describe the prelude to an undying passion . . .'

But he saw the point. The girl wasn't specially pretty, though a certain virginal air gave her charm; it was the mother who made her daughter, by contrast, a ravishing beauty. She was also, obviously, the girl's chaperone, escort and gaoler.

'Not this time,' said Alec gently. 'Not even you could get that one, Stan.'

'There must be a way, my friend.' He was feeling the strain of the pose but he had to stay with it till the girl looked at him. At the moment she was dutifully listening to her mother, whose black velvet neckband was jerking to the flow of words. 'There must be a way,' said Stan broodingly.

Their *Canard à l'orange* was served in a flourish of napery and silver dishes, and Stan was obliged to break his pose in any case because cramp had started in one leg. The girl looked at him too late, with a passing glance that took in the two waiters and the orchestra-leader with equal interest.

'Spurns me, does she, the little jade?' He picked up a fork and toyed petulantly with his new garden peas, now and then cocking the famous eyebrow at the next table but one.

Chris leaned over and cut the meat for him. 'They're English,' she warned him.

'You must be joking! A French *grande dame* with her little *demoiselle*, see it a mile off.' He took back his fork. 'Bless you, my love.'

'I'd say you're about right,' Mike told him. 'She's sixteen if she's a day.'

'Are you serious? That old trout's in her early hundreds for a start. Right out of the French Revolution with a neckband to cover the scar where she got the chopper. Now what were they thinking of, screwing a head like that back on?'

It was going down well and even Ron was smiling. The sixth bottle of Moët et Chandon had been uncorked and the seventh was beside them in the ice-bucket.

'Send her a note,' Mike suggested.

'You don't suppose it didn't occur to me? It'd have to include the old battle-axe.'

Alec said: '"Would you two charming ladies do me the honour of joining me for coffee in the lounge?"'

'Jesus, the old crone would pack her daughter off quick as you like an' drag me bodily in the lift an' then where would I be?'

'On your way up, boy, she's probably a countess.'

A laugh came from Ron and they glanced at him without thinking. They remembered, each of them, the way he had laughed so much more easily before, in what they thought of now as the 'old days'. It was probably the champagne tonight; but it didn't matter what it was; it sounded the same.

'I know what I'll put,' Stan said with a look of high cunning. '"Dear Miss Glorious, this is Agent 0007. I've just heard on my secret collar-stud radio that your mother's won the consolation-prize at Cruft's. It's a revolutionary brand of flea-killer containing instant-arsenic and it's waiting for her at the desk. P.S. You won't be lonely while she's gone because —"'

'*Stan*,' Fay nudged him, 'they're *English*.' The orchestra had stopped and his rich bass tone carried on.

'" – Because once I've got you under that table you'll know you've got company . . ."'

'One more word,' murmured Chris, giggling because of the wine, 'and I shall leave.'

Stan put a hand over hers. 'You wouldn't desert your poor Uncle Stanley just when he's going to order you a bowl of fresh strawberries and Neapolitan ice-cream with whipped *Crème Chantilly au Grand Marnier*, would you now? You don't know which side your Toast Melba's buttered, I can see that.'

'They're out of season anyway.'

'No, to be quite honest,' Stan said reflectively, 'I really think our master-plan lacks boldness.' He saw the *grande dame* turn her pince-nez in the direction of his voice, and offered her a graceful bow of his head. 'I think it calls for a concerted effort, men. We'll just go across and Mike can take the feet and Alec the arms and I'll take the head in case it comes off again and we'll throw the entire object through that plate-glass window – make sure it's shut, of course – and the rest of you can distract the daughter's attention with a suitable line in small-talk while we're doing it – how pretty the flowers are, and isn't the music nice now it's stopped playing, that sort of thing, so she won't notice.'

Chris made a pretence of carrying out her threat, half-rising, but Stan hissed in her ear – '*Not yet!* You don't start the small-talk till the action's on!'

She subsided weakly and he called it a day, signalling the waiter to open the next bottle. Laura was laughing into her hands and Ron hadn't looked so relaxed for a long time. The cork popped and the glasses frothed and Stan looked round the table.

'The Old Firm,' he said, and waited for them to drink with him.

A three-piece band had taken over and the main lights were dimmed; a dozen couples were on the miniature dance-floor in front of the dais.

Alec and Fay were among them.

'You've never looked lovelier.'

Her eyes were shining and he had forgotten how beautifully she danced.

'It's because I'm with you.' The wall-lamps circled and she closed her eyes for a moment and let the warmth and the wine and his gentle hands carry her through the dark. It didn't matter what they said; no one could hear.

'You've changed, Fay. Did you know?'

'We both have, haven't we? We all have.' His hands were so strong, so steady. 'I never knew how much I needed you, Alec. I suppose I never had to know.'

It still felt strange to him that someone should want to give themselves into his protection; he'd so long been used to Laura's capability.

'I'll always be around,' he said.
'Will you?' Her step faltered.
'Somewhere.'
'Yes. As long as you're somewhere. It doesn't have to be close, not even as close as this.' She opened her eyes because it mustn't seem too like a dream. 'But there's nothing I can do for you, Alec, or be to you.'
'Just go on losing things, and you'll be everything I need.'

They were alone at the table. Mike was dancing with Laura, and Alec with Fay. Stan had gone off to pay the bill where no one could see him in case they wanted to chip in.
'I love you,' she said.
'It's not right, Chris. It's —'
'No – I don't deserve you, Ronnie, that's what isn't right. But it doesn't stop me loving you, and I'm going to look after you from now on. I've spent so much time – so much of *our* time – looking after strangers, people who didn't mean anything to me really, ever since we got married.' She was holding his hand but there was no response in it and she knew he didn't want her to touch him; but he must learn. 'I ought to have spent my time with you, Ronnie, not all the other people. It was because I fancied myself once as Florence Nightingale and when it turned out I was no good at it I went running about trying to be a bloody little foster-mother to everyone in sight —'
'You mustn't say things like —'
'I should have said them a long time ago and taken a bit of notice.' Her head felt swimmy because of so much wine but she was thinking straight enough. 'And all the time there was you, left on your own just as if

you'd never married me – and that was the most wonderful day of my life, you know, when we sat in the little car you'd polished up to take me home in; it came on to rain, remember, in the park, and you said you wanted to marry me and the rain looked all silver suddenly and I cried. You don't remember, but —'

'Yes. Yes, I do.'

Her hand tightened on his. 'Well it could have been a wonderful day for you too, but I let you down. I had a husband but you didn't have a wife. We should have made a home together and had babies instead of using that damned pill – that's what you married me for, to make a home —'

'It was because I loved you—'

'Then don't stop, Ronnie, don't stop loving me now. It's not too late, and we'll have a home and babies – we'll have the big life from now on. It might seem small enough to other people but it'll be big enough for us.'

'But *Chris*,' and his head went down and he squeezed his eyes shut, 'if only you'd *blame* me for what I've done, what I've done to you and the rest of us and – and him, and *him* . . .'

'It doesn't need two of us, Ronnie. You'll go on hurting yourself for such a long time, and that's going to be part of what I've got to do for you as your wife, help you to live with it till you've punished yourself enough, till you're ready to see what you can't see now: that you didn't mean it.'

'What difference does that make?'

'All the difference, Ronnie. You can't see it yet, and it's going to be a long time before you let yourself. But one day you will.'

Gently she took her hand away from his and let it lie alone between them on the banquette, knowing that this must be the first step, that he must come to see that however bitterly he hated himself he could always reach out and touch someone who didn't hate him at all, who thought that he was good.

His head had lifted and he opened his eyes, slowly blinking as if even these soft lights were too bright for him after the dark of the nightmare thoughts.

'There's never been a wife like you. There never could have been. Taking it the way you have. I can't understand it, someone as small as you.' He was looking at her in a kind of bewilderment. 'So big.'

'I'm not much yet. But I'm growing.'

He moved his hand over hers. 'You're all the world to me.'

'I love you, Ronnie.'

They walked home together in the moonlight, taking the road by the sea the way they had come. They had all drunk too much but Stan didn't break out in song, and apart from some slight swaying about where the road was uneven they managed well enough.

It wasn't altogether the wine, though Stan had ordered three more bottles to last them till the band packed up. Tonight they had come close to forgetting, and the release was heady for them. Tonight they had seen themselves almost as the people they remembered from the other years, the people in the album that was on the shelf between the Ronald Searle and *The Decameron*. Walking arm in arm through the lane from the sea where now the trees reared black among brilliant stars, they were half-aware that tonight was timeless for them, that this year might be any of the other years, and that it didn't matter which. Time was where they were, and they were here.

Their voices were low and sleepy.

'That's the most beauful . . . most beautiful tree in all the world. Did you take a pho – a photograph of it?'

'Yes.'

'This year? A pho – tograph?'

'I take one every year.'

The small round pebbles crunched under their shoes, except for Laura's because she had taken them off. 'My God I'm tired . . .' She stood for a moment with her eyes shut and her face to the sky, drawing her fingers through her hair. 'All over. Even my hair feels tired . . .'

'You needn't brush your teeth, tonight.'

It was what they said sometimes to Mandy.

Quietly Mike said: 'You were a good boy. A very good boy.' Most of the effort Stan had made at the table had been to cheer up Ron.

'Who me? I'm a right bastard.'

'That's fair enough, a lot better than a wrong bastard.'

They came to the porch, where all the swimming-gear was piled.

'Has someone got my shoes?'

'I have.'

'He's the most won – the most wonderful man in the whole world, and you'll never lose anything any more.'

They opened the door.

'*Sh!* We don't want to wake anyone.'

'There's no one here, 'cept us!'

'I mean in the other houses.'

The girls went into the shadowed hall and the others followed. Someone's foot touched the note that had been pushed under the door and it was sent skimming, but nobody heard it.

CHAPTER 17

Most of them slept late but Stan was out of the house before nine, going the back way and across the grass so they wouldn't hear him on the gravel.

They'd think he was mad, rushing out like this after what he'd said yesterday.

He walked as quick as he could and didn't notice the women when they passed him. The shop was in the big square and it was open, thank Christ. He banged his right arm in the doorway and pain shot through the bone and he had to stand still a minute. The Doc had said he'd got to go round there again today and make sure the plaster was all right but there was only one thing to do and that was wait till the bloody thing healed up, they all said you'd got to see them again when they wanted the money.

The pain was bad and he stood gritting his teeth over it and a girl with glasses was watching him.

'*Vous vous êtes fait mal, m'sieur?*'

'What?'

'You have made hurt?'

'Hurt? Oh yes. No. I'm all right, I just bashed it, that's all.' He tried to steady up. The thing was to act normal, they'd all agreed on that, or they'd call attention to themselves. 'Have you got the papers? The *journaux anglais*, yes?'

'*Pas d'aujourd'hui, m'sieur.* It is too soon.'

'No. Yesterday's. *Dimanche.*'

She was looking sorry for him and he wished to Christ she'd get on with her job and give him the papers.

A thin man smoking a Gauloise inclined his head and said courteously: 'Excuse me, sir. The journals of Sunday will not arrive until today afternoon.'

'They won't? All right, Saturday's – what about Saturday's?'

The thin man looked at the girl. She said: 'I think we have not any remaining, *m'sieur*.'

'But you must have.' The sweat was running on him.

'Wait, please.'

She went into the back of the shop and spoke to someone else.

'It is so annoying,' the thin man said. 'Some of them are printed in Paris, of course, but the time is still long for them to arrive.' He took out a tin box from his pocket and put his cigarette-end into it. 'I have many English friends here. They always complain with the subject of the journals, yes.'

'They do?' He'd get a drink, soon as he could.

The girl came back. 'There is only one of them remaining, *m'sieur*. It is —'

'I'll take it.'

'So!' The thin man beamed in delight. 'You are the lucky one!'

'What? Yes.' He gave the girl some change. 'That's all right.'

'Oh but please. It is too much.'

He didn't want to open the paper but the headline was nothing about it, Common Market or something. The girl was shutting the till and he took the money and shoved it in his pocket. 'Thank you. Kind of you.'

The thin man said something to him as he went out but he didn't catch what. The sun was hot and he crossed the road to where there was a café with tables under the trees.

'*Cognac.* Double.'
'*Café-cognac, m'sieur?*'
'*Oui. Deux fois,* the *cognac,* eh?'
'*Grand café-cognac, tout de suite!*'

He still didn't open the paper. It didn't matter what was in it. Anyway it was Saturday's and plenty could have happened since then. They should have bought a new radio before the shops shut Saturday afternoon and got it rigged up instead of that clapped-out bloody thing of Madame Dupont's, then they could have got London.

But it didn't matter. It had come to him in the night, couldn't sleep, and a bit of luck, that, because he'd done some straight thinking instead. It was all very well saying they must stick together and keep smiling – he'd said it himself, must have been barmy – stick together and wait till the whole thing blew over. It'd never blow over, this lot. You kill a copper and you'd have them after you for the rest of your life, never give up, they wouldn't. Well he hadn't killed a copper and he wasn't going to take the can back for it and that was a fact.

It was all very well for Mike. He was in the game, a professional bloody crook, might as well face it, call a spade a spade. Mike'd got them all into this lot and didn't have the guts to admit it and no one had so much as blamed him. Ron had got something coming to him but after all it was him that did it, fair's fair, and he couldn't expect other people to cop out for him. It was a bloody shame, he was a good kid gone wrong, but it was a bloody shame for that poor sod Goddard and his wife and kids, no one ought to forget that.

The light hurt his eyes and he turned his chair round and got a cigarette and lit it and opened the paper before he could stop himself.

Swift Developments in Goddard Shooting.

It was learned early today that the Yard's Murder Squad team headed by Det.-Supt. J. M. Braithwaite, investigating the shooting of Police-constable James Henry Goddard late on Friday night, are following several leads they describe as 'promising'. It now seems almost certain that the four men wanted for questioning were involved in a raid on the premises of Bayliss and Tyndall, City brokers, that took place at about the same time as the chase that led to the shooting. These premises, where a safe was blown open and emptied of 'considerable funds', are within a mile of Courier St where the chase began. In an interview at Holborn police-station, temporary headquarters of the murder team, Cmdr Norman Straker, one of the senior Yard officers engaged in the investigation, said: 'We now have a good deal more to go on, and this will make things much easier for us.' Questioned about the murder weapon, he told reporters: 'It hasn't been found yet. But if that gun is still anywhere in London we will find it.'

Cmdr Straker's tone of grim determination is echoed by almost every member of the police who are asked for a statement. The general feeling is that the wilful shooting down of a policeman strikes at the very heart of law and order, and that if superhuman effort is necessary to discover and bring to book the men responsible, then it will be made. But beyond this there is the more special feeling – and it has spread spontaneously throughout the whole population – that this act of murder is 'most particularly foul', since the victim held an enviable record for public service and devotion to duty. It will be remembered that P.C. Goddard only recently saved a little girl from drowning in a reservoir.

This feeling is being expressed by all members of the community. The fund set up by Councillor Tom Fairleigh, Mayor of Holborn, for the dependants of P.C. Goddard, has already reached nearly £2,000. There has been a steady stream of people with donations at Holborn police-station, and many postal gifts reaching Scotland

Yard are being pooled with money collected at police-stations throughout Britain. Schoolchildren at Acton, where P.C. Goddard lived, have set up stalls in the street to sell their toys and raise money for the fund.

Meanwhile it is learned that the funeral of P.C. Goddard will be delayed 'for at least a week'. In a statement to the Press, Mr Edmund Moresby, the City of London Coroner, said today: 'In a case of established murder such as this, it is usual to allow the defence counsel to examine the body if a man has been charged with the crime. As yet, nobody has been charged, but since there have been strong indications by the Yard that such an event may be expected very soon, I am under no pressure to issue a burial certificate.'

Although the Yard has revealed nothing substantial in its reports on progress in the case, it is generally expected – in view of the Coroner's statement – that criminal proceedings against a man or several men will not long be delayed. The nation-wide hunt for Goddard's killer has now reached massive proportions, and it is thought unlikely that he can escape its net.

The sunshine threw reflections in the café window and he saw himself sitting there, a man at a table with a newspaper. He moved his head. Yes, it was him. One of the 'several men'. Reading the paper, having a drink. No one'd ever think it. You passed people in the street, you never knew.

The boy in the white jacket was going by and he caught his arm. 'Same again. *Encore.*'

'*Grand café-cognac, m'sieur?*'

'What? No. Skip the coffee. Just the *cognac*. Double.'

'*Grand cognac, hein?*'

'Go on then.'

So they'd get him. Ron.

That was a bloody shame but you'd got to look at it

practically. Kill a copper and that's your lot, no use trying to struggle. Poor little sod but it was his own fault, and bloody Mike's. A couple of bad 'uns when you looked at it straight.

Take the can back for them? He wasn't daft. South America for him, thank you very much. Take his share and turn it into francs and get out quick. Mike couldn't refuse, he'd promised him a third, that was the offer and fair enough. It was in the spare room, in the croquet box. That's why he'd shifted the thing, the cunning bastard.

I'll have my share now. All right with you?

A bit late, isn't it?

What's that got to do with it? I'll have it now.

What for, Stan? What are you going to do with that much cash?

Look, it was a fair deal, remember? A third, that's what we said.

Not thinking of running anywhere, are you, Stan?

You think I'm going to sit here on my arse till they come and get us? It's every man for himself now, it was bound to happen, you know that.

If anyone runs, Stan, he's going to drop the rest of us in it. We've agreed on that much.

It's too bloody late now! This is Saturday's paper, you can read, can't you? Today's Monday. You think they knocked off, Sunday? Christ, they're even keeping the poor bastard on the slab because they know they'll get us!

You're not running, Stan.

We all are if we've got the sense! Now do I get it or don't I?

You get it, Stan. It was a deal. But you're not running.

Who's going to stop me?

None of us.

'Voilà, m'sieur – un grand cognac!'

The voice made him jump and he picked up the glass the minute the waiter had gone.

Brazil. Buenos Aires. Sunshine like this.

They wouldn't stop him. Even Mike wouldn't. Big enough to break every bone in his body but he hadn't started on him because of that, it was what he'd said about Ron.

Copacabaña Beach, all the lights at night. Set up a cosy little salon when the money ran out, a good crimper could make a living anywhere. And the women. Christ. Spanish ones. Tourists, shiploads of them.

Stan, you're on your way.

Alec had taken a couple of aspirins because he hadn't slept well and the onset of a hangover had brought depression with it in the early hours, the hours when everything looks black at the best of times.

Laura was already up, but didn't change out of her dressing-gown.

'We'll have to go on the beach,' he said. The eau-de-Cologne stung his face; he'd cut himself shaving.

'I couldn't face it.'

'We booked for the week. They must have wondered why we weren't there yesterday.'

'I can't help it, Alec.' There were blotches under her eyes and she wouldn't look at him.

'Then you might as well go back to bed.'

'I've spent long enough in bed, thinking.' She folded another shirtwaister and laid it at the top of a valise.

'Are you packing, Laura?'

'I suppose so.'

'We don't have to, yet.'

'We'll have to, some time. We shan't be here for ever.'

He went back into the bathroom and took a cold shower but the shock of it didn't throw the night-thoughts off. He kept remembering Jim; not Jim the boy he'd swopped catapults with at the East Cheam Grammar but Jim the man with a tired wife and four kids, coming up for sergeant in 'D' Division. He'd have no time for the Turkish baths this week because the paper had said they'd called in every available policeman in the London area.

Jim would be looking for him now, working the clock round with thousands like him and going home dead-beat and bloody-minded and telling Phyllis, *We'll get them, it doesn't matter how long it takes, we'll get those bastards.* They all felt the same, thousands of men like Jim, because any one of them could have been Goddard.

And if it all went wrong, Jim would one day tell Phyllis: 'We ought to go and look in on Laura. Laura Bromley. Take her something. She won't have so many friends now.' It would be like Jim to do that. But it wouldn't help much because they'd have to mention him some time – 'Going on all right is he, Alec?' And Alec would be passing his time away in the cells and corridors with nothing to do but sew canvas and take his turn at the buckets and sometimes try to get a glimpse of the sky when it was spring and the trees were in bud. And Laura would have to thank them for coming.

The water-pipes banged as he turned the tap off and reached for the towel. When he went back into the bedroom he looked at Laura and knew he should talk to her and say a lifetime of things while there was a chance.

She was leaning at the window looking out.

He said: 'Would you like some coffee?'

'If you're making some.'

He went downstairs.

It was Fay who found the note that had been pushed under the front door, because she was nearest when Madame Chaumond called, and went to open it. Madame Chaumond was Marcel's mother, a wistful-looking woman with a young face aged by trouble or the fear of trouble.

Fay asked her into the salon, putting the note unread on to the little Florentine table.

'Mais quelle merveille, cette pièce! C'est vraiment splendide – mon petit Marcel n'exagérait pas!'

Luckily Alec and Laura were there with a tray of coffee, and Fay left it to them. Laura's French was the best and she threw them the gist of it from time to time. Madame Chaumond was extravagant in her thanks for their looking after her *petit* Marcel, and wished them to know how he always spoke of them as his dearest friends. They listened politely and Laura said she had children of her own and she'd miss them more than she did if it weren't for the pleasure of Marcel's company down here, and so on. It took a little time for the real subject of Madame Chaumond's visit to come out: Marcel had seemed *'un peu distrait'* on Saturday evening after they had brought him so kindly back from the beach, and he was 'not himself' all yesterday, yet would say nothing other than that the hot weather fatigued him. It just occurred to his mother that perhaps by some chance he had said something to them on Saturday that might help her to 'divine the cause of his unease', which was worrying her.

Laura appealed to Alec and Fay and they shook their heads and she translated for them: no, they hadn't let him stay too long in the sun or the water, and he'd seemed as *'insouciant'* as ever. But perhaps – Laura took a lead from Alec – it was *they* who had been the trouble. The night flight had disorientated them as it always did and she herself had been obliged to keep to her bed the whole day; the others had gone to the beach partly to sleep in the shade of the parasols and thus avoid disappointing Marcel by staying at the Villa. Their lassitude may well have been depressing for a lively youngster; at Marcel's rather critical age they tended to be extra sensitive to people's moods.

It sounded plausible and Madame Chaumond did a lot of nodding, so Laura elaborated further to convince her and seemed to succeed. There were repeated declarations of gratitude as she left them; it was fervently to be prayed that if *le petit* Marcel was not his usual self they must understand that it was no fault of theirs; on the contrary he was fortunate to count such generous and sympathetic people as his friends.

She seemed as troubled when she left as when she had come; but perhaps the despair on her still-young face was permanent now.

No one spoke for a minute or two in the ornate room. Fay took the tray out to the kitchen and came back, and Laura lit another cigarette.

'I suppose,' she said, 'there's nothing we can say to him?'

'What like?' Alec opened the shutters. It was better they should be open.

'I don't know. Try to persuade him that he's got it wrong. That we were – we were acting a play or something, rehearsing a play.' It sounded so stupid and she dropped wearily into a chair. 'Oh, God ... I can't even think any more, and there's so much to think of.'

'It might not be that,' Fay said hopefully. 'It might be the heat or the business with Ronnie when he swam out too far – Chris was frightened, we all saw that.'

Alec moved back from the window out of the sun.

'We might as well face it. He heard enough to worry

him. Then he saw the headlines when I bought the paper. And it tied in. He knew he'd heard right.' He pressed his fingertips to his temples, circling them, because that was where the ache was worst. 'And there's nothing we can do about it now.'

He was still in the salon, alone. Fay had gone upstairs and Laura was in the garden. The aspirins were taking effect and the physical ache was going, but the sunshine playing into the room dispersed none of the thoughts that had kept him awake in the dark hours. They were of the same pattern and contributed to one thought that was dominant: the mistakes had begun.

He'd been concerned with London, before, with the people there: Dolly knew about Stan's tonsillitis but Laura's mother didn't and there was a slight but dangerous chance that Dolly would come down here. There might have been other mistakes they'd made without knowing it: had anyone mentioned Stan's wrist in the postcards they'd sent? If Dolly and Mother got into touch it would make things worse – a broken wrist? But he told me it was tonsillitis ... Had Laura given anything away when she'd phoned last night, by a word or even the tone of her voice? She hadn't wanted to phone, to feel herself in touch with London where so much was going on.

He had stopped thinking about London now. They'd begun making mistakes down here. Dr Giraud had made no comment on the story about the 'falling bottle' that had done the damage; it must have sounded as thin as it had to Chris, who'd had nursing experience. And Giraud has asked after 'the lady who is ill' at the Villa Mimosa. How had he known Laura had spent the day in bed? Marcel must have told his mother. 'Then she must be made a visit from Dr Giraud,' he'd said when they were going down the lane to the sea. His mother must have mentioned it to Giraud: they were neighbours and probably friends. One of them ill; another with a wrist broken by a 'falling bottle'. And Ron 'swimming too far out' – how much had the *maître nageur* suspected? He would have missed them down there yesterday and would miss them again today.

And tomorrow. They wouldn't be going on the beach again.

He knew what Laura had meant when she'd said she couldn't think any more and there was so much to think of. Behind all the other thoughts there was one blacker than the rest, shapeless but overpowering; and they couldn't consider that one. It was in Laura's mind; he knew that. And in his own.

'Where's Stan?'

He opened his eyes. He hadn't even heard anyone come into the room.

'Hello, Mike.'

Mike looked at him critically. 'Anything wrong?'

'Wrong?' He got up and poured a full glass of Perrier. Flush out the liver, too much champagne last night. This was morbidity, that was all, a hangover. 'No. Nothing's wrong.' They'd agreed not to tell the others about Madame Chaumond's visit because it would only worry them.

'Where's Stan?'

'I've not seen him.' Mike seemed worried. 'Why?'

'I just wondered. Had breakfast?'

Alec smiled ruefully. 'I couldn't face it. He's probably still asleep, Mike.'

'No. His door's ajar so I thought he'd come down.'

'Maybe he went for a walk.'

'That's right.' He wouldn't say any more.

'There're a few eggs left in the fridge.' Mike had drunk less than the others last night; he never drank much.

'It's an idea.'

He nodded and went out, but not down the passage to the kitchen. He went up the staircase and Alec listened for a minute or two. Mike wasn't noisy but he wasn't taking any trouble to be quiet either. It was the spare-room door he'd opened; it had a squeak in the hinges because it was the least-used door in the house. He wasn't in there long. When he came down he saw Alec still standing with the glass of mineral water in his hand.

'Do you want some eggs too?'

He'd had to say something because the staircase was opposite the double doors of the salon and he couldn't go along to the kitchen without Alec seeing him.

'Not for me, Mike.' More quietly he said: 'He'd never do a thing like that.'

Mike came into the room a little. His breathing was heavy. He was a big man but in good condition, and the stairs wouldn't have got him out of breath. His face was stony as he looked at Alec.

'He wouldn't?'

'No. It's still there, isn't it? All of it?'

Mike had told him where the stuff was.

'It's all there, yes.'

'You shouldn't have looked, Mike.'

'I shouldn't?' He half-turned towards the kitchen. 'You trust everyone, don't you.' It wasn't a question but a criticism.

'Everyone here. If we don't, we're done for.'

She had changed before coming down, and brought her bag. She wasn't thinking very clearly but it had seemed necessary to lie, saying she was going into the garden.

The post office was crowded and there was an actual queue for the telephones but she stuck it out because it was difficult in a bar to ask for London; they weren't used to it.

Last evening she'd felt a kind of dread and had to stop for a minute by the wall in the reception-hall, and the man had come back to see what the matter was; and all the time she'd been talking she knew her voice wasn't right. That was because Alec had suggested it; she'd been almost forced into it, knowing he was right and that she ought to reassure Mother.

Now it was her own idea and she'd hurried all the way and stood here with the cigarette trembling in her fingers. The dread was the same, worse if anything. It was her own idea but she'd still been forced into it. She had to know.

The connection took almost half an hour and just before they told her Cabin 2 she had turned to go, go without even telling them to cancel it; because her voice would sound as shaky as the frightened tumble of thoughts that were colliding through her head. But it made no difference. If she'd gone she would only have come back. She had to know.

'Mother?'

The line was shocking. People's voices in the background.

'Is that you, Laura?'

'Yes, Mother!'

'What's happened?'

She hadn't even thought of anything, any reason, hadn't even realized her mother would ask.

'I – we were cut short, a bit, last night. There was someone waiting. For the phone.' There was nothing she could do about her voice; she was shaking all over and couldn't stop. 'How – how is everything?'

The line crackled and she couldn't tell if her mother had answered.

' – there, Laura?'

'Yes. Yes I'm here.'

' – time?'

'What?'

'Are you having a nice time?'

'Marvellous!' She pressed herself against the wall of the booth. Perhaps if she could stop her body shaking her voice would be better. 'Are – are they all right?'

'Of course they are.'

Her mother's voice was suddenly very clear. The gabble in the background was cut off.

'What's – what's happening over there? In London? I mean anything exciting?'

'We're all fine, Laura.' Perhaps the line was bad in one direction. Her voice was puzzled.

'Oh, good! What's the – the news today, over there?'

'Laura?'

'Yes?'

'You don't sound well, dear. You sound upset. I'm sure —'

'No, it's the line, bad line.' Her own voice vibrated against her ears in the booth and she knew she couldn't go on half-shouting much longer; she'd have to get out; there was no air in here; it was stifling her. 'Is there anything in the papers, Mother?'

'The what?'

'The papers!'

Begging for news, pleading to be told, because once she was told she could cope with it, the worst would be over.

'Laura?'

Very far away now. Alec would be appalled if he knew what she was doing. Nobody in London must suspect

241

anything. He could be appalled, then. Angry with her, afraid, anything he liked. She had a right to do what she thought best. *Couldn't she phone her own mother now?*

'Laura? Hello?'

God knew she had the right, they were her children and if anything happened she must be there to cope with it all, protect them from it if she could, as much as she could, it was the least he could allow her. *Once he's been caught I can cope.*

It frightened her and she pushed herself upright again. There was no air. I don't mean that, I mean once I know, I can't be expected to face things I don't even know, I don't want them to catch you, you didn't do anything bad, it was that bloody little fool —

'*Vous avez terminé?*'

'No! No, don't cut us off – *ne coupez pas!*'

'Laura?'

'Yes! I'm here, Mother!'

You were trying to protect him, they'll realize that, but did you have to, couldn't you think of me first, try to protect *me?* He was always ready to look after me from the beginning but I didn't fancy a lifetime of wet-nursing.

'Fay! Don't go! Can you hear me?' Not Fay. Mother. London. '*Tell me what the papers say!*' The frightening thud of her heart suffocating. Line bad, people's voices. 'Mother?' People's voices, people's voices.

'*Vous avez terminé?*' Voices. 'You have finished?'

She was my mother.

'Yes. I've finished.'

The door shuddered open and a man caught her, a man with a surprised face, caught her, spinning away.

CHAPTER 18

Last night they had made love.

She had slept afterwards, for quite a long time. In the night it didn't seem she was sleeping much, tossing and turning; but now she knew she must have slept quite a lot. She felt almost fresh and almost happy.

It had been difficult. He was so sensitive. But in the restaurant she'd at last got him to hold her hand, to reach out and touch her. That had been the first step, making him see he wasn't some kind of a monster and that people didn't mind if he touched them, especially her.

It hadn't been all pleasant because he was so sensitive and they couldn't sort of do it knowing they were going to do it. She had to use tricks and behave like some awful little gold-digger trying to seduce a sugar-daddy, and that had been beastly but it was the only way. Then he suddenly seemed to believe her when she said it, 'I love you', over and over again, whispering it, because suddenly he relaxed and managed it, so quickly that he was through before she was, before she was anywhere near it; so she pretended and they lay quietly. It didn't matter that it had been so one-sided; she had done what she'd set out to do and it was the first time they hadn't used the pill.

She could hardly think about it yet, but at the back of her mind she knew that today was the second most wonderful day in her life.

When they came downstairs they found Mike in the

kitchen, just standing with his huge shoulders against the cupboard, his arms folded.

'I came to do some eggs,' he said, looking at them and not really seeing them.

Ron wondered what had happened, and nearly asked Mike, 'What's happened?' but stopped himself, not wanting anything more to have happened.

'There's only three,' said Chris, looking in the fridge. 'And there's no milk.' She shut the fridge door and took one of the string bags from the hook, untangling it from the others: there must be a dozen of them, a lot of them still with dried bits of brussels sprouts and bean-pods clinging to them. 'Come on, Ronnie, we'll pop into the town and get a few things in. We'd better take two of these because of the milk.'

On their way past the salon they called out to Alec, telling him they were just popping round to the shops. They left the front door open so the sun could come in, and Ronnie took her hand as they crossed the porch and saw the police-car coming down the drive.

The *garçon* was standing in the doorway fiddling with a toothpick, glancing at him now and then.

The sun was hot, bouncing heat off the pavement. The trees were shady but the air was hot everywhere, sticky. The traffic went roaring round the square filling the place with blue gas, it was enough to choke you.

'Right. Let's have the bill.'

The *garçon* came over.

'*Comment, m'sieur?*'

'Bill. *Addition.*'

He took the three tickets off the table and shuffled them. '*Ça fait quinze soixante-dix.*'

'Keep the rest.' He put a couple of ten-franc notes down.

The leg of the chair got caught on a join in the pavement and he nearly went a purler because of his arm being in the sling, couldn't balance himself.

'*Merci, m'sieur! Faites attention, hein? 'Y a beaucoup de circulation!*'

You must be joking.

The edge of the iron table had caught him across the thigh and it didn't make him feel any better.

You think you're going to see me fall flat on my arse and get up and walk straight under a bus, don't you? All on three doubles? You must be joking, boy.

The exhaust-stink came up at his face and he turned along the pavement instead. There were yellow lines on the corner and they couldn't knock you down without getting run in for it so you had the laugh on them in the end even if they had to come and scrape you up with a bloody shovel.

The pain had stopped, the pain in his wrist. It was the answer all right, better than all your barbiturates and hydrocortisones and that lark, the blood of the grape, my friend, that is most definitely the final and unargufiable answer, and this is Stanley telling you.

Black gas out of a diesel bus, enough to blind you. Tyres screaming – I'm on the yellow bloody ladder can't you see you wild lot of garlic-bashing bloody maniacs?

'*Allez prendre du café, vous!*'

'Bollocks!'

But you'd got to watch it and that was a fact, they'd have your teeth round your tonsils as soon as look at you.

Heart thumping. My heart's thumping, Doctor, now what you think that is? It's quite probably a valvular defect, my boy. Well, you're bloody wrong, it's because I nearly got run over so it shows how much you know, doesn't it?

It was cooler nearing the sea. Sea-breeze.

Christ, he'd almost done it, scarpered. But that was all very well, all very well that was. It wasn't nice, thinking about what he'd been thinking about. Forget it.

He sat for a long time on a bench by the sea, breathing in the air, under a tree where it wasn't so hot. Felt better now, much better.

Escape the net. Now that was a rotten bloody way to put it. Poor little sod caught in a net.

The sea was blue. It'd look like that along Copacabaña way, lights all along at night. Lots of lovely Spanish girls and tourists by the shipload, cruise down there in a dirty great Cadillac and pick 'em up by the dozen, now get in the back my beauties and unfasten your seat-belts for Stanley.

While they were putting the poor little sod in the dock.

He felt much better. The sweat had poured off him sitting outside the café. It was the first time he'd ever hated anyone, hated their very guts, put a knife in their guts and twisted it. Mike. If he'd never walked into that bastard's office that day he'd have been in the clear now, enjoying his holiday, her down here with him, Dolly. *Bloody Mike.*

The sweat had poured off him. He'd wanted to get up and throw that table straight through the café window, one hand and all, see it smash, see that kid in the white jacket running for his life. He'd never felt like that before, ever. Got on well with people. But by Christ it was all he could do to stop himself breaking out, going wild. Sitting there with a broken wrist and reading about what they were doing over there, trying to find him, trying to find *him* and put him in the dock with that poor little sod. Nice bloke, Mike Owen, dropped you in the shit and then broke your arm when you complained. A nice bastard.

He didn't want to think about it any more. Been the heat of course and the bash he'd given himself in the doorway and the shock of what it said in the paper.

You'd got to think straight or you wouldn't like the look of yourself in the mirror. Mike hadn't used any persuasion. They'd been talking about the job, that was all, very amusing, a nice change from listening to that bunch of stupid little whores twittering away and losing him a customer every time they opened their trap. And what was it Mike had said? He wouldn't be getting all of the stuff away, but he wasn't worried, didn't want to push his luck. That was Mike – careful, a real pro.

Well, isn't there something *I* can do?

I wouldn't like to ask you.

You haven't asked. It was my idea.

Then I should forget it.

That's how it was, near enough. Couldn't let well alone, though. Had to stick his neck out. All right, let's face it: *he'd* persuaded Mike to let him in on it. Because he'd been ready for it, ready for something like that, a bit of a lark, fed up to the back teeth with that crowd of sooty-eyed little cows and the stink of the setting-lotion all day long day after bloody day. Ready for it.

The sea was a lovely blue. He felt much better now.

You've been a fool, Stan. A big one. Say that for you, always do things big. But don't you go putting the blame on other people. You're a fool but you're not a squealer.

There were boats on the sea with their sails well over in the wind. You wouldn't think there was a wind out here.

He got off the bench and looked at the sea and the boats. The air was a tonic, that was a fact. It was as if he'd been ill and was over it now. The beach went in a long curve just here and he could make out the place where the sheds were, the place where he'd seen the blue boat propped up by the palm tree last year, the notice on it: *A Vendre*. He must go along and have a look tomorrow, see if it was still there, see if it was sold or not. Tomorrow, or some day.

Alec did his best with his French but after a minute the Inspector started talking in quite good English.

'I was in England once, yes. When we have the war. I was at the town named Sout'ampton. Do you know that town?'

He was a short compact man with a lined face and iron-grey hair and hooded blue eyes, older than his colleague, who sat stiffly on the edge of the Louis XVI chair and watched. They were both in uniform and had taken off their silk-lined kepis, putting them diffidently on the floor beside them in the way policemen do, knowing they are not guests but intruders.

Alec sat facing the Inspector. His mind felt chilled and his thoughts were clear. It was perfectly natural for Marcel to have gone to the police. He had heard them talking about it when he had stood outside the shutters, and he had seen the headline in the newspaper. He would be a hero now and make many more friends. It might seem extraordinary that although they had known he must have overheard them and had seen the headline they had done nothing about it, made no attempt to think up an explanation that a boy of twelve might accept. But it wasn't extraordinary because they had made so many mistakes and if this one wasn't the fatal one there would be others and they would be too tired to think their way out. At some time in the recent past it had started to be too late.

Laura knew. She had lain the shirtwaister carefully on

top of the other things in the valise. Perhaps the rest of them knew.

Mike stood by the windows. The sun had moved higher and only a thin angle of its light fell across the blue-and-white tiles. Chris sat near Ron, the two string bags still empty by their feet. Fay was still upstairs, probably sleeping, or she would have heard the police-car and come down to see who it was. Nobody had seen Stan or Laura for some time.

'We must notice reports like this, you see.' The Inspector shrugged with his hands. 'Many times it is nothing, of course, but we must notice such reports.'

Alec nodded absently. Even when a twelve-year-old boy went to them with a story like this they must investigate.

The Inspector had been looking sleepily from one to another with his hooded blue eyes. 'It is the *maître nageur* at the Midi Plage who makes this report, and I have inquired from him about this.' He was looking – as if by chance – at Ron. 'It is you, *m'sieur*, who was bathing too distantly?'

Alec shut his eyes just for a second. There was silence. He heard himself helping Ron. 'Swam out too far.'

'Yes,' Ron said. 'Yes.'

'So. And did you do that before?'

'I beg pardon?'

Alec said mechanically: 'Have you ever done it before?'

They knew it was Ron from what the *maître nageur* had told them: he would have said 'the small man' or something like that.

'No. I don't think so.'

'Why did you do this thing?' His forehead was puckered into thin folds below the iron-grey hair and his eyes brooded, half-closed.

'I don't know.'

Alec leaned forward. 'It shook him up, you know. It upset him. We were all upset; *agités, très agités*. That is why we did not go on the beach again today. We do not like thinking about it.'

The attempt was automatic: the attempt to correct the mistakes and explain why they all looked like this. Even though it had started, some time ago, to be too late.

The *maître nageur* was a registered life-guard. He had fetched people back to the shore a hundred times like that and he knew an imprudent swimmer from a would-be suicide. Maybe he'd not been sure though, because it was Mike who had got there first and Ron had probably calmed down a little before the life-guard reached them. So he'd slept on it. Then they hadn't shown up yesterday although they'd booked for a week, and that had decided him; it was his official duty to report a matter like that: attempted suicide was attempted murder. And he would have noticed the mood they were in, quiet all day, none of them going into the water except 'the small man'. He didn't know where they were staying but the police had found out, or maybe Marcel had wandered down there yesterday hoping to see them – the house had been empty and he didn't know they were shopping at the market – and the life-guard had asked him where they were staying.

'Of course,' said the Inspector. 'I can understand that such a matter made you *très agités*, as you have said. It has not been agreeable for you, oh no.'

Then Chris spoke. 'Are you always told when someone goes out too far?'

Alec remembered that she didn't know.

'Not always, *mad'moiselle*. Only if there is any thought that it is made *exprès*. Deliberately.'

'Deliberately.' It was a flat repetition as if she couldn't

take in his meaning. Her eyes were large, watching him.

The Inspector glanced at Alec. 'Perhaps I have not —'

'Yes, that's right, it's the right word.' He didn't look at Chris. There was nothing he could do for her.

She was laughing suddenly, a light trembling laugh, and her hand touched Ron's knee, resting on it. 'I see, yes. I see what you mean. But you're wrong. This – is my husband and he's got everything to live for.'

'It is very evident, *madame*.' The sleepy eyes smiled as he corrected her title.

'Thank you. Yes, he's – he's got me, and much more than me. He's got everything in the whole world.'

Alec, hearing her sudden light laughter, had turned his head; and now he watched her in admiration, a flood of wonder coming into him. She knew now what Ron had tried to do; she might have suspected it but now she knew, knew it was true and denied it at once, taking the shock and throwing it off in the same instant, defeating a sick truth by refusing to recognize it, killing it off by a flashing statement of faith.

He had never seen such a thing before, and couldn't for a moment look away. She sat with her small hand on Ron's knee, her eyes glowing.

'That's right,' Ron said. 'I've got everything in the world.' His hand moved and covered hers. His face was strained but he was smiling a little, as if unused to it. 'Her name's Chris. It's – short for Christine.' There was nothing arch in what he said; he didn't mean that the name of 'everything in the world' was Chris, though that was true; he simply wanted the stranger to know her name and how pretty it was.

The Inspector inclined his head. 'That is a nice name, *très jolie*, yes. We have that name in France. Perhaps

Madame Christine is just a small part French? I like to think so.'

He glanced at his colleague and they picked up their smart silk-lined kepis. It was Alec who showed them out and they stood talking for a minute on the porch where the beach stuff was piled.

The Inspector was sure that the *'m'sieur trop courageux'* had learned his lesson, yes, and that he would no longer bathe too distantly. It could have been a tragedy, of course, and they realized this thing, and so they should now forget it, and thus enjoy their vacation.

Alec waited until the police-car had left the drive. Chris and Ron had come out of the house, carrying a string bag each.

'We'll go to the shops now.' She smiled.

'Watch the roads,' Alec said, 'and remember the cars come the opposite way.' He watched them go up to the lane, and wondered again where Laura was.

Mike was still in the salon.

'Did they twig?'

Alec said: 'They're not stupid.'

'What do they think?'

'I'd say they think it was true: he tried it. But Chris convinced them he wouldn't want to try it again.'

'Will they do anything?'

'Eventually.' He stood looking through the doors at the mimosa tree, not seeing it. Eventually they would do something; they'd have the Interpol report already. Four men. But not four men in a holiday party with their wives. Behaving unusually. It would take a little time, hours, days, but eventually they'd link it up.

'What's the answer, Alec?'

'There isn't one.' He turned away from the doors. 'It's not on, Mike. It never was.'

CHAPTER 19

Stan came back a little before Laura.

Mike saw him come in, because he'd been waiting for him, not believing he'd come but waiting just in case, trying to convince himself that Alec was right.

Stan's face shone with sweat and he stood in the hall with his feet carefully apart. Mike had come out of the salon, hearing his footsteps.

'I am pissed.' He stood looking at Mike. There was a kind of pride in his deep voice. 'I am ever so slightly fuckin' inebriated. And how is my good friend Michael?'

'I'm glad to see you.' His big arms had been folded but now he freed them and shoved his hands into his pockets. The bottled-up laugh was coming out of him, the one that Stan had often mimicked for them all. Stan didn't mimic it now.

'I'm glad to see me too.' Slowly he tilted his head back until he was eyeing Mike with deliberate accuracy, sighting along his nose. In a sing-song tone he said: 'You thought I'd run away, didn't you? Like a naughty little boy, didn't you?'

'I did?' His laugh went on, like a stifled whimper.

'Yes, my good friend, you did. Now that was a nasty thing to think about your good friend Stanley, wasn't it?' He lowered his head and levelled a look of deep reproof at Mike, starting off again down the hall and coming past him, putting one foot with caution on the bottom stair. 'It just goes to show the highly rep – reprehensible state of your dirty rotten mind, does it not? It does indeed, my good Michael.' He went up the staircase with deliberate care. 'Mind you,' he said conversationally over his shoulder, 'you were perfectly right. Perf – perfectly correct in your stinkin' bloody assumptions. Yes indeed.' Mike moved to the bottom stair and leaned there, ready in case he lost his footing on the marble. 'But it was such a hot day, you understand.' He kept his right arm carefully away from the banisters. 'And it seemed such a fright – frightfully long way to anywhere.' He had safely reached the top. 'When the only place that really int'rests me is the jolly old lavatorio.'

The man who had broken her fall in the post office had insisted on taking her home in his car and she had been too feeble to refuse; but by the time they had reached the sea-front she felt well enough to walk, and asked him to drop her off.

He tried to persuade her to let him take her right to the house; his Gallic *galanterie* had been fully aroused by having an attractive English lady faint into his arms and he wished to make the most of it; but she quietly assured him that thanks to his great kindness she was perfectly all right again – '*C'était le manque d'air dans la cabine —*'

'*Mais bien sûr, ça devient insupportable, cette vague de chaleur!*' He got out of the car and trotted round to open the door for her.

'*Vous m'avez montré une gentillesse extrême, m'sieur.*'

'*Chère madame, c'était un rare privilège . . .*'

He stood by his car, watching her into the entrance of the lane to assure himself she was fully recovered.

She walked in the scented shade of the eucalyptus trees, not angry but resolved. She had the right and she would use it. They could argue with her, try to shame her, plead with her, but she would use her right. They'd got themselves into this mess and they'd have to get out of it themselves: she'd had no part in it and she wanted no part of it now.

A branch of the mimosa had fallen, broken off by a cat or a child perhaps; the yellow blooms lay in the dust, already shrivelling.

She was a woman and she had her children and her mother and her home and that was where she had to be now, for their sake and her own. Nothing else counted.

The small round stones were scattered by her shoes, where last night she had walked in stockinged feet, so tired that when she had drawn her hair back and faced the moonlit sky she had almost fallen asleep where she stood.

She wasn't tired now. It was different now; she had something to do, somewhere to go. Home.

Passing the open doors of the salon she saw Mike standing by the windows, his back to her. There was a slackness about his massive body as if something had defeated him; he was so lost in his thoughts that she was climbing the staircase before he turned, hearing her. She was glad. She didn't want to talk to anyone, listen to anyone, argue the point with them so they'd be made to realize it wasn't wilfulness or a brainstorm but the calculated exercising of a human right. She didn't want to have to be angry with them, and that was what would happen if she was forced to talk. She could feel the anger simmering inside her, ready to boil up.

She opened the door of their bedroom and saw Alec. He was stooping over a valise on the bed, snapping the locks. He turned and she saw the same attitude in him that she had seen in Mike just now.

'Hello, Laura.'

She pushed the door shut behind her.

'Hello, Alec.'

'I'm glad you're back. I was getting worried.'

'Were you?' She looked at the valise. It was a black one, one of his. 'Are you packing?'

'Yes.'

'Are – are we going?'

'Yes.'

She leaned her back to the door; the sudden passing away of the anger had left her weak. In a moment or two she asked: 'What happened?'

'Nothing, really. I don't think we can stay, that's all.'

'We knew all along, didn't we?'

'I expect so.'

She went to him and put her brow against his shoulder, and he held her, stroking her long hair.

They had talked on the way back, keeping to the shade where they could and sometimes stopping to rest the two bags on a bench or a low wall. Ron had the heavy one with the milk in it. They hadn't bought much, just enough for a meal for all of them.

The woman at the shop had said they must put the milk into the *frigo* as soon as they were home, or the heat would turn it. Chris thanked her and said they would do that.

Neither of them had said anything particular about it; they were suddenly just talking. They had known already, last night. There had been something final about it all, the way they'd let Stan talk them into going 'on the town', the way they'd drunk too much. And then, later when they were alone, the way she had coaxed him.

She had stopped crying inside a long time ago, this morning when it was just light and she had watched his sleeping face, thinking to him 'I love you', as she did at the beginning of every new day. She had cried because she had realized, some time in the dark hours when she couldn't see him, how lonely people were. Even people with wives and husbands and children, people in love, people with lots of friends, were lonely.

She loved Ronnie and would do anything for him, anything in the world, good things, bad, hard things, desperate things, if they helped him and helped her to look after him no matter what happened. They could run away and hide somewhere, far away, abroad, and she would save him from anyone or anything that tried to hurt him; she would charm people, persuade them, force them, *make* them help and give them shelter till one day they could stop and look around and see that they were safe and could rest, and begin life all over again. It was a silly way to put it, but she was his sword and his shield, ready and fierce by his side for always, for always.

But he didn't want that. He wanted to go back and he thought it was right, so she couldn't try to stop him. And that was what loneliness meant.

'Do you love me?' she smiled.

They had stopped again, this time at the corner where the last shop was, a shop selling novelties, straw hats and beach-balls and plastic rafts with transparent panels in the bottom so you could look down and see the fish. There was a bench here and they rested their string bags.

'Yes,' he said, smiling back. 'I love you, Chris.'

He'd always answered like that, never saying 'you know I do' or 'of course I do', because he seemed to know it was the actual word that mattered, 'love'.

He loved her; she knew that; and he'd do anything to make her happy. He would even let her talk him into running away and hiding so they could stay together for as long as they could, as long as it lasted. But he had enough sense for both of them and he knew it wouldn't work. She wouldn't be happy with him, seeing him having to 'live with it', hating himself and exhausting his nerves, jumping every time someone knocked on a door or called to him in a street. He wouldn't be the Ronnie she knew and loved, after a time. All she wanted in the whole world was to be with him, and that was what he couldn't give her, however much he loved her. So he was lonely too.

Everyone was. They were locked up inside themselves and couldn't reach out and touch other people when they wanted to, when it was all they wanted. Only sometimes. Not always. She'd cried, last night, for everyone.

'Let me have them both,' he said again.

'Not likely.' She smiled. 'You've got the heaviest one as it is.'

They started off again hand in hand, and she stopped thinking about it. There was always a point where she had to stop, a kind of brink; she didn't know what would happen if she went too near; she just knew she mustn't. There was the future on the other side, the years ahead of them where they wouldn't be walking hand in hand any more, and she couldn't let herself think about that, or something would happen to her.

'Are you hungry?'

'A little bit,' she said.

'Then we'll have a fry-up, shall we?'

'Yes.'

The handle of the string bag was cutting into his fingers but they mustn't stop again. There were things they'd got to talk about and this wasn't the place, with all the sunshine and blue sky and everything. He still couldn't seem to get over it, how she'd agreed like that, even though he'd sort of known she would last night. He didn't have to tell her what was in his mind; she just understood. He felt better now, much stronger, because of her, the way she'd agreed. He could face it now, knowing she understood what he felt.

He'd done a terrible thing to that poor man, and it might make his widow and his friends feel a bit better if they could see him in the dock. It was as much as he could do and he wanted to do it as quick as he could. He owed that man everything he could pay.

It was shady in the lane with the tall trees and they didn't stop again till they reached the gates.

'Oh look, there's a bit of mimosa come off.' She picked it up.

'It won't last.'

'It might, if we put it in some water.'

They went down the stony drive, but now she had the string bag in one hand and the mimosa in the other, so she let it fall and took his hand again instead.

Fay had come downstairs and was helping Chris and Laura in the kitchen. Ron had gone up to start packing.

Stan was with the other two in the ornate salon. He'd had a cold shower and dozed off for a bit and then had another shower. He was more like himself now, though his hands weren't steady when he lit a cigarette and he spoke in a flat dull tone when he spoke at all.

He knew what was on. No one had said anything but the feeling was all over the house; it was like the feeling you got in a ship just before it was abandoned. But they told him about Ron.

'He tried to drown himself,' Alec said. 'The day before yesterday.'

'*He what?*' The cigarette was jerked out of his mouth. 'Why didn't you tell me?'

'What could you have done?'

Stan stood looking at nothing, his breathing shallow

and quick. 'That's right. That's quite right.' He looked at Mike. 'When you went out there, was it, after him?'

'Yes.'

'Poor little *sod* ...' He dragged on the cigarette with shaky fingers. 'That's why you broke my wrist, was it? Shouting the odds about him, wasn't I? Should've broken my bloody neck.'

'Another thing you ought to know, Stan. The chap on the beach reported it. He twigged it. The police have just been.'

'*Christ.*' He looked from Mike to Alec. 'That's why everyone's packing, is it?'

'Not really,' Alec said. 'It's given them a lead on us and we can't stay here. But we could move on if we thought fit, and give ourselves extra time. We could break up now and take a last chance.' He was watching Stan closely. 'You've no commitments, no wife, nothing you've got to go back for. And we're going back anyway so you wouldn't be letting us down, not now.'

Stan wasn't looking at either of them. He said suddenly and harshly: 'I don't fancy it.'

'You ought to think about it, Stan.'

'I've thought about it. I tell you I don't fancy it, isn't that good enough for you?'

'Yes,' Alec said.

Stan flicked the cigarette spinning through the doors. 'I'm a Londoner, me. I'd miss the bloody place. Going to turn himself in, is he?'

'That's what he wants to do,' Alec said. 'It's the only thing that'll save him.'

'Save him?'

'As a person.'

Stan turned away, his energy driving him. 'That means the lot of us, does it?'

Mike had taken out his nail-file and was using it. 'Once he's in,' he said, 'they'll be on to us very quick.'

Stan's breathing was painful to hear; every breath sounded an effort. 'Got to go back, has he?'

Alec said: 'He thinks he's got to, and that's the same thing.'

'Well they'd nail him anyway, wouldn't they, down here? Sooner or later?'

'Sure. Unless he runs. But he doesn't want to run. He wants to go back, not get taken back; he's not a kid any more.'

Stan couldn't keep still. 'That's our lot then.' The sweat ran down his face.

'Yes.'

'All right.' He took out his gold cigarette-case and opened it and snapped it shut and slung it on to a chair. 'All right.'

Mike looked up from his nails. 'You'd better not go making any big gestures, Stan.'

'You can shut up for a start.'

'You'd better give some thought to what we've got coming to us.'

'I know what's coming to us. The chopper.' He picked up his cigarette-case and took one and lit it. 'Keep smiling. Maybe we'll get a soft judge.'

'A *what*?'

They were startled and looked at Mike quickly. His eyes were bright and his smile was terrible, a baring of teeth. It was a moment before he spoke again and Alec knew he'd first had to get himself under control. He didn't raise his voice; it was softer than usual and he spoke slowly and every word had weight.

'You can get a good jury or a bad one, but good or bad they're human people. And they're hamstrung. They're going to be asked if we're guilty or not guilty of committing a crime or helping in it. Breaking a safe. And it'll be "Guilty" because we've got no defence. They'll be there to acquit or convict but nothing else. They won't give the sentence. That's for the law to do. The judge. The one in the wig and the red robes, the one in fancy dress. And the law says that if we committed that crime we killed a man too. The law says that. Not the jury.'

He looked down from Stan's face and began using the nail-file again, his fingers pressed together to keep them steady, the blood leaving them.

'The jury's hamstrung. It knows what the law says but it can't say anything itself. Those twelve people can't say, "We think they're guilty of robbing a safe but only one of them killed the policeman because only one of them had a gun."' He looked up suddenly. 'Take Alec. He was trying to look after a friend that night. He knew the job was illegal but he wasn't in it for gain. He wouldn't have been there at all if it wasn't for trying to keep Ron out of trouble. You think if a jury could give the sentence they'd send Alec down for thirty years? For what he did? Thirty years? The judge will. And they can't stop him. He's the law.' The nail-file was busy again, gouging at the white fingertips. 'I had a brother once, couldn't stop nicking stuff. Third conviction, seven years. He'd nicked more than a hundred quid that time. Big stuff. Seven years, to teach him not to steal, see? Put him in with people like himself so they could learn from each other how not to steal. Makes sense doesn't it. But he didn't like it in there. Seven years seemed a long time to a kid of twenty-two. So he smuggled a bit of sacking out of the workshops and strung himself up in the cell. You won't get a soft judge, Stan. You'll be up against the full majesty of the law and Christ help you.'

A crimson spot was forming under one of his nails and he put the file away.

'A brother?' Stan couldn't look away from him.

'That makes no odds. It could've been anyone.' He folded his big arms. 'This time it's us.'

Stan took another turn round the room and Alec was reminded of something in a cage and wished he'd keep still.

'Well I'll never say you didn't warn me. That fair enough?' He came and stood in front of Mike. 'Do him a bit of good, won't it, young Ron, if we're all there in the dock? Keep him company, right? I'm on. I'm on. They can put me away but not for long. I've got funds. Got friends. So've you. So's Alec. Get Ron out as well if we work at it.'

'No, Stan,' Alec said. 'He'd not walk out even if you left the door open.'

Stan swung on him. 'If that's how he wants it.'

'It is.'

'All right. Then it's us. Did we shoot a man down? Did we have a gun, did we *ever* have one, did we ever *want* one, would we kill a man, would you, would Mike, *kill* a man?' He was still sweating but his voice had lost its dull flat tone and he could keep still at last.

They knew now that he'd go back with them. He thought there was a future and that the clang of the door wouldn't be the end. Whether he'd ever try it on or whether the months and the years would pile on him and stifle even his brand of energy and turn him into one of the grey-faced apathetic lags the prisons were crowded with, they couldn't know. He knew, or thought he knew, and that was all he needed.

'So they'll have a job. Keeping us lot inside. Have a job. And I don't think they can do it. You with me, are you?'

'Sure.'

'We'll be with you, Stan, in or out.'

They all had some eggs and bacon, sitting in the salon, some of them on the terrace just outside, the plates on their knees. They talked now and then.

'I never thought I'd be hungry,' Fay said.

'You're not doing too bad.'

Stan dropped a piece of bacon, having to manage with one hand. 'It's not like the English.'

'And that's Danish.'

'Not the stuff we get. Greenback.'

'I'd miss London,' Chris told them.

'That's what I said.'

'Did you, Stan?'

'I wasn't born for foreign parts. All this monotonous bloody sunshine, it gets in your eyes.'

Some of them laughed.

When they had finished the girls cleared away and Laura went up to help Fay with the last of her packing while Alec and Mike went round all the shutters and turned off the Butagaz and locked the doors.

Then they were all downstairs and there didn't seem anything more to do. It was Laura who asked: 'What's this?' and picked up the envelope from the Florentine table.

'I'd forgotten it,' Fay told her. 'Someone slipped it under the front door, I don't know when.'

Laura opened it and took out the note. When she had read it she gave it to Alec without saying anything and went across the room to the windows, her hands going up to her face for a moment.

Alec glanced at the signature. 'I'll read it out, shall I?'

'Yes,' Chris said. It couldn't be bad news. There wasn't any more.

Alec read slowly:

'"*Dear Friends, I know what is happened to you, I think, yet there is a mistake, because I know that you are the wonderful people of the world and are good. Do not think, please, never, that I will tell people of this thing. It shall rest my secret, this I avow in my full heart. If you go away, I must think of you with no pausing, and will look never at La Villa Mimosa without thought of you there, because you are always my loved friends. I have the Honneur to be Yours Truly, Marcel.*"'

They took a train from Antibes station. The packing and clearing up had kept them too late for the afternoon flight and they all agreed they couldn't stay another night now they knew they were going. There was no hurry and they'd see some of the countryside, which they never could from the plane. They always agreed on things like that, without any discussion.

Alec had left the key and a note with Dr Giraud to give to Madame Dupont. The note said that urgent reasons had called them home but that they had enjoyed their short stay in her lovely house. With much regret they didn't think they would be coming again next year.

Then he walked up the lane through the eucalyptus trees to fetch the two taxis.

The others had nothing to do, and didn't talk about anything important. Laura said they ought to have cleaned the place up a bit better than they had, but Mike said the woman would be coming and it was provided for in the rent. Stan tried a joke as they stood about waiting, drawing his thumb across the strings of the guitar on the wall, saying Handy Stanley, the One-armed

Guitar-player. Nobody laughed; they listened to the notes dying away.

All the cases were in the porch; the beach-things had been taken back to the spare room. Laura was in the drive to listen for the taxis, and wondered how the broken branch of the mimosa had got there, halfway along. Then she saw the first taxi turning in from the lane.

'They're here,' she called.

Stan had been trying to think of something else funny because Chris had gone very pale and Mike was humming a tune, which made it sound even more quiet, with no one talking. He was relieved when Laura called out. He picked up the first valise.

'Come on,' he said. 'This is no place for the wicked.'

Now they had gone. The sun was shining but there was only a half-light in the ornate salon because the shutters were closed. Reflection from the terrace glowed on the varnish of the guitar and the inlay of the little Florentine table with the wonky leg.

A full pack of cards lay on top of the escritoire, and someone had left their cigarettes on the arm of the Louis XVI chair. There was nothing else to show that anyone had been here except the empty basket at the bottom of the staircase, the one the apricots had been in.

The four angels floated in the high corners of the salon; the two that were opposite the windows caught more light than the others, and they were reflected minutely in the drops of the chandelier, so that there seemed to be many of them, a flight of small angels passing.

CHAPTER 20

The ordeal of the journey was no worse than they had expected, but it was different.

There was no pattern to it, no order. The headlong running of the wheels under them gave no peace, and talking was sometimes difficult, so that things that must be said quietly were half-shouted and took on a different meaning. The wheels and the rocking made them aware that they were going in the wrong direction and too fast. They were like the people who take their seats in a roller-coaster and afterwards wish they hadn't.

Day changed into night and that was different too; the dark is less sure than the light, and flickering bulbs are no help. They caught sudden glimpses of themselves in black windows, the yellowish light and the movement making their own faces unfamiliar; and the seeming loss of identity frightened them.

They had meant to sit together at adjoining tables in the dining-car, eating something to pass the time; but although the train was not crowded (most people were coming out on holiday, not going home), the other passengers had already spread themselves among the tables and they had to sit with strangers and couldn't all see each other, or talk.

There was nowhere they could be together, so that the evening was spent between the restaurant-car and their sleeping-compartments in little groups, some of them staying in the corridor and hanging on to the rail to stare through their reflections at the lights that went swinging past in the dark outside.

Because of the speed that bore them along they felt that time itself had accelerated, leaving them less than they needed for things to be said; so they said them tonight instead of the next day, fearing they might never be said at all.

'Don't worry. You won't miss me after a while.'

'You mustn't ever think that, Mike.' But she had thought the same thing only yesterday: that she'd been more alone since they'd married than before. She'd not realized he had known. 'I'll never stop thinking of you.' Especially when she danced with someone, because no one could dance like Mike. It was how they'd first met, dancing.

'You'll have the business,' he said. 'Mrs Hallowes can go on running it. She's very efficient.'

'I can help her in the office.'

'If you want to.'

'Of course I will.' But he didn't think she'd be much help to Mrs Hallowes when she couldn't even catch the right bus or keep track of her purse.

The wheels rolled, racketing under them.

Laura had made up the bunks in the sleeping-compartment and sat with a cigarette. Alec had taken off his jacket because of the heat.

'I rang Mother today. This morning.'

'I wondered where you'd gone.'

'I was desperate for some news, that was all. I'm not good at turning my back on things.'

'Was she all right?'

'She was till I rang.' The corners of her mouth turned downwards; it was an expression that had become a habit in the last few days. 'The line was shocking and I wasn't exactly in control of myself. It worried her, so she'll be glad to see me tomorrow safe and sound, if that's what you can call it.' She wondered if he'd ask her what 'news' she'd heard from her mother.

'She's a good woman, Laurry. They'll be all right with you, and her there as well. Try and get her to stay for a while.'

She thought of the empty twin-bed in their room.

'I suppose, Alec, this is what being "destroyed" means.'

In a moment he said reflectively: 'No one can ever be destroyed, not even when they die.' He was turning the watch on his wrist, playing with the reflection of the lamps in its glass; she could see the flicker of light across his eyes. 'No, this is just something we've got to face, and the thing that matters is how we face it. We've never had anything bad happen to us before. A lot of people don't; they go through life with nothing to worry about; they're the people you see in "good" hotels on the coast, sour-faced and down-in-the-mouth, nobody but themselves to think of; give them a tough piece of steak or tell them the chemists are shut and they think it's the end of the world. It's not really their fault; they've just had nothing to face.'

She put her cigarette into the ash-compartment and snapped the lid down sharply. 'Then we're lucky.'

'We might turn out to be, in a way. That's up to us. We could turn out better people, one day.'

The train crossed a network of points just south of Lyon, jarring everyone's nerves. From the corridor people could see the Rhône glinting and the white wake of a barge.

Fay had gone to lie down, hoping to sleep. She hadn't taken any pills; she'd thrown them away, all of them, first thing this morning, and this morning she'd dropped off to sleep without any trouble; she could remember Alec smiling to her, remember him as clearly as if he'd been there with her, saying, 'Nothing will happen if you doze off for a while. Everything's all right.' And she'd felt better when she'd woken up, and even felt hungry for the bacon and eggs, which had surprised her.

In the corridors a few people, 'promenading' after their meal, clung to the rail as the train crossed the points.

'You may find it useful, Stan.'

'That bloody stuff?'

'You may change your mind one day. You earned your share. There wouldn't be that amount there if you hadn't given me a hand.'

'A lot of things wouldn't be where they are now if we'd done differently, though I don't blame you, you know that.'

'You know where it is.'

Once Mike got on a subject you couldn't make him talk about anything else.

'It can stay there.'

'You've got to be practical, Stan. There's plenty of people done worse than that, still doing it. Top people, too. Government ministers, popes, presidents, one hand on their heart and the other in the till, some kind of till even if it's not the kind you keep cash in. Though it's mostly that kind. They're smarter than us, that's all, though I'd bet none of them could blow a peter as neat as I can.'

They were swung about as the train took a curve, and Mike moved his big hand to stop Stan's right arm from hitting the window.

'I can stand up, for Christ sake. I'm not pissed.'

'Well that's a change.'

'You blow those bloody bars out then. That'd be something smart.'

'That's what I'm talking about, see? You ever get over

the wall and you'll want somewhere to go to, and you know where your share is, might find it useful. It's in the croquet box.'

'Well there's a place to leave it!'

'Safer than any bank. There wasn't room for the stuff till I cleared out the cobwebs.' In the yellowish phantom face on the window the red eyebrows jerked up. 'You play much croquet, Stanley?'

'You're a downright reprehensible bloody immoral son of a whore, you are.'

'Is that a fact?'

There were fewer people in the corridor now and most of the compartment doors were shut. A businessman wandered the length of the train in a crumpled suit and with ash falling; sometimes he stopped and brushed the worst of it off his lapel.

An attendant leaned near the galley, talking to one of the cooks, their faces glum with the news of a rise in the price of bread.

A boy held a girl, a young soldier with his kit on the floor beside them; they swayed together, saying nothing.

A mirage flew against the long dark windows, clouds of steam curling from tall metal spouts, a glow of light where men quarried with machines. Nobody saw them. It was getting late.

It was a pretty ship. The *Invicta*. The sea was dead calm with mist along the horizon.

They could still see France, a pale blue line with patches of pink where the watery sun picked up white walls and coloured them. The spire of Calais stuck up from the mist and there was a small cloud of smoke above the rail-yards.

Chris and Ron had stayed on deck; they stood watching the seagulls swooping across their wake.

'They're French seagulls, Ronnie. I wonder if they call in French?'

She was cold. The air was warm and rather damp but she was shivering. It was no good going inside because it would still feel cold.

'I don't know,' he said. 'We ought to go downstairs.' His arm was round her shoulders, trying to warm her.

'No, I like it up here with you.'

'Well I'd go down too.'

'I know. But it's nice here. If you like it.'

'Yes, I do.'

A pleasure-boat went past and people waved.

'Ronnie, I'm going to have your baby. I didn't use the pill, last time, on purpose. Isn't that wonderful?'

He didn't know what to say, quite, because the idea brought so many things to mind, all terribly important. She knew that, and didn't want him to say anything. But he felt he must say something, and he chose the most important.

'He'll remind you of me.'

She drew in her breath sharply as if there was a sudden pain she couldn't stand, and he pulled her closer against him, thinking he shouldn't have said it. It had been a silly thing to say.

The sky rocked against her eyes and she shut them quickly; she wasn't going to fall, because he was holding her tight; but it would take a minute to get over it and she couldn't speak. It was the feeling she'd had once or twice in the train, not fainting exactly, and not wanting to be sick. It was like walking into a cold sea when the water came over your stomach and you didn't think you could bear it.

She listened to the wash of the boat and the gulls, the French gulls. In a minute she opened her eyes, feeling better.

'It's not that, Ronnie. It's silly of you to think I did it for that.' She heard herself laughing a little bit. 'I don't need reminding of you. It's something we can think of and look forward to, both of us. They can't stop it; nobody can; it's ours and nobody can ever take it away from us. And it's the biggest thing we could have, you see.' She smiled, thinking of it. 'As well as the smallest. You like my idea, don't you?'

He wouldn't have believed he'd got room for any more feelings, what with the dreadful itch to get there and tell them and let them do what they wanted to do so he could start paying back, and the sort of burning that he knew was anger because of what he'd done to the others, Alec and the others. But he found there was room for a new feeling, though it wasn't a feeling exactly at first, it was just a picture in his mind, her with a baby, smiling at it and making it smile back. It was so easy to think of Chris with a baby in her arms that he wondered why he'd never thought about it before, why they'd never had one.

'You'll look great,' he said, 'great!'

She turned her head against his shoulder and looked up at his mouth and strong sharp nose against the sky. He was smiling.

'I didn't do it so that I could *look* like anything!'

'You will. You'll look great.' Then the feeling began. 'And he'll be ours.'

'That's what I said. That's what I meant.'

The other thoughts were going away and they didn't seem so important now. 'It's the most wonderful thing in the world, your idea. I'd never have thought of it.' He was surprised how it grew on him; they'd only been talking about it a minute and everything seemed different already. It ought not to, and he was half-trying to stop it, because it hadn't changed all the other things. But he could think about them later. And he could think about this too, he didn't have to stop thinking about this. It was right what she said; nobody could take it away.

He swayed her gently in his arms as he sometimes did when they stood close like this; they called it their 'dancing bears'. 'You'll have to look after him, Chris.'

'I'll look after him, and the others. He won't be the only one. He's the first though. That's why he's important.' She closed her eyes again, but quietly this time, just letting them close. The shivering had stopped. 'You don't know how busy it's going to be, Ronnie. There'll be so many things we'll have to think of, there won't be time to think of anything else.'

They hadn't talked about it, except for the details of how it had to be done. They were all of the same mind.

Alec didn't know that he could do it at all but he knew he'd have to because it was best. Also it would be easier, however hard, however almost impossible, and they owed it to everyone to make things easier, as well as to themselves.

This would be no atmosphere to take into a home. Mother would have to be told and it would take time and patience. Mandy and Toops would know something bewildering had happened, just by his face and his voice. And at the end he wouldn't be able to leave without saying goodbye, and wouldn't be able to say it. It would be hard on Laura, but less hard than if he went there and had to leave again so soon.

Mike had no one he wanted to see. He could give Mrs Hallowes the instructions later.

'I'm easy,' Stan said. He'd had a last drink at the bar. Double.

They knew what Ron wanted to do.

It was gone five o'clock and the ship was in sight of landfall. The gulls were already out from the cliffs. People were going on deck to look.

Ron and Chris had come down, finding the others in the saloon. They talked sometimes. Fay said Stan must go and see a doctor first thing and have his wrist checked on, and he said yes. Chris said she'd send a letter to Marcel, and some postcards from time to time, Beefeaters and the Changing of the Guard. Then Alec left them quietly and went along to the radio room.

CHAPTER 21

The radio-telegram was received at Dover Police Station at 5.16 p.m. and the signals clerk took it straight in to Superintendent Ross. He was alone in his office.

He read it twice and got up and went into Inspector Finlay's room, where there was the smell of Sloane's Pain-killer; Finlay had toothache and couldn't get to the dentist until tomorrow. Finlay wasn't there. The Superintendent went across to the door on the other side.

'Where's Inspector Finlay?'

'Operations, sir.'

'Ask him to be good enough to come down right away.'

He went back to his desk and picked up a telephone, glancing at his watch. 'I want a priority line to the Yard, Detective-Superintendent Braithwaite. No – Braithwaite. Now get me Operations.' He put the receiver down. 'Brickman!'

'Sir?'

A door opened.

'Find Sgt Tomms.'

'I don't think he's come in yet, sir —'

'Yes he has. Find him.'

A lot of other doors began opening and there were footsteps on the Ops staircase. Someone was calling for Sgt Tomms and someone else asked what was up.

Operations was on the internal line when Inspector Finlay reported to the Superintendent, who was talking into the phone.

276

'Four cars, normal crews, rendezvous at the Admiralty Pier immediately, ferry berth.' He looked at Finlay. 'Read that.' He asked the switchboard for lines to Port Special Branch, Rail Police and Waterguard Officer of Customs.

Finlay read the radio-telegram. REFERENCE GODDARD STOP WANTED PARTIES ARRIVING DOVER 17.30 IN INVICTA STOP WOULD APPRECIATE ESCORT.

'Who sent it, sir?'

'Can't tell. It looks as if they did.' He got up and took his cap from the stand. The phone rang and he said: 'Take it, George. You know the drill. I'm going down there now. There's a call booked for Braithwaite at the Yard so make sure he gets the message.'

'Right. We're holding them till the Yard sends someone down?'

'Well we're not taking them to the pictures, are we?'

Finlay answered the phone as the Super went out.

There was quite a lot of noise in the building now. No one knew what had happened but it was obvious that something had. It was as if a gust of wind had risen.

'Where's Tomms?'

'On his way, sir.'

'Tell him I'm outside in a car. Quick now.'

After Superintendent Ross had left for the Port, Inspector Finlay gave the telegram to Sergeant Waring while he was busy handling the calls. Within ten minutes everyone knew. An air of satisfaction settled through the building and people looked in on each other.

Inspector Locke was on his way from the C.I.D. office to the Operations Room. Two constables were calling to each other in the corridor.

'So we've got the bastards.'

'About bloody time!'

'Baker!'

'Yes, sir?'

'They've not been tried yet.'

'Quite true, sir.'

The Inspector went up the stairs.

More quietly Baker said: 'It's a bloody shame we've stopped hanging just the same.'

The *Invicta* reversed screws and came in stern first. The mooring crew stood by with the lines and people watched from the main deck. The mist was thicker, clinging below the cliffs. Dover Castle was only just visible high above the town.

The passengers were gathering near the gangway as usual but two of the ship's officers were keeping them back.

The radio room had informed the master and there had been a short discussion as to whether the four men should be invited to go into No. 1 Cabin. They had been observed in the main saloon shortly after the radio operator had identified the passenger who had sent the telegram. The party he was with seemed quiet enough, and two Immigration Officers handling foreign and Commonwealth people offered to keep watch.

Fay said it was for the best when Alec told the girls.

They had been jostled into a corner of the mid-deck area as the other passengers crowded past. Nobody noticed them there.

Chris had the feeling again and couldn't get her breath for a minute but Ronnie was there and he cupped her cold face in his hands and kissed her. The others were kissing each other too, and then Alec turned away because he could hear the gangplank swinging into position. Stan was by his side. A man came up; they'd seen him before and Alec said:

'Are you looking after us?'

'That's right.'

'Somewhere out of the way, then.'

Mike and Ron joined them and they went through into the main saloon, which was deserted now.

As soon as the police party had come on board the crew began getting the passengers off.

Friends and relations had come to meet people and the Admiralty Pier was fairly crowded near the Customs hall. The platform for the London train was filling up and the porters were busy.

Two children wriggled through a knot of grown-ups and scampered towards a worried-looking man in a plaid hat. 'Uncle Billiam! Uncle Billiam!' His face cleared.

A boy with a peeling face and a straw sombrero threw his arms round a thin girl in jeans. They stood together for minutes.

'Oh, Bob! I don't *believe* it! What a *fantastic* tan!'

People were waving and laughing, finding each other in the commotion.

'Did you see anything of Anna down there? She said she'd look out for you!'

A transistor was playing.

'Oh, much the same since you left. Drizzly, you know.'

The gulls screamed in the narrow waterway; someone had thrown them a half-empty bag of crisps.

'Hello, darling. Good crossing? Gosh I've missed you!'

A young man with a guitar saw his friends and gave a sudden whistle.

'Mummy, what's that lady crying for?'

'I don't know, darling. I expect she's lost something.'

The gulls screamed.

From near the ship's gangway the black cars drove off towards the town.